*Extraordi*

*Se*

"As long as there are writers like Sean Doolittle out there, American crime fiction has got a sterling future ahead of it. *Rain Dogs* is tense, evocative, and anchored by a main character, Tom Coleman, who I'd love to see more of. A terrific novel." —Dennis Lehane

"*Rain Dogs* is a full-press body-parts exerciser: a heart-stopping, gut-clenching, eye-opening, brain-tingling effort." —*Chicago Tribune*

"A superb, suspenseful tale filled with the droll expressions and ambiguous gestures of Nebraska natives . . . A beautifully written work with idiosyncratic humor and a lot of heart." —*Wall Street Journal*

"[Readers will be] drawn in by the quality and authenticity of the writing. Doolittle's lean, mean prose evokes the hardscrabble territory of the Nebraska badlands that serves as the story's setting. His style is likewise stark and spare, casting the story in the hard-boiled tradition of James M. Cain and Jim Thompson." —*Chicago Sun-Times*

"Sean Doolittle is a young writer with serious chops. With *Rain Dogs* he brings it strong." —George Pelecanos

"Doolittle's style is clipped, his dialogue terse, but the story is lifelike and nuanced. *Rain Dogs* will satisfy fans of hard-boiled fiction and classic noir, as well as any crime fans who don't like their plots tied up too tidily."
—*Booklist*

"A terrific, complex thriller, and Doolittle can write hysterically funny prose even as he breaks your heart."
—*New London (CT) Day*

"Sean Doolittle creates characters that will break your heart. You'll care about these people."
—Victor Gischler, author of *Suicide Squeeze*

"Fast-paced and noir . . . [with] a good bit of humor."
—*Mystery Lovers Bookshop News*

"Good character-driven mystery." —FreshFiction.com

"As lean and gritty as they come . . . A refreshing break from more run-of-the-mill, testosterone-driven crime fiction . . . a very, very good crime novel because it is, in the first place, a very, very good novel."
—James Clar, author of *The Mean Streets*

## BURN

Gold medal winner for mystery in *ForeWord* magazine's Book of the Year Award
A Best Crime Fiction of 2003 pick from *January Magazine*

"An exceptionally well-crafted and well-told tale of arson, police work, misplaced zeal, bad relationships, good relationships, family bonds, and, oh yes, exercise videos. Quirky, compelling, intelligent, and funny . . . If you like Elmore Leonard, do yourself a favor and pick up *Burn.*"
—*Lincoln Journal Star*

"Sean Doolittle has been winning high praise from crime fiction readers, and *Burn* will show you why—it's deftly written, tense and intelligent, and bound to make you scramble to find his other work."
—Jan Burke, author of *Nine*

"A cult writer for the masses—hip, smart, and so mordantly funny that the casual reader might be laughing too hard to realize just how thoughtful Doolittle's work is. Get on the bandwagon now."
—Laura Lippman, author of *By a Spider's Thread*

"[A] twist-filled crime caper." —*Publishers Weekly*

"Dryly funny . . . [a] writer to watch."
—*Omaha World Herald*

"Sean Doolittle combines wit, good humor, and a generosity of spirit rare in mystery fiction to create novels that are both engrossing and strangely uplifting. He deserves to take his place among the best in the genre."
—John Connolly, author of *The White Road*

"Doolittle's prose style is smooth, his plotting fast-paced and addictive." —*January Magazine*

"A pleasure to read." —*Drood Review of Mystery*

"Textured and tasty . . . far beyond the typical thrillers . . . Doolittle is a true Crimedog, and *Burn* is his thesis. And you can see it all over this nine millimeter of a novel that his best is yet to come." —*Plots With Guns*

"Doolittle expertly weaves [his] themes into a tight plot populated by memorable characters. . . . Having read hard-boiled mysteries for over thirty years, it has been exciting to watch young turks become grand masters. I certainly hope that Sean Doolittle has a long, exciting career." —*Mystery News*

"Doolittle has managed a somewhat genre-bending feat in the mystery realm—he's written a feel-good hard-boiled mystery . . . that is wholly original. Smooth and stylish, combining wit and intelligence . . . Doolittle is adept at balancing a suspenseful, well-paced mystery story with realistic and humanistic characters." —trashotron.com

"The cast of characters [here] is second to none in diversity, peculiarity, and hilarity. The dialogue is sharp and energetic, and the narrative is spare and spot-on. . . . Sean Doolittle shrugs off the sophomore curse without so much as a stuttering blink. . . . If you want something new to read, something fun, something *good*, then your search is over. *Burn* is the book for you. Highly recommended." —*Cemetery Dance*

"An estimable addition not only to the publisher's list but also to crime fiction . . . Doolittle delivers a briskly plotted hard-boiled mystery that has its roots in the Elmore Leonard school of dark comedy."
—*South Florida Sun-Sentinel*

# DIRT

An Amazon.com Top 100 Editor's Pick
A Book Sense "Book of the Day"

"Uproarious." —*Publishers Weekly*

"It's very rare for a first novel to be perfect; to have a great story, sparkling writing, interesting layered characters, a carefully balanced and realized setting, a beautifully modulated pace, and not a single misstep. This first novel comes very close. . . . Doolittle is a writer with a story to tell and the skills to tell it well—clearly a writer to watch." —*ForeWord Magazine*

"A really top-notch thriller . . . the book is a delight."
—*Lincoln Journal Star*

"Doolittle gives us a great comic-noir romp . . . one of the best noir novels of the year. It's a creative and quirky tour de force." —*Plots With Guns*

"[Doolittle] balances realism and authenticity with the twists and turns of a mystery thriller." —*Reader*

ALSO BY SEAN DOOLITTLE

**RAIN DOGS**

**BURN**

**DIRT**

A DELL BOOK

THE CLEANUP
A Dell Book / November 2006

Published by Bantam Dell
A Division of Random House, Inc.
New York, New York

This is a work of fiction. Names, characters, places, and incidents either are the product of the author's imagination or are used fictitiously. Any resemblance to actual persons, living or dead, events, or locales is entirely coincidental.

All rights reserved
Copyright © 2006 by Sean Doolittle
Cover design by Craig DeCamps

If you purchased this book without a cover, you should be aware that this book is stolen property. It was reported as "unsold and destroyed" to the publisher, and neither the author nor the publisher has received any payment for this "stripped book."

Dell is a registered trademark of Random House, Inc., and the colophon is a trademark of Random House, Inc.

ISBN-13: 978-0-440-24282-6
ISBN-10: 0-440-24282-7

Printed in the United States of America
Published simultaneously in Canada

www.bantamdell.com

OPM 10 9 8 7 6 5 4 3 2 1

For Neil Smith and Victor Gischler

A Plot with Guns

# PROLOGUE

## $AVEMORE

# 1. MEAT AND FROZEN

Worth couldn't get over the looks people gave him. It seemed like an easy question.

"Um, paper," the woman said. "I guess."

He swiped open a sack and went to it. Beside him, Gwen skimmed her cheat sheet for produce codes. Up and down the line, scanners beeped. Groceries clattered. Tinny Top 40 swirled in the rafters.

The woman finally leaned across the checkout stand. "Forgive me for asking, but don't they have employees who do this?"

Worth did his best to ignore the way her breasts pressed together above the zipper of her jogging top.

"I don't mind," he said, already lifting the first sack into the cart at the end of the stand. Square. Stable. Not too heavy.

"Hey," said the woman. "Wow."

Worth touched a salute and quickly reduced the left-over rubble to three neat bags. He saved a little room at the top of the third, nestled a loaf of bread in the space. The woman was smiling now.

"Say . . . do you think you could put the meat in plastic? And the frozen stuff?"

"Meat and frozen stuff in plastic." He nodded to the young boy at her hip, drawing his baton. "Okay with you, partner?"

The boy shrank, staring, chewing on the neck of his soccer shirt. Worth kicked himself for showing off. He raked the new pile forward with the side handle, leaned the stick out of sight beside his knee.

Gwen struggled along, scanning with her good hand, running the keypad with her bum wing. Soon the cart was full, the total totaled. The woman scribbled a check.

"Is that a real gun?"

He smiled down at the kid, who now gazed at Worth's gear belt closely. "It's real, kiddo. But it's only for emergencies."

"Have you ever shot somebody?"

"Not even once."

"Ethan. Don't bother the officer."

Worth fished a Jolly Rancher from a vacant Mace holster. "Here you go, pal. That's official candy. Omaha PD."

Ethan looked to his mother. The woman slipped Worth a grin, gave kiddo the nod. Worth handed the candy over. He finally spotted one of the regular sackers sauntering back in from a carry-out, twirling his apron, nowhere special to be. Worth flagged him while Mom admired her cart.

"You know," she said, "you're pretty good at that."

He held up his hands. "Long arms of the law."

She laughed and tried to tip him. Worth took Ethan's

empty wrapper instead. Something in the boy's newly fascinated expression depressed him a little. He dropped the kid a wink.

When they were gone, Gwen closed her drawer with a hip and batted her lashes. "You're so good at that."

"Don't start." He nodded to the wrist she'd sprained playing volleyball in some bar league. She'd come on shift with a brown club of bandage for a right hand; by now her long slender fingers looked like spoiled knockwursts. "You should go home and put ice on that."

"It's okay." She flicked his elbow with her good hand. "How come you're here so early? No life?"

"Law enforcement is my life."

"My hero."

He liked seeing her smile.

Gwen pushed him out of her stand with his own baton. Worth strolled back to his spot by the cigarette case. He reholstered the stick, hooked his thumbs in his belt, and tried to look like a cop for a while.

## II. GWEN

Once per session, usually during a lull, Dr. Jerry Grail would take a hand mirror from his middle desk drawer and hold it up in front of Worth's face.

"Describe what you see. Use only nouns."

Sometimes it was adjectives. Once it was animals. It always felt canned, insipid, a little bit demeaning, but Worth needed the grade, so he did his best to play along. Sometimes Dr. Grail scribbled something in his case folder. Sometimes not. Half the time Worth felt pretty sure the shrink wasn't even listening.

One afternoon, when he saw Grail's hand moving toward the drawer, Worth said, "No offense, Doc, but don't we pretty much know what I look like by now?"

Dr. Grail stopped his reach and leaned back. He had a narrow face, a shell of thinning hair, and a way of looking across the desk that always made Worth feel like he was letting the guy down.

"The mirror is only an exercise, Matthew," Dr. Grail said.

"You say that like it's a positive thing."

"Does it make you uncomfortable?"

"Not really." No way was he falling for that one again.

Grail ran a finger around the inside of his watchband. He did it ten or twelve times an hour. Worth sometimes counted.

"Last week you mentioned feeling concern for somebody at work." The shrink checked his folder, flipped a page. "Gwen?"

Worth wished he'd never brought it up. "Right."

"Would you like to talk further about that?"

"I guess not."

Grail scribbled a note.

"By that I meant I guess there isn't much to say."

She was a nursing student at Clarkson and worked a combination of graveyards and swings. Weeknights, she kept a battered textbook under the register with a pack of Dorals and a highlighter pen. She had big gray eyes, a sly sense of humor, and a manner that seemed feisty and fragile at the same time. The first time he saw her, Worth thought of the bird that once came in through the chimney and tangled itself in the fireplace screen.

He wasn't about to tell Dr. Grail that he'd grown to look forward to the shifts he worked with Gwen. That sometimes, watching from his spot by the cigarette case, he found himself entertaining pathetic fantasies.

Worth imagined coming to her rescue. More than once, in the long dead hours after midnight, he'd passed the time constructing elaborate scenarios in which he demonstrated steely-eyed heroism. Occasionally, he caught himself making adolescent, X-rated, cop-and-checkout-girl movies in his mind.

Ultimately, he drove back to assembly after sunrise feeling like either a sleaze or a sham.

Worth didn't kid himself. He probably never had been hero material, but he wasn't typically a letch. He was just lonelier than he'd realized. And he really didn't know Gwen at all.

She sprained her other wrist in September. One night, she came in with a limp. Sorensen, the night manager, told him that Gwen seemed to play volleyball all year round.

"Rough sport," Worth suggested.

Sorensen stood quietly in his tie and shirtsleeves. He scribbled something on his clipboard, met Worth's eyes briefly, then agreed that it must be.

By then he'd already found himself in the habit of going for coffee when she took her breaks. One night she caught him off guard.

"I found stuff out about you."

It messed up his regular small talk. "Stuff?"

"Mm." Gwen looked up from her textbook. She took a drag from her cigarette and watched him through the smoke. Even in the harsh light of the employee break room, her gray eyes caught a warm glimmer. "I asked around."

Worth went to the counter and worked a foam cup from the stack by the coffee machine. He suddenly felt clumsy. "Stuff like what?"

"Stuff like what. Hmm." Gwen tapped her highlighter against her chin. "Let's see."

"You shouldn't tease the police."

"That's what I hear."

"How's that?"

"I heard you punched another officer."

He stopped pouring, tightened his jaw. Ricky.

Or Curtis. He couldn't keep them straight. He didn't know what the hell was the matter with him lately, telling macho stories in the stockroom for those two knuckleheads.

Gwen said, "Is that really true?"

"Not really."

"I wondered," she said. "You don't seem like the type."

Worth slid the pot back. "I punched a detective."

Now she closed her book and leaned over it, elbows on the table, cigarette trailing smoke beside her ear. "You did not."

"Unfortunately."

Vargas in Homicide. He'd told the Modell brothers, Ricky and Curtis, only about the Vargas-on-his-ass part. Worth hadn't mentioned the part where Vargas came back up, feinted left, and shattered his nose with a straight right. He hadn't even seen it coming. Just thinking about it was humiliating.

"Why did you punch a detective?"

"Poor impulse control."

"Ah."

"It's a long story." It was a fairly short story, actually. Pretty simple.

She nodded along. "Is that how you ended up here? Keeping me company?"

Going on ten weeks, he'd realized coming on post tonight. The store had reported a rash of shoplifters in June and an unarmed robbery the first week in July; some crankhead from Fremont had jumped two checkout stands and run out the front doors with a cash tray under each arm, trailing loose coins.

Worth's lieutenant had manufactured the detail when he'd initialed the reinstatement papers. Six months, A-shift, SaveMore at Saddle Creek and Leavenworth. Provisional duty pending a fitness sign-off from psych.

"More or less," he told her.

"That's interesting."

"It's not that interesting."

Gwen sat back. He liked the way she smoked: thoughtful, slightly awkward, one eye pinched. He'd never really seen anybody with eyes that color. They sort of fascinated him.

"I heard something else," she finally said.

"Boy. What else did you hear?"

"You're a faker."

He burned his tongue on the coffee. "Sorry?"

Gwen looked at his left hand. It took a moment

before he got it: the wedding ring. Worth chuckled, felt his ears get hot.

"Right," he said. "That."

"How long?"

"How long was I married? Or how long have I been divorced?"

"Whichever."

"Marriage, ten years," he said. "Divorce, eight months."

"Ah."

"It was over before that, I just didn't know it."

"I'm sorry."

"Don't be."

She nodded as though she understood. "Still hung up, huh?"

"It's complicated." It wasn't.

Somebody came in then, and they both looked. Worth recognized LaTonya, one of the other full-time checkers, cornrows beaded tonight, smock draped over her shoulder. She went to the clock, punched out, and slid her time card back into the slot on the wall. She hung the smock on a hook.

"Night, Gwennie."

Gwen smiled. "See you tomorrow, babe."

"Night, Supercop."

"Good night, LaTonya."

LaTonya glanced at Gwen, chuckled a little, and walked out humming.

When she was gone, he said, "What was that all about?"

Gwen had already gone back to her textbook. She shrugged, uncapping her highlighter with her teeth. "Who knows with that girl?"

## III. SUPERCOP

Lately, he'd been thinking about something Sondra once said.

*You want to know your biggest problem?* This had been a few months before she'd left him for Vargas in Homicide. *It's not the job. It's not the department. Christ, Matthew, news flash: It's you.*

He'd written the comment off at the time. She'd been pissed because he hadn't put in for the sergeant's test, decided to get mean about it. At some point in their marriage, Sondra had grown disappointed. He hadn't even seen it coming. Just thinking about it was humiliating.

Lately, even Worth was beginning to see the irony.

His great-grandfather took a bullet in the ribs when the courthouse fell to the mob in 1919; the way all the stories told it, Mort Worth had gone on bleeding and cracking heads even after they set the building on fire. His grandfather worked Boss Dennison's funeral in '34. A great-uncle made captain in the Southeast. His father gave the force thirty years and his liver; his older brother Kelly gave three and his life.

He was the last in four generations of Worth men to wear the shield in this town, yet somehow it had taken the SaveMore to remind Matthew Worth why he'd wanted to become a cop in the first place.

This store had been a Food 4 Less when he'd worked here as a teenager, but mostly it felt the same. Back then, he'd always been the one zero his age who actually enjoyed having a part-time job at the supermarket.

He'd enjoyed sacking people's groceries. There was something satisfying in fitting a mountain of shapes and sizes into a few uniform packages. He liked helping folks out to their cars, getting them on their way. It made him feel good when they said thanks and meant it.

Over the past few weeks, Worth had come to accept the sad facts:

He was living in a world where tired soccer moms were so accustomed to watching some apathetic teenager drop the milk jug on top of the eggs that they wanted to tip you just for trying to put a little extra "serve" in Protect and Serve.

And he probably felt more useful wearing an apron and a name tag than he'd ever felt wearing a gun belt and a badge.

Anyway, he only kept wearing the wedding ring because he knew it burned the shit out of Vargas in Homicide.

The last week in October, a cold front sliced down from Canada like a blade.

Worth hadn't listened to a forecast for a couple of days. The night the weather turned, he took his 2 A.M. spin around the perimeter with his jacket collar up, bare hands in his pockets, watching his breath form frosty clouds in the drizzle. He heard her before he saw her.

"Russell, please."

The lamps out front cast a faint blue sheen over the oily wet surface of the parking lot. One of the lamps had gone dark. As he rounded the last corner of the building, Worth ID'd a tricked-out GTO parked askew in the shadows around the base of the pole. Muscle era, glossy black, rear spoiler, mag wheels. Vanity plates stamped *BadGoat*. Cute.

Gwen stood half-bent at the driver's side.

"Honey, I'm sorry," she said. "Okay? You're hurting me."

Worth saw the driver's hand, clutching her arm through the open window. He lengthened his stride.

Whoever sat behind the wheel spotted him coming. Gwen got her arm back just as Worth reached the car's front fender. He rested one hand on the butt of his stick as he came around the driver's side.

"Everything okay over here?"

Gwen folded her thin arms and looked at the blacktop. "Hey, Matthew. Just finishing my break. Everything's fine."

Worth put his hand on the Pontiac's roof. "How about in here?"

In the driver's seat fumed a lean, muscular guy in jeans and a tank top. The guy gripped the wheel and stared straight ahead, stubbled jaw shaded amber in the panel lights of a custom stereo.

Russell, he presumed. Warm air laced with cologne blasted from inside the car as Worth's fingers grew numb against the cold wet steel.

He said, "It's not polite to ignore people when they ask you a question."

"Man, you heard her. We're fine."

Worth straightened and turned to Gwen. Looking at her just then, he thought of Tiffany Pine. Unpleasant images flashed in his head.

He shook his head and said, "Walk me back inside?"

Before she could answer, the car roared to life. A

sudden assault of headbanger metal came blaring as headlight beams leapt through the mist. Russell dropped into gear and gunned toward the nearest exit, leaving the two of them standing alone.

Worth waited until the GTO's taillights disappeared around the curve, tires whining, before he asked her again if she was okay.

Gwen looked at the blacktop. Everything suddenly seemed too quiet.

"You shouldn't have done that," she said.

"Gwen, that's why I'm—"

"No. I mean you *really* shouldn't have done that."

Gwen didn't have a coat. He was halfway out of his tac jacket when she turned, hugging herself, and walked back toward the entrance of the store alone.

He found the Modell brothers clowning around in the break room, throwing box cutters at empty soup cases. They'd scrawled crude bull's-eye targets on the sides of the boxes, presumably with the Sharpie marker now stuck behind Ricky's ear.

Most nights Worth didn't mind the guys. Good-natured, blond-headed tree stumps, both of them, stocking shelves full-time since losing university wrestling scholarships to a combined grade point average somewhere in the high decimals. But they had manners. They went out of their way for people. Either one of them would lift a car if you asked them to.

Tonight, he nodded them toward the door.

Ricky didn't get it. As he stood there, blinking, Curtis

punched him in the shoulder hard enough to dislodge the Sharpie. "Wake up, Debbie."

Ricky reared back, rubbing the spot.

"You're an ass-head," he said.

Curtis ignored him, grinning at Worth on his way out the door.

Ricky caught up, nailed his brother a payback shot. Worth couldn't help noticing the way Gwen flinched at the sound of a fist smacking flesh.

When he took a chair, she stubbed her cigarette in the grimy tin tray by her hand. She fished in her pack, lit another, finally gave him a weak grin.

"Take a picture, it'll last longer."

*Hey,* he almost said, thinking of the DV bag in the trunk of the cruiser. *You read my mind.*

He said, "I want you to do me a favor."

"What kind of favor?"

"I want you to file a report."

"A report?"

"With me."

"I'm not sure what you mean."

In the weeks he'd known her, Worth couldn't remember seeing Gwen wear so much as a smudge of lipstick. Tonight she'd caked her face with so much makeup she might as well have worn a Halloween mask. He could still see the shadow of the bruise beneath, high on one cheekbone, cupping her eye.

"If you need a place to stay, I can arrange it."

"A place."

"Somewhere you'll be safe," he said. "If that's what you need."

Gwen still wouldn't look at him. She crossed her

arms, holding her cigarette near her lips. "I guess you know where you can find a place like that?"

The graveyard shift ended at seven. Worth went to the break room at 6:30 and waited by the time clock.

At 7:15, he went looking for her.

At 7:25, he circled back to find that she'd punched out and slipped away.

## IV. VOLLEYBALL

Gwen Mullen called in sick her next two shifts in a row. Sorensen, the night manager, told Worth she hadn't missed a shift in the two years she'd worked for him at the store.

The second night, during roll call, Worth's cell phone buzzed. Assuming it was Sondra, calling about the house, he let it go.

After muster, he checked his voice mail. It was Sorensen.

"She wouldn't talk to me," the manager said on the way up.

Worth nodded. "I'll give it a try."

"She wouldn't take off her coat."

"Okay."

At the top of the rough pine staircase, outside the door marked ASSOCIATES ONLY, Sorensen lingered. It seemed like he wanted to say something more.

Some of the employees made fun of the guy. He was around Worth's age and lived with his mother. He had an average build but tended to look a little dumpy, and he'd probably never been much in style. He had a strange cowlick and a bit of a dandruff problem. Told the same lame jokes all the time.

But he was a good guy, from what Worth could tell. He seemed to care. The grocery man clicked his ballpoint, looked Worth in the eyes.

"I'll talk to her," Worth told him.

Sorensen sighed. He finally nodded. In a moment, he turned and went back down the stairs.

When the manager was gone, Worth tapped the door twice with a knuckle and stepped inside.

The office had three bland walls lined with file cabinets, then a bank of one-way windows overlooking the front of the store. Gwen stood at the windows, narrow shoulders hunched, an arm wrapped low across her waist. Worth could see the cigarette trembling in her other hand from where he stood.

"Hey," he said. "How are you feeling?"

She tried to smile. She might as well not have bothered.

"Been better," she said.

From the doorway, Worth looked her over. She wore a silky blouse that looked like it went with a stylish business suit, not sweatpants and muddy shoes. She'd taken off her thin fleece zip-up, just not in front of Sorensen.

Worth's number came over the radio on a crackle of static. *"Baker 52, Adam Double Zero."*

Lardner and Sanchez. He ignored the call out of experience.

When it came again, he squeezed the com set strapped to his shoulder. "Three Adam Zero."

Crackle. Beep.

*"Yeah, um, Double Zero, I need a price check."* Worth could hear Sanchez snickering in the passenger seat. *"That's Kotex with wings. Um, UltraThin. Advise, over."*

Goddamned children. He reached to his hip and cut the radio.

When the silence settled, he said, "Hey?"

She finally looked at him. The remains of her shiner stood in yellow smudges against her dishwater complexion. Her hair hung limp around her face. He'd noticed at times that her eyes almost seemed to absorb her mood, the color of the room around her. Tonight they seemed flat, pale, twin chips of dirty chalk. The tremble in her cigarette seemed to climb up her wrist.

"What happened?"

She said, "Can I show you something?"

Worth reached back and closed the door.

She took half a minute to stub out her cigarette. She moved slowly, keeping her arms close to her body. At last she straightened, turned her back to him, and began to undo the blouse.

By now he had a pretty good idea what was coming. He had an idea why she'd chosen a soft, loose-fitting top. Still, when she finally let the blouse slip from her shoulders, Worth's heart sagged.

Gwen's slim back was a boiling thunderhead. The worst of her bruises practically seeped blood. Around the edges, he saw knuckle marks like grubby fingerprints.

Somebody had been using her as an ashtray. Worth brushed aside a length of her hair and saw a burn mark, a crusted sore at the base of her neck. More between her shoulder blades.

He'd never gotten a true sense of her figure in the shapeless smocks she wore at work. Gwen was even thinner than he'd realized; he could count her ribs, each knob of her spine.

At the same time, from where he stood behind her, Worth saw the V of her waist, the top flare of her hips. The suprising outer swells of her breasts. Her previously concealed features seemed at odds with the willowy design of her frame; even under the horrid circumstances, Worth felt a slight spark of arousal. He hated himself for it.

With one hand, he carefully peeled down the waistband of her sweatpants on her left side, leaving an imprint of elastic in the soft flesh beneath. The contusions crawled over a filigree of tattoo ink at the small of her back. More bruising around the jut of her hipbone.

"I'll take you to the hospital," he said.

Gwen began to cry. Worth lifted her blouse up as gently as he could.

That was when she turned, and he saw the dry vacancy in her eyes, and realized that she wasn't sobbing but shivering.

She said, "Can I show you something else?"

# 1

# PLASTIC

# 1

In retrospect, announcing himself in the hallway almost seemed funny. *Police. I'm opening the door.*

The small bedroom in the back of Gwen Mullen's apartment felt like a meat locker. Worth understood when he reached down and felt cold iron: She'd valved off the radiator in here. She'd also opened the windows. Plastic blinds clattered on the chilly breeze.

He raised the Maglite to eye level.

Russell lay naked in a twist of sheets. In the beam of the flashlight, Worth caught glimpses of white amid ragged red pulp. He guessed he was looking at molars. Maybe jawbone. He wasn't sure.

Moving the light around the room, his own breath foggy in the beam, he passed over the nightstand and noticed a dark square centered in a thin layer of dust. He found the lamp on the floor beside the bed, cord trailing, still plugged into the socket near the peeling baseboard.

The lamp came on when he flipped the switch by his elbow, throwing shadows up the cracked plaster wall. By some trick the bulb had remained intact; dark clots of stuff had congealed around the chunky glass base.

Worth automatically reached for the mike on his shoulder. The words sat in his throat, pushing their way up: *Three Adam Zero, Three Adam Sixty.* His sergeant's car.

He wondered how long the guy had been here like this. He wondered how many times she'd hit him with the lamp.

At some point, he realized he'd released the call button without speaking.

Worth found Gwen sitting on the floor in the living room, staring at nothing, arms around her knees. A dime-store jack-o'-lantern the size of a Weber grill hulked in one corner, bathing the place in cheap orange light.

He slid a stack of magazines out of his way and sat on the edge of the low coffee table in front of her. There was a big ceramic ashtray shaped like Texas, heaped with butts. None of them looked like Gwen's brand.

"In the bedroom." She pointed. "Back there."

"Gwen," he said. "You showed me."

No response.

"Can you look at me?"

If she could, she didn't.

"Can you tell me what happened?"

"Didn't you see?"

She drifted again, and Worth let her go. In the reflection of a framed race car poster on the wall he could see the jack-o'-lantern standing sentry over his shoulder, jagged mouth leering. For some stupid reason, he found that he didn't like having the thing at his back.

He stood and took a better look around.

Cracked woodwork, water stains on the ceiling. A fist-size hole in one wall, exposing slats like broken ribs. Between two tall windows, mismatched sheets tacked up for curtains, an enormous, expensive-looking flat-screen television sat on milk crates.

Back in the bedroom, standing over the fish-bellied body on the bed, Worth couldn't decide what depressed him most: the bludgeoned corpse, the image of Gwen Mullen raising the lamp and pulling it down, or the thought that he could, conceivably, wind up playing officer-on-scene to that miserable prick Vargas in Homicide.

He keyed the radio. The beep made him think of the checkout scanners at the store.

Just then a soft gasp drifted in from the other room, toward him down the short dark hall. Worth followed it back.

Gwen had finally lost her grip. Fat tears squeezed beneath the heels of her hands, leaving slick trails; her cheeks glistened in the gaudy Halloween glow.

Worth got down beside her, cuffs rattling, silent radio digging into his side, not sure where he could touch her that wouldn't hurt.

She covered her face and slouched against him. It was as if she had no weight. He felt her tears, her steamy breath.

"I didn't know what to do," she whispered.

He stroked her hair. "It'll be okay."

"How?"

Worth didn't kid himself.

# 2

Eddie Tice was officially done fucking around.

"You'd better be dead in a ditch," he said into the phone. It was the last message he intended to leave. "You hear what I'm saying, smart guy? Because if you're walking around out there? Thinking you're a smart guy? I'll find you, is the first thing. Don't even think I won't find your stupid ass."

He longed to slam a phone down and hear its guts jingle like you used to be able to do. Instead, he thumbed the button and threw the Wi-Fi handset against the wall. Batteries and shards of cracked plastic were still hitting the carpet when Troy Mather stuck his head around the door.

"Um . . . hey?"

"What?"

"Okay to come in?"

Tice took a deep breath. "Come in, Troy. Please. Let me extend a personal invitation."

Troy pushed the door the rest of the way open and came inside. Derek Price followed, hung a left, and fell into the sofa sectional in the far corner. Price grabbed the remote and punched on the wide-screen Eddie had taken off the showroom floor and put in the office. Last year's model.

"By all means," Tice told him. "Be comfortable."

Derek held up a thumb, flipping through channels until he landed on *SportsCenter*.

Troy had plopped himself into the discontinued leather glider on the other side of Eddie's antique desk.

"Well," he said.

"Well what?"

"He ain't anywhere."

"He's somewhere," Eddie said.

From the sectional: "Maybe he just forgot to charge his phone."

Tice folded his arms and leaned back in the tall chair. He'd already checked with the state cops between here and Chicago. No reports involving the GTO so far.

He'd check again tomorrow. Benefit of the doubt. Possibly a whole different set of problems to worry about.

Troy nodded along with the whole cell-phone idea, then said, "But just to be, like, devil's aggregate?"

Eddie Tice sighed. "I'm listening."

"Okay, me and Derek got the idea to check his girl," Troy said. He sounded proud of himself. "Right? So I remember she got the Modells a job where she works. The SaveMore there on Saddle Creek. Curtis and Ricky. Remember those guys?"

"No," Eddie said.

"Big beefy dudes? Kinda stupid? They worked for me, I dunno, couple months. I think they might be those kind of twins that don't look like each other."

*Worked for me.* Troy liked to feel as though he had a little authority at Tice Is Nice Quality Used and Discount Furniture. At least in the warehouse. Eddie Tice let him feel as though he had a little. "Keep telling your story, Troy."

"Anyway, we go there," Troy said. "I already know she works Fridays, being Russ normally comes to poker night, but she ain't nowhere around there tonight. Talked to Curtis and Ricky, nothin' outta them. Talked to some other dude pushin' a mop on the way out. He said the girl hasn't been to work in, like, a couple days."

While Troy Mather rambled, Eddie's mood about the situation began to darken. He realized he still hadn't taken off the thermal FootJoy Windshirt he'd been wearing on the thirteenth green at Tiburon twelve hours ago. Now his back ran with sweat.

"Does she have any other jobs?"

Troy opened his mouth, then shut it.

Eddie moved on. "But she definitely wasn't home."

"Um . . ." Troy said. He glanced over toward the corner. Derek wasn't even paying attention. "We didn't know what kind of car she drove."

"What happened when you knocked on the door?"

"Well, it's Friday night, man, so we figured . . ."

"Didn't go to the apartment, did you?"

Troy's face darkened. He was blushing. "Shit, Eddie. I mean, like, why the fuck would he be at the apartment, right?"

"It's okay," Eddie said. Thinking: *Holy Lord.* Troy was dependable if you didn't give him too much to think about; Derek Price didn't weigh more than a buck twenty, tattoos included, but he had some street sense and knew how to keep his mouth shut. The two of them together didn't quite equal a Russell—who, until tonight, Eddie Tice had always looked at as a candidate for bigger and better things. "I'll call Tony."

"Aww, come on." Troy hopped up out of the chair. "Let us handle it. Seriously. We'll go back there right now."

"I said it's okay," Eddie told him. "You guys did fine."

"Eddie—"

"Quiet," Tice barked. When he saw the wounded look on Troy's face, he softened. "Look. Do you want to help?"

"You name it, boss." Troy cracked his knuckles. "We're on it."

Eddie Tice pulled off the Windshirt and tossed it aside. He leaned forward, opened the middle left drawer of his desk, took out a bottle of Eagle Rare and a rocks glass, grabbed his BlackBerry from its charging cradle, and said, "Go down to Electronics and bring me back a new phone."

# 3

Tiffany Pine had led the news for a sad string of days in December his first year sworn.

Worth had been fresh out of the academy, still rolling with his FTO. She'd been twenty-two, a Metro student, working her way toward a two-year associate's degree in early childhood education. It was Christmastime.

No one who knew her claimed to understand why she'd stayed with the guy so long. By all accounts, he was a hothead with tendencies, nonviolent coping skills not prominent among them.

Pretty girl. Ugly situation. For too long she did everything people did, and then she did everything you were supposed to do. None of it mattered in the end.

They'd found her on the front steps at Helena House, throat slit, pregnant belly hacked apart. To Worth had fallen the task of setting up a tape line around their remains: adult female, infant male, two young bodies slowly freezing in a slushy pool of blood-melted snow.

He still remembered what it felt like to be a cop in the

weeks after Tiffany Pine. It didn't feel very much like he'd thought it would.

---

Problem number one: supplies.

Gwen had a roll of cheap garbage bags in the cupboard under the kitchen sink. Russell's toolbox, same cupboard. Worth cracked the lid and found a roll of silver duct tape in the bottom.

Problem number two: Russell T. James.

There was a mangy area rug in the living room. Worth moved the coffee table and took the rug up. The fake pumpkin watched.

Back in the bedroom, he stopped what he was doing long enough to think, one last time, of the camera kit in the trunk of the cruiser. He could get digitals of Gwen before the Henry units arrived; he'd take the photos in good hard light. *Call it in.*

Russell James probably had been considered a good-looking guy. T for Thomas, according to the driver's license he found in the wallet on the nightstand by the bed. Twenty-five years old. He'd given the DMV a cocky grin.

Good hair, nice straight teeth. The kind of face that made you try to think which young movie actor he resembled. Worth remembered something Sondra once told him about how women couldn't help being drawn to men with dark eyes.

Bloody meat.

That's what good-looking Russell looked like now. Scraps of meat, pieces of bone, a slick cap of dark tangled hair.

The prosecutor's office would secure photographs of

their own. Worth tried to see the big picture, all the angles, the possible outs, but all he could think of was that he and Sondra had lived in an old building like this early on. No air-conditioning, no thermostat, finicky heat. Once, in the dead of winter, the power had gone off for nearly thirty-six hours. But they'd been fine, huddled together under heavy blankets, finding ways to pass the time. That was one thing about these old iron radiators: They'd stay warm for at least a couple of days.

The radiator in Gwen's bedroom was cold as a morgue tray.

No matter how he played it out, standing there, looking at the mess in front of him, Worth kept running up against the unavoidable fact:

She'd beaten a guy to death with a lamp. While he slept. She'd crept out of bed so she wouldn't wake him, and then she'd hit him until his face was gone.

Afterward, she'd opened windows. She'd even rolled up a bathroom towel along the bottom of the door.

You didn't have to be a lawyer to imagine how it would play in court. Russell James was the victim now. Not the other way around.

For Gwen, even with a back full of ugly bruises, self-defense would be a tough sell. He imagined the prosecution's arguments: Had the defendant ever attempted to leave the victim? Had she ever filed a report? Could the defense offer any proof that the defendant had suffered her injuries at the hands of the victim in the first place?

If she'd been able to slip out of bed undetected, why had she chosen to bludgeon the victim to death in his sleep instead of simply leaving the apartment and finding safe haven?

She'd eventually reported the crime. Maybe she'd helped herself there. But in this town, she'd still be above the fold in the papers, a lead-off on the six and ten. A juicy burning-bed story. She'd be there again at trial time.

Worth thought of Gwen, working bad shifts, knuckling over textbooks during her breaks. He thought of all the waste-of-space Russells he'd encountered on the job. He thought of Tiffany Pine.

An overwhelming sadness swept over him, like a wave that had been building from a great depth.

Even if she caught the outside odds, some sort of clemency, starting now, this girl's life was off the rails. And for what?

He hadn't known he was capable of thinking this way. Worth wondered how his older brother Kelly would have handled the situation. He thought he knew the answer, and it didn't really help.

He wondered what Dr. Grail would have written in his case folder.

By the time he'd taken off his gear belt and started unbuttoning his winter duty shirt, Worth had moved beyond all that. Past logic, past speculation, past the right or the wrong, finally on to something he found simpler to grasp:

Strategy.

In that sense it came down to nothing more or less complicated than sacking groceries. A big pile of problems. A few tidy solutions.

Russell had been a good-looking guy.

As it happened, he'd also been just about Worth's size.

• • •

The alley separated Gwen's building from a sagging two-story house next door. In back, a cross alley ran between a row of overflowing Dumpsters and the backs of two other apartment buildings. Nothing to the north but a fractured pad of asphalt, fenced off from the street by weedy, trash-clogged chain link. Tenant parking. Currently vacant but for one dark, orphaned GTO.

Worth had parked the cruiser out front. As if from a distance, he saw himself hoisting a rolled rug into a fireman's carry, descending a wooden fire escape in back. He wore a dead guy's clothes, black ball cap stitched with a NASCAR patch pulled low over his eyes. It was like watching a murky scene in some movie. A movie about bad people. Dumb bad people.

But if anybody with a view happened to look out a window, they wouldn't see a uniformed cop hauling a bulging bundle out the back of Gwen Mullen's apartment after midnight. If anybody in the building was paying attention, the presence of the squad unit would most likely draw their attention toward the street.

If anybody who knew Russell came around the corner, or up the fire escape, Worth didn't know what would happen.

Nobody did.

Problem number three: vehicles.

Even with beer and Vicodin, John Pospisil hadn't slept through the night in ten weeks.

He hadn't done much of anything except sit around and hurt since the middle of August, but the past few days had been a new kind of fun. Guys at the hall had told him he'd feel it when the weather changed.

He was feeling it.

A guy didn't want to complain. Not after his tie line breaks and he goes to the hospital with a busted leg instead of zipped up in a bag.

John had been framing a skylight on a million-dollar new build out west when he'd opened his eyes and realized he'd fallen three stories onto flat concrete: through the rafters, into an open stairwell, all the way down to the poured basement floor.

Thirty years as a carpenter, he'd lived around job sites without so much as stepping on a nail. The safety guys always said it only took once.

He still didn't remember slipping. One minute he was

marking a chalk line; the next, they were hauling him out of there with a shattered tibia and a six-inch shear of fibula sticking out of his knee.

Two surgeries, three rods, a stainless steel plate, and half a bucket of screws later, he had enough hardware down there to sink a bass boat, and he wasn't done yet. Ten weeks along, he still sported what the doc called an external fixator. The insurance company called it an even three grand. It looked to John like a twenty-four-inch bar clamp drilled into the side of his leg.

It made a decent weather gauge, too. John swore the thing conducted every tick of the barometer straight down into the bone.

The clock by the bed said 12:25 when he finally called it quits. He wished he hadn't followed the doc's advice and popped the Ambien; he always woke up anyway, and the stuff only made him feel dizzy and strange. He sat on the edge of the mattress until he thought he could stand without falling over in a pile.

Doc wanted him to keep a walker by the bed. A damned walker.

*Thirty years.*

John Pospisil sighed, hauled himself up, gathered his balance, and crutched his way along the well-worn path through the dark to the La-Z-Boy recliner in the living room.

It was quiet in the house, and a little cool. Light from the streetlamp came in through the gap in the drapes, striping the floor. John stopped at the thermostat and turned the dial just enough to kick the furnace on. He rested another few seconds, then gimped along, finally steadying himself against the recliner at the end of the trail.

Outside, a car passed on the street. While John stood there, the muffled sound of the engine grew into a souped-up grumble that seemed to slow and linger in front of the house. Headlights passed across the curtains.

He raised a crutch and moved the curtain a few inches to the side.

Across the street, a black car idled in the driveway behind Helen Worth's house, waiting for the garage door to rise. Old sixties Camaro, it looked like. Something along those lines. Sharp, whatever it was. Driver door open. Dome light on.

While John watched, a guy in a black ball cap and a denim jacket came out of the garage. He got in the car and pulled inside. The garage door came down.

It was Matt living there now. Helen's grandson, a city cop just like old Joe and his sons. Good guy, took care of the place. John had seen him leave for work in his pickup a few hours ago; he didn't see the pickup in the garage now.

Must have had some company staying. Maybe he'd call over in a little while. Kill a few minutes, make sure everything was kosher. Maybe he'd mind his own business.

Hell. He probably wouldn't be able to remember what he did or didn't do. He wished he hadn't taken the Ambien.

---

From the house, Worth walked to the GitGo on Center Street. He called a Husker Cab from the pay phone outside.

He used the name Tom Smith, kept the ball cap low, stood with his back to the security camera mounted outside the store.

Three blocks from Gwen's apartment building, he got out of the cab and paid the driver in cash. He walked with his head down, hands in his pockets.

By the time he finally climbed the rear walkup back to Gwen's apartment, it was after one in the morning. The trip home and back had taken fifty-one minutes; since he'd left the SaveMore with Gwen, an hour and a half had passed.

A long stretch. He could nudge the time in his reports, but not by much. He'd need to claim it had taken time to assess the situation. He'd claim the subject had required special handling.

At the least, he'd surely take some sort of informal reprimand for sloppy radio procedure. No matter what, he'd end up looking bad.

Ironically, given his record at this point, looking bad was practically its own explanation.

The fact that he'd left his post instead of turning the call over to a field unit presented potentially larger problems. But his detail was a joke, and everybody knew it. He hadn't caught a call-worthy incident at the SaveMore in weeks. As long as nobody decided to rob the place at gunpoint in the next few hours, his initiative toward conducting a little actual police work related to his limited jurisdiction would likely be forgiven.

The clock was still his biggest problem for now. As soon as he changed back into uniform, he'd hit the radio. Car 300 to dispatch, en route to the ER at UNMC. He'd call in a description of the GTO.

Nothing in progress, no reason for other units to respond to the apartment. The thought of leaving the apartment in its current state kicked his stress levels into high gear, but he didn't have time to deal with it now.

He'd have to come back. First thing in the morning, after finishing his shift. In broad daylight.

First things first.

On the third-floor landing, he sorted through keys until he found the one that opened the back door.

---

Gwen Mullen hadn't entertained the possibility that she'd snapped until her dead boyfriend came home.

Seeing him felt like a punch in the chest. She understood that her mind was tricking her, but just for an instant, there he was. Looking like a sexy redneck. Like nothing had happened.

"Gwen," he said, shattering the illusion.

She looked up into Matthew's troubled eyes, feeling overwhelmed, flooded with relief and disappointment both. For the past hour, waiting alone in the empty apartment, she hadn't been able to decide what she was feeling. Everything had changed.

"I'm going to change back into my gear," he said. "And then we'll go. Okay?"

"I wasn't asking you for this," she said. It was the truth. "I would never ask you to do this."

He touched her face. The warmth of his hand felt comforting. "We're going to fix it."

She took a breath.

"I'll just be a minute. Okay?"

Gwen felt herself nod.

She'd already decided that she didn't like seeing Matthew wearing Russell's clothes.

# 5

Little by little, cold morning light filtered up from the east, slowly revealing a gray slab sky.

Worth stopped by the SaveMore in his street clothes after coming off shift. He found Sorensen in the office doing paperwork; his own hand still ached from filling out the reports on Gwen. He was bone tired, and he had a hard bright headache. He didn't feel like talking to anybody.

But he tapped the open door with a knuckle. "Morning."

Sorensen raised his head. The night man didn't look so fresh himself. Seeing Worth in the doorway, he took off his glasses, rubbed his eyes, and said, "How is she?"

Worth told him the truth. "It could be worse."

He wanted to take a seat but he was afraid he wouldn't be able to stand up again. He'd never felt so thoroughly drained. Every part of him seemed heavy.

"Does she have a place to go?" Sorensen settled his glasses back onto the bridge of his nose. "I know she doesn't get along with her family."

"She's in the hospital," Worth told him. "For now."

"The hospital?"

"Clarkson UNMC," Worth said. Right up the street. "When I left the ER, they were talking about keeping her a day or two."

According to Gwen, the last beating had come more than twenty-four hours ago. According to the resident on duty, she was still urinating blood. Worth didn't mention that to Sorensen.

He didn't mention any number of things. He only said, "I've seen it worse."

Sorensen clicked his pen. He didn't seem satisfied, but Worth didn't have anything else for him. "That's the status at this point. I thought you'd like to know."

"Yes," Sorensen said. "Thank you. I do appreciate it." He paused a moment, then added, "What about the . . . person who put her in the hospital?"

"We're looking for him."

"I hope you find him."

Worth felt a quick slither in his gut. "I hope so, too."

After another pause, Sorensen went back to the inch-thick blue-bar printout on the desk in front of him. "I hope you accidentally put *him* in the hospital."

Worth couldn't think of anything to say to that.

Eyes on his inventory sheets, pen making tick marks again, Sorensen said, "I'll have Floral send her a basket. From everybody."

Worth told him that sounded like a nice idea. Before walking out he kicked in a ten-dollar bill.

Down below, the SaveMore was jumping. Even for a Saturday morning, the place was a zoo. Customers clogged the aisles, wrangling carts, loading up on food and batteries, decimating the big new display of ice melt up front. Worth hadn't caught the new weather predictions until he heard the guys talking in the locker room back at Deer Park.

A forty-percent chance for novelty flurries had become a national winter weather advisory overnight. Whiteout country from the Rockies to the Mississippi, and outside the leaves were still changing color. The whole town was scrambling. Battening the hatches.

Worth felt disconnected from all of it.

It had become a small pleasure, stopping by the store on his way home in the morning after work. The elaborate new HyVee on Center was closer, and there was a No Frills a block from the station house.

But he liked coming back to the SaveMore, off duty, in his own vehicle and clothes. Replenish the staples, pick up something for dinner later. It made him feel like anybody else.

This morning he only wanted out of there. Worth grabbed a basket from the first stack he passed and took a quick spin through Aisle 9. Cleaning products. Your sprays, your powders. Your bleach.

He picked up a little of everything he could use. Then he scanned the front and picked out a checker he'd never seen before.

On the way up, he saw a two-for-one special on heavy rubber dish gloves. Worth stopped and threw those in, too.

---

Tony Briggs kept an eye on the stairwell while Ray Salcedo picked the dead bolt and carded the latch.

The address they'd been given had brought them here: a crumbling, mossy brick three-flat off Jackson. The building had probably been a decent little property once, but decent had come and gone a while ago.

They'd cased the place before entering and hadn't seen a sign of life in half an hour. No sounds coming through the doors inside the building, either. No televisions, morning coughs, fights, flushing toilets. Just a dusty warped staircase that groaned beneath them like it might collapse anytime.

Tony didn't even know why he was standing around, looking out. If anybody came up, they'd hear it.

"There it is," Ray said.

He opened the door and went in. Tony followed, closed the door behind them, and threw the bolt again. Ray went on through the entryway, into the stuffy living room.

"Man. What a dump. Your uncle must not pay shit."

"He pays *in* shit, the way that stairwell smells."

"You could fix a place like this up, though." Ray ran a finger along the edge of a door frame. "All this woodwork. Built-in bookcases, hardwood floors? That's leaded glass, too. You could fix this up."

"In this neighborhood?" Tony snorted. "Why?"

"You think like a yuppie."

"You dress like one."

Ray jerked a thumb toward the television sitting on milk crates between the main windows. "Think your uncle knows about that?"

"Hey," Tony said. Besides the big, ugly plastic Halloween pumpkin in the corner, the television was the first thing you saw coming in. Tony walked around the coffee table to take a closer look. "That's the same as mine."

"Yeah?"

"Yeah, man. Samsung. High-def. Eddie gave it to me for Christmas last year."

Ray Salcedo started chuckling.

"Son of a bitch," Tony Briggs said. The slick bastard had probably fudged an invoice or something.

"Your uncle gave you a hot TV," Ray said. He was laughing now. "I love it."

"Man, who cares about that? This has to be a fifty-incher."

"So?"

"That son of a bitch only gave me a forty-two."

Ray Salcedo laughed even harder. He actually dabbed at his eyes.

"Think that's pretty funny?"

"Man, check the phone." Ray headed across the creaky bare floor toward the hallway to the back, unzipping his black leather jacket, the whole time still chuckling to himself. "I'll go see if there's anything left in the closets."

Tony took a last look at the Samsung. He finally turned the bill of his cap around backward and went to work, thinking: *That shit is irksome.*

The phone sat atop one of the built-in bookcases Ray thought were so cool. They went about rib-high and divided the main room from a smaller dining area that led back to the kitchen. There were schoolbooks and papers stacked on one shelf, old issues of *Entertainment Weekly* on another. A few picture frames, a couple half-dead plants, a half-burned candle. Nothing much there, but nothing looked missing.

He paged through the screen on the base unit of the phone, wrote down the last five outgoing numbers and the last five coming in. He was just about to play the messages when he heard Salcedo's voice from down the hall.

"Ho, baby."

"What's up?"

"Dude."

Tony headed that way, past the tiny bathroom, to the doorway at the end of the short hall. Ray stepped aside for him.

"Holy shit."

The top half of the bed looked like a used maxi pad. Tony scanned the small room. He saw a glass lamp on the floor, tucked away in a corner. It looked like it had been dipped in a bucket of blood.

Ray said, "Thoughts?"

"Just out of curiosity," Tony said, "what's that closet look like?"

Ray wedged past, around the end of the bed, and pulled open the slatted folding doors. There was a bar full of clothes still on hangers. Shoes piled up in the bottom. A half-zipped suitcase spilling underwear shoved up against the back.

Ray pulled the sleeves of his turtleneck sweater past his cuffs. He used them to pull the doors shut again, then wiped off the knobs.

Tony said, "The fuck you figure happened here?"

Before Ray Salcedo could respond, they both heard the sound of a key sliding into the dead bolt on the front door.

"Shit," Tony said.

They looked at each other. Ray moved first.

Tony followed his lead, back down the hall, both of them pigeon-stepping past the ugly pumpkin, through the gap in the bookcases, toward the doorway on the other side of the dining space.

A short, cramped pantry led to a kitchen the size of a postage stamp. Ray was slipping out the back door to the fire escape just as the front door rattled open behind them.

Tony Briggs followed right on his heels. They made the landing outside; Tony eased the back door shut without clicking the latch. They each took a side, backs up against the cold brick, breath billowing in the frosty morning air.

"Now what?" Ray whispered.

Tony put a finger to his lips.

The door had a window. From his angle, he had a sliver of a sight line through the curtain still rippling on the inside.

Footsteps. Creaking boards. In a minute, a guy in jeans and a brown suede jacket appeared in the kitchen. Tony couldn't quite catch his face.

The guy dropped two bulging plastic sacks on the counter. Tony saw a spray nozzle poking from the top of one of the sacks. He saw a white bottle with a blue cap.

The guy knelt and pulled a roll of garbage bags out from under the sink. Then he stood and grabbed the sacks from the counter. Headed back the other way.

Ray motioned with his hand. *What's happening?*

Tony ducked under the window, tiptoed over to Ray's side, and whispered, "I think the janitor's here."

"How do you want to play it?"

"I dunno. You?"

"It's your uncle, man."

"Shit," Tony said. "Let's bust in. Shock and awe his ass." He paused, thought about it, and said, "Shit."

He tilted his head toward the stairs and took the lead. Together, they made their way as quietly as they could down the rickety fire escape to the parking lot below.

On their way toward the nearest corner of the building, Ray glanced back the other direction and said, "That Ranger wasn't there before."

He was right. Dark red Ford, engine still ticking under the hood. Without speaking, they reversed course, went over.

Nebraska plates. Tony wrote down the tag number.

Ray went around to the passenger door. He jiggled the handle. Tony took a look around in the empty bed. Ray went around the front and said, "Hey."

Tony looked over his shoulder, then right and left. He headed over.

"Whatcha got?"

Salcedo pointed, and Tony saw what he was talking about.

Inside bottom of the windshield on the passenger side: one of those plastic contact decals. Blue circle with a buffalo head on a red center.

Omaha Police Union, Local 101.

He looked at Ray and said, "The cleanup guy's a cop?"

They sat around the corner in Ray's Expedition for a solid three hours, watching the trashy lot behind the building. No vehicles came in or went out. Just the Ranger and a rusty little Tercel that had been there all morning. Tony had already written down both tag numbers.

Other cars drove by. Leaves blew along the sidewalks. Eleven o'clock on a Saturday morning, and the whole street was like a ghost town.

This was bullshit. By the time anything happened, Tony Briggs was cold and ready for a cheeseburger and about bored out of his skull.

"Here we go," Ray said.

Down the fire escape came a guy hauling a load of bulging garbage bags over his shoulder. White, mid-thirties, dark hair. He went maybe five ten, one seventy-five. Same brown jacket Tony had seen before.

The guy looked all around, then headed across the lot toward the Ranger. He tossed the bags in the bed and got in behind the wheel. The reverse lights came on. Exhaust rolled from the pipes in a cloud.

"Finally," Tony said. "I'm about starved."

"Maybe he'll stop at McDonald's."

"I wanted Bronco's."

Ray started the Expedition. He waited for the Ranger to corner out of the alley onto Jackson, then pulled away from the curb and tailed along.

# 6

It was almost noon by the time Worth finally pulled into the detached garage behind his grandmother's little house on Martha Street.

In the adjacent stall, beneath a heavy blue tarp, sat a 1971 Pontiac GTO, the owner's garbage-bagged, rug-rolled corpse still in the trunk.

He knew what was waiting for him and still it seemed like a surprise. Worth grabbed his bag from the passenger seat, thumbed the button clipped to the visor, and got out of the truck. The garage door lowered behind him, grinding and banging in its track, slowly cutting off the outside light.

In the dimness, dust-flecked slivers of daylight slipped in around the edges of the black landscaping fabric he'd put over the windows a few hours earlier. Worth grabbed the claw hammer from its spot on the pegboard and went around pounding in more tacks.

Strategy.

He couldn't risk getting caught in any kind of weather

with the idiotic street-drag tires on the GTO. Worth didn't want to take the car out before dark. But if he waited, and the snow came like they said, he and his new buddy Russell could wind up with trouble.

He wanted to sleep so badly it hurt. The headache was worse, and he couldn't seem to concentrate. Stress. Mental exhaustion. Worth knew the signs. People made mistakes if they weren't careful.

Tools caught his eye.

When he finished squaring up the windows, Worth traded the hammer for a ten-pound sledge. He grabbed a corner of the tarp and peeled it away from the back end of the goat, just to see.

There was a decal on the trunk lid, same as the ones behind both front wheels, all of which he'd noted in his report. Two words in wavy cartoon letters: *The Judge.*

Standing there, feet spaced, balancing the weight of the sledgehammer in his hands, Worth saw a liquid reflection of himself in the car's gleaming black finish. He heard Dr. Grail's voice in his head: *Tell me what you see.*

A dozen stiff jabs and one passing swing with the sledge knocked the spoiler off the back end in a loud clatter. Worth stopped and picked the splintered fin up off the cold concrete. He tossed it in the backseat, next to the spare tire he'd had to remove from the trunk to make room for Russell.

His stomach rumbled. He looked at his watch. He looked at the car, pondering decals. Trunk lid, front quarter panels, matching accent stripes over all four wheels: instant identification.

Worth leaned against the handle of the sledgehammer, thinking it through. He tried to remember where he'd put the heat gun he'd bought that time the gutters froze.

He tried to focus, jumping inside his own skin at the sudden sharp rap at the side door.

# 7

"Matthew?"

He stood still, brain seizing.

"Hey." The knock came louder. "Open up, it's me."

When the doorknob twisted, Worth lurched from his spot. The sledgehammer's handle slapped the concrete behind him, sharp and startling. He made the door just as Sondra poked her head inside.

"Are you—"

"Oh," he said, backing her up, stepping on her feet. "Hey."

"Jesus, let me get out of the way."

Worth turned his back as he pushed across the threshold, boxing her out. He pulled the door shut behind him, feeling a snag at the pocket of his jacket.

"Ow!"

*You didn't lock it.* Twenty minutes he'd spent covering all the windows, imagining remote possibilities, and he hadn't locked the goddamned door.

Mistakes.

Sondra wore a pained wince. She hiked a brown leather sling purse up on her shoulder, sucking the tip of her left thumb.

"What's wrong?" He could hear his voice. Too urgent.

She gave him an exasperated look. "You bent my nail back."

"Are you okay?"

"I think it's still attached." Sondra glanced at her thumbnail. Coffee-colored polish, freshly chipped. "Damn."

"Let me see."

She shook her hand, already over it. "It's not even bleeding. What's with you?"

Worth took a breath. "Sorry. Long shift."

"You're just coming off now?" She checked her watch. "I thought you'd be asleep already."

*Then what the hell are you doing here?* Worth thought, but he let it go. Even in the midst of ball-squeezing panic, seeing her brought a small sad tingle.

Sondra looked terrific. Snug jeans, a fitted sheepskin jacket that stopped at her waist. Her hair was longer than he'd seen her wear it, loose cinnamon curls nearly touching the wool collar of the coat. Lips the same shade as her fingernails. Her pale skin always flushed in the cold.

"I didn't know you were coming over," he said.

"Hello to you, too. I rang at the house, then I heard all the racket out here." She looked beyond his shoulder. "What are you doing in there, building something?"

"Car trouble," he said.

She tried a smile. "Maybe if you pounded on it some more."

Worth became conscious of his hands, suddenly jittery,

adrenaline tremors creeping along his fingers. He shoved them in his jacket pockets. "What's up?"

Her smile became an expression he didn't know how to interpret.

"It's freezing out here," she said. "Can we go inside?"

She'd met with the Realtor an hour ago.

For some reason it was imperative that she stop by, unannounced, knowing his schedule, to accomplish what on any other day they'd handle by answering machine.

Worth could feel himself cratering. He'd been on autopilot for hours, and now he was running on fumes. Impatient, mind still in the garage, he fried two eggs and a slab of ham at the stove while she ran the deal points down for him.

"We can close next week," she said.

"Okay."

"You're fine with the offer? We can counter."

"Yeah."

"I think I'll take my pants off."

When he realized that a long silence had passed, Worth looked toward the kitchen table. "What?"

"Jesus," she said. "You're on Pluto. Are you okay or what?"

"I told you, I'm fine." He glanced through a gap in the curtains above the sink, toward the sky. "Just tired."

"That's the fourth time you've looked out the window. Who are you waiting for, anyway? Hot date?"

"Just the snow."

"Well, I'm not staying long," she said. "You could at least pretend to listen."

Worth sighed. He snapped off the burner, slid his breakfast onto a plate, and sat down at the table across from her. "Okay? I'm listening."

"Never mind." Sondra reached for her purse. "I'll just call you later."

"Jesus, sweetie. Give me a break."

The endearment hung in the air between them, awkward. *Sweetie.* Still automatic.

"I just thought . . ." She dropped the purse strap, slumped against the back of the chair. "It's such a gorgeous house. I don't know."

Worth didn't know, either. He started eating. What did she want him to add?

They'd wanted a place with some character, in one of the neighborhoods, near a decent school. Her parents had helped them with the down payment on a drafty foursquare in Dundee—a beautiful fixer-upper with more space than they'd needed, a price they couldn't pass up, and a mortgage they could just afford.

Sondra had stayed there alone through the separation, even after the divorce. For a while, Worth had deluded himself into taking that as some sort of hopeful sign.

"I mean, whatever," she said. "It's still our home."

"It's our house," he said.

"Matthew, don't say that."

"What do you want me to say?"

Last month, she'd moved into some cookie-cutter minimansion with Vargas, out in Pepperwood. *I thought you never wanted to live west of Seventy-second street,* Worth had said. She'd just sighed into the phone like she was tired. *We thought all kinds of things.*

He'd been living here, in the house on Martha.

Renters had trashed the place, and it had sat vacant most of the winter. Those first weeks, Worth occupied himself hauling out carpet soaked with cat piss, scrubbing mold and nicotine from the walls, fixing what was broken or throwing it out. Midsummer, he'd spent his one-week duty suspension replacing the old fuse box with a new breaker panel, pulling all the old wiring, fishing grounded Romex to every room.

It hadn't ever been much. A little cross-gabled Cape Cod: eight hundred square feet with a half-story attic, an unfinished basement, one small bathroom on the main floor. But it sat on a nice corner lot with big old trees and lots of yard. This spring, his grandmother's flower beds still bloomed through the weeds.

Sondra watched him wolf down the last of the eggs, polish off a glass of milk. The food only made him hungrier.

Just as he pushed away, heading back to the counter for seconds, she reached across the table. In the dry air, a light snap of static electricity nipped his wrist where she touched him.

"It's been a year," she said. "Are we really still enemies?"

A year. "It's been nine months. And I've never been your enemy."

He took his plate and went back to the stove. When he looked back and saw her expression, something wilted in his chest.

As much as he'd wanted to imagine otherwise, there was no denying the obvious: The divorce had been like medicine for her. Fresh in from the cold, Sondra looked like a summer morning. It was the first time they'd talked face to face in two months, and she looked ten years younger.

As a matter of fact, she looked radiant.

It took him just that long to put it together. And then he understood. He didn't know how he knew it with such certainty, but he knew it. Sondra wasn't here about the house at all.

"You're pregnant," he said.

He hadn't intended to say it out loud. The words fell out of him. Sondra looked up, eyes suddenly glassy. Worth stood at the counter, skillet in hand, stove burner glowing hot behind him.

"Really?"

She nodded.

"Wow."

"Mark and I are getting married," she said. Her voice gained a quiver, but she took a breath and laid it out. "Tahoe. In January, New Year's Day. We just found out about the baby. We weren't even going to start trying until after the wedding."

Tahoe. Mark. The baby.

"Congratulations," he said.

"You don't have to say that. I know you don't mean it. I just needed to tell you, and I've been trying to decide how, and there's no good way."

Worth only heard bits and pieces. *The baby.* He couldn't get past the words. Five years, they'd knocked themselves out: doctors, money, strain, exhaustion. Quiet defeat. Vargas got it done without even trying.

"I got up this morning sick as a dog," she said. "And then I had the appointment with the agent, and . . . I don't know. Everything just seemed to crash together. I felt like I couldn't let another day go by."

You wouldn't have known she was crying by her voice.

Just a clear tear or two, caught in her eyelashes, the faint blush at the tip of her nose that meant either she'd been crying or she'd had a glass of red wine. Worth thought of Sondra sitting at this same table the day of Kelly's funeral; she'd cried then, too. These were different tears entirely.

"I'm not asking you to be happy for . . . me." *Happy for us.* She'd edited herself just before saying it. "I know I can't ask you that. But I needed you to know. I'm sorry for just showing up like this. It's not really fair."

"Don't apologize."

"I know it's not fair."

"It's not your fault," he heard himself say. "You deserve to be happy."

Sondra made a quiet sound.

When he looked, she was up from her chair, halfway around the table. At the stove, she took his face in her hands and looked in his eyes.

She kissed him. One good kiss, warm and full. When it was over, she put her damp salty cheek next to his.

"Even if you're lying," she said, "I love you for saying that."

Without thinking about it, he put his arms around her. She let him draw her in, and they stood there awhile. Worth could feel the faint flutter of her heart beating. He imagined he could feel an extra pulse of warmth where her flat belly pressed against his belt line. It was the first tender moment between them in as long as he could remember, and every second of it broke his heart.

Eventually, Sondra leaned back and said, "You smell like Clorox."

"Yeah?" For a few minutes he'd actually forgotten what he'd been doing all morning.

They agreed it must be the pregnancy. She claimed she'd been walking around smelling all kinds of things that weren't really there.

---

The mystery woman came out the front door of the little house about forty minutes after they'd both gone in the back together.

Sexy little thing. Tight jeans, high-heel boots, great hair. Cute little jacket, wool trim. All warm and toasty.

"She is fine," Ray Salcedo said, watching her cross the street.

"That's called a shearling jacket."

"Huh?"

"That coat she's wearing," Tony said. He'd been paging through the clothing catalog he'd found on the floor of Ray's SUV. He pointed to the picture. "Shearling. Bet you didn't know that."

"You're gay."

"It's your catalog."

They watched. She tossed some hair back, dug in the purse on her shoulder, came out with a set of keys. A point, a click, and she got into the silver Land Rover parked along the opposite curb. She buckled her seat belt.

"Good girl," Ray said. "Safety first."

Tony wrote down the plate number beneath the house number. To keep it straight, he scribbled *(babe in land rover).*

She sat behind the wheel for a moment, doing nothing. The side windows of the Rover had a smoky tint, but from their angle, they had a partial view through the windshield.

She put her hands over her face. After a bit, her head and shoulders began to bounce. Just a little.

"Awww," Tony said. "There, there."

"Hey, girl. Why so sad?"

Tony glanced back at the house and said, "Damn. Guess our boy's got some game."

The mystery woman sat like that for a minute or so. Then she finally straightened up and rubbed her eyes. She leaned over, came up with a tissue, and blew her nose.

As soon as she was finished, she started the Rover and pulled away.

"Shit," Ray said, slouching down in the seat.

Tony pulled his cap low and did the same.

At the stop sign, she turned right and drove past them, steering with one hand, still wiping at her eyes with the other.

"So, what," Ray said. "You want to sit on the house, or find out where that one's heading?"

Tony thought about it. The mystery woman was probably nothing. The way it looked, their boy had sent her packing. This was a guy who had things to do.

On the other hand, who the hell knew what was what? The more they knew, the better.

Then again . . .

"She's turning."

"Shit, I dunno. What do you think?"

"It's your uncle."

*Fuck it.* Tony nodded up the street. "We know where the janitor lives. Follow the babe in the Land Rover."

An hour before dusk, the first trace of sleet began to patter against the windows like fine white sand.

Worth finished cleaning up in the basement and laid everything out on an old towel to dry. He grabbed a shower and another plate of eggs and headed back out to the garage.

He pulled all the masking tape, the newspaper with it, and shoved the whole wad into a garbage bag. He turned off the space heater and the fans and gathered up the half acre's worth of drop cloths he'd used to line the garage. He left the blue tarp draped over the Ranger.

In the adjacent stall sat a 1971 Pontiac GTO, minus a spoiler, clad now in a tacky coat of American Home Interior Satin. Tawny Barnwood, Prairie Earth Collection.

Worth went to the workbench where he'd left the inventory of items he'd collected from the interior of the car. Title and registration. A fat padded folio of CDs. A loaded .38 revolver, a sleeve of unopened rubbers. A handheld Bearcat police scanner. Half a pack of Dentyne.

He put everything but the radio scanner and the pistol into a zippered kit bag, shoved the bag back under the seat.

Outside, the temperature had dropped. The wind had picked up, and the sleet grew coarse. Worth checked across the street and stepped back into the garage.

He used his cell phone to call the number he'd copied from the phone book inside the house; after a few rings a voice answered, thick with sleep.

"Yeah."

Worth said, "Ricky?"

"Curtis." A yawn. "What?"

"This is Matt Worth."

"Who?"

"Officer Worth. From the store."

"Oh." Another yawn. "Um, hey man. Shit. We late for work? What time . . . hey. It's snowing."

"Curtis, do me a favor, okay?"

"What's up?"

"I want you to call this number. Got a pen?"

"Pen. Hang on." Silence. Rustling. Footsteps thudding away, thudding back. "Yeah, go."

Worth read him the other number he'd written down inside the house. "Ask for somebody and play dumb for a couple minutes. Figure out you dialed the wrong number by mistake, but take your time about it. Okay?"

"Who do I ask for?"

"Doesn't matter. Just pick a name and burn a couple minutes."

"Yeah, I got it. How come?"

"Just playing a joke on a buddy," Worth said. "Omaha PD thanks you for your cooperation."

"Whatever you say." Curtis paused. "Hey?"

"Yeah."

"We heard Gwen was in the hospital."

"She is."

More silence. Worth looked at his watch, already spending more time on this call than he'd intended.

"Hurt her pretty bad this time, huh?"

"Bad enough."

Curtis sighed into the phone. "Ricky wants to go kick the holy shit outta that fucker."

"I didn't hear you say that."

"Maybe polish that car he drives with a brick."

Worth glanced at the freshly spray-painted trunk of the GTO. He was beginning to feel queasy now. The second round of eggs wasn't sitting well. He could hear the patter of sleet on the roof, clicking against the east windows.

"Probably best if you let us handle it," he said. "Listen, Curtis, I'll fill you guys in later. Promise. Can you help me out?"

"Right, operation crank call. Forgot."

"Just keep the line busy a couple minutes."

"Play dumb," Curtis said. "No prob."

Back outside, hands in his pockets, sleet stinging his cheeks, Worth squinted toward the house on the corner lot across the street. John Pospisil. Good guy, a fellow in divorce, laid up at home after a nasty fall. John was the only neighbor with a clear view of Worth's garage; he'd been standing on the front porch in his quilted flannel overshirt for a half hour, leaning on one crutch, drinking a beer and watching the sky.

He saw Worth and raised a hand. Worth waved back.

John looked at the sky, shrugged. *Nebraska weather, right?* Just then he cocked his head and listened.

His shoulders seemed to sag. In a moment he waved again, turned, and hobbled into the house. It looked like slow going. Hard to manage the screen door. Worth hated to do it to the guy.

He hustled into the garage, hit the button. The door opened slowly, hauling in a swirl of sleet.

He forgot to grab the remote from the visor of the pickup to close the door again behind him. He had to go back and get it. Fifteen seconds wasted.

Little mistakes.

He backed the GTO out of the garage, into the turn-around, and scooted down the narrow driveway to the street. Sleet scoured the roof of the car, filling the interior with soft white noise.

Worth checked both ways and headed south, past John Pospisil's empty porch, palms slick on the icy wheel. His pulse thudded in his neck, receding gradually as he pulled out of view.

At the end of the street he turned west, then south toward the interstate, the first crackle of chatter from Russell's cop scanner emerging from the steady whisper of flash-frozen rain.

---

"Hello?"

"Is Scotty there?"

John Pospisil sighed. All the way in he'd come, thinking it would be his son or daughter calling, checking on him.

They got nervous if he didn't answer. Liz especially.

She'd pack up the kids and drive all the way up from Plattsmouth if he let the phone ring more than five or six times.

"I think you have the wrong number," he said.

"Oh. This isn't 555-0102?"

"Nope, sorry. This is 555-0120."

"Hey, no, I'm sorry. I must have mixed up the numbers."

"That's okay. Happens all the time. Bye, now."

"Um . . . wait a second. Hello?"

John sighed again and hopped on his left foot, wedging the crutch under him a little better. He needed to remember to carry the cordless around with him. Especially outside.

Though the way his leg was yelling at him, maybe he didn't need to be going outside anyway. He got so that he felt so cooped up in the house that some days anything seemed worth a gulp of fresh air. But one step out the door, and the icy air slipped right through the cracks in his bones. It felt like somebody working on his leg from ankle to hip with a hammer drill.

"Sir? Hello?"

"Yes?"

"You said this is what number?"

"Five-five-five," John said slowly, "oh-one-two-oh."

"And Scotty isn't there? Scotty Sullivan."

Jesus. He needed three Vicodins, a shot of Jack, and a long nap. "I'm sorry, son. Try it again."

Outside, John heard a rumbling engine. He moved the curtains and saw a curious sight.

Across the street, at Helen's place, a car backed out of the garage. Sixties Camaro, or something along those lines. Sort of an odd, puke-tan color. A back end that looked . . . wrong. John couldn't quite put his finger on it.

He suddenly felt all muddle-headed. Something about the car seemed familiar and off-kilter at the same time. He could see Matt Worth's pickup covered up in the other stall, a bright blue tarp showing through the sleet.

The garage door came down.

"Five-five-five," the voice in his ear repeated, "oh-one-oh-two."

"Zero-one-two-zero," John said, struggling with his temper now. "Son, change the last two numbers around and try it again. I've got to go. You take care."

He hung up the phone and watched the car pull away down the street, thinking *Goddamn sleeping pills.*

# 9

Junk Monkey Scrap and Salvage sat across the river, an hour northeast into Iowa, bunkered among the tall wooded bluffs overlooking the spine of the Lewis and Clark Trail.

The weather let him go at the river. Even with the improved visibility, Worth doubted he'd have found the place in the dark if the directions he'd been given hadn't held up.

Eight miles down a winding road tunneled over by gnarly burr oaks, he marked the turnoff in his high beams: a pair of tires bolted to fence posts on either side of a long rock driveway. On each tire, runny hand-sprayed letters spelled the words JUNK MONKEY in reflective white paint.

The driveway followed the curve of a dry creek bed, then up a small rise, to a three-story farmhouse surrounded by various outbuildings. From the slight elevation, Worth could see jagged shadows of the scrap yard in the clearing, spreading back to the trees. Yellow light spilled from the open entrance of the largest of the buildings, a corrugated machine shed down the slope from the house.

Worth took a fork in the driveway and followed it down the hill, rocks crunching beneath the tires.

As he rolled up to the machine shed, a burly silhouette appeared at the edge of the big bay door. Thick shoulders, shaggy hair and beard, heavy Carhartt coveralls stained with grease. The man raised an arm, shielding his eyes from the glare of the GTO's headlights. Worth braked to a stop, idling in the pond of light from inside the building.

The guy gave the car a long once-over.

When he finally stood aside, Worth pulled in, off the rock and up onto smooth concrete. The sound of the engine changed pitch as he entered the shed, doubling back on itself, gaining an echo in the hangar-size space.

He parked behind a super-duty pickup, a snow blade braced up on jacks. The bay door closed behind him, a cavernous rumble that drowned out the growl of the GTO.

As he cut the motor, it was as if a cinch strap loosened. Neck, shoulders, hands—all suddenly ached with relief, as though he'd carried the car here on his back.

But he was here.

And now there was that. Worth killed the lights, took a breath, and got out of the car.

"You found the place."

If they'd seen each other on the street, Worth wasn't sure he'd have known him.

"Vince," he said. What else? Nice to see you? How have you been? "You look like Charles Manson."

Vince Worth, Jr., stood a few feet away, hands shoved

deep in the pockets of the Carhartts, expression hidden behind the overgrown shrub of beard.

Matthew said, "How's Rita?"

"In Phoenix," Vince said. He looked past him, toward the GTO.

The quick-and-dirty paint job had taken a beating on the way out of town. The sleet had scoured the front end back to the air intakes on the hood, leaving the car with tattered hide and a slick black snout.

But the half-assed camouflage had served its purpose. It had gotten him here—out beyond the storm, across the state line, past two Iowa state troopers, and into the hills, miles and miles removed from Gwen Mullen and the scene of Russell's demise.

Vince said, "Bad goat, huh?"

*Christ,* Worth thought.

Just then realizing, after all the rigamarole, that he'd never once considered swapping out the personalized license tags on the goddamned car.

Vince Junior used his thumbnail to scrape soft paint away from the trunk lid, revealing the decal beneath. He opened the driver's door and poked his head inside. He grabbed a hook light and got down on a knee with a labored sigh, head disapearing beneath the undercarriage for a minute or two.

He eventually hauled himself back to his feet, nodding vaguely, as though everything checked out.

"Not custom," he said, answering questions Worth hadn't asked. " '71 Judge. Last year they offered the option."

"Vince—"

"Four hundred bucks got you the four-fifty-five high output, ram air hood, the suspension and wheels. Fin on the back, the decal set. Less than four hundred made. BadGoat here's got the original factory build sheet."

"Vince, forget about the car a minute."

"Guess it's sorta custom now," he said. "Where'd you find it?"

"That's what we need to talk about."

With that, Vince gave him his full attention. Worth didn't know quite what to do with it. He groped for a way to get this off the ground, finding that he had no idea how to explain himself to this grizzly, middle-aged ex-con.

He finally stepped to the car, keyed the lock, and popped the trunk lid. After a moment, Vince ambled around the back bumper, face still unreadable. A glowing industrial heater warmed the immediate area; Vince tugged the zipper of the coveralls to the waist as he moved, showing the cracked tongue and chapped red lips of an ancient Rolling Stones concert T-shirt beneath.

Standing in proximity, amid the shop smell of grease and gasoline, Worth caught a vague, not-unpleasant body odor—a day's work mingled with the cling of stale cigarettes, a hint of Old Spice, a thread of whiskey breath. It took a moment before he placed the strange familiarity: Vince smelled like Dad.

They stood together, looking into the open trunk of Russell James's one-in-four-hundred GTO. Worth's mind returned again to the muffled snap he'd felt, throwing his weight against the job, straining to cram the cumbersome roll into the space.

From where he stood now, the way the rug had ended

up in the trunk, bent at a sickening, lumpy angle, he could see into one end through the fringe. Gwen's cheap garbage bags hadn't held; in the overhead light he glimpsed a crown of dark sticky hair a few inches down. For some reason he flashed on the childbirth video he and Sondra once watched together, immediately wishing he could unthink the image. Or that he'd double-bagged.

"Guess now would be the part where you explain why you called."

When he looked up, he found Vince watching him, casual as a vacation day.

Worth forced himself to meet his eyes. "I need help, Junior."

"I got that," his oldest brother said. "Skip to the part about needing a goddamn incinerator."

# 10

When Worth was a kid, maybe seven years old, he'd jumped off the rail of the deck in back and taken a header into the concrete footing of the nearest clothesline pole.

He'd been trying to catch the crossbar, imagining a fluid, Spidey-style vault. Maybe landing somewhere over near the peony bushes in a precision crime-fighting crouch.

Primarily he'd been trying to impress Kelly, four years older, only that summer deemed old enough to stay home in charge. They'd been horsing around in the backyard, weekday bored, thinking up dumb little ways to outdo each other, not exactly keeping score. Worth hadn't known to start bawling until he'd seen the look of stricken panic on Kelly's face. Completely unaware, until that moment, of the blood pouring out of his own.

To this day, he had a clear memory of Vince showing up as if by magic, wading into the chaos, sorting them up and herding them both into the back of his dented Thunderbird. Two hours later, an ER nurse walked Matthew back out to the waiting chairs at UNMC with his first set of stitches: six tight black whiskers across the bottom of his chin.

He remembered Vince scruffing his head and telling him he looked like a tough guy. Matthew had smeared blood all over the seats getting in and out, but Vince hadn't seemed to care. On the way home, he'd stopped at the Goodrich on Saddle Creek and bought them all ice cream cones.

Thinking back, Worth guessed Vince must have been dropping in on Mom, knowing Dad rolled second shift, not knowing she'd taken a day job looking after Mrs. Stillmock up the street.

All he could say for sure was that it was the first time he could remember hearing his mother lie. She'd changed the names and times on the accident report she filed with the old man later, editing herself into the story, Vince out, describing their trip to the hospital down to a fabricated mix-up with the insurance card.

He and Kelly had listened through the air vent upstairs and gone to bed grateful for the fib.

Thirty years down the line, Mom and Kelly were gone. The old man might as well be. Junior was into his fifties by now. And Matthew still couldn't grow real whiskers over the scar he'd earned that day he'd opened his face in the backyard.

They loaded Russell James into the cargo bed of a mud-spattered GATOR 6X4. Worth had barely climbed in shotgun when Vince dropped the UTV into gear.

They headed out of the machine shed and out over bumpy ground. Worth bounced along, folding his arms against the cold, the main buildings receding behind them, the starless night growing darker all around.

A few hundred yards down the hill, Vince stopped at a padlocked gate and trudged into the beam of the headlights. He popped the lock, unwrapped the chain.

They rolled on, into the shadows of the scrap yard, through the weed-choked bones of junked cars. Vince steered the Gator along a bald winding track—through a huddle of eyeless schoolbuses, ranks of pastured farm machinery, great black mounds of old tires.

Soon they approached a clearing, where hulking silhouettes rose up from a rubble-ringed plain. A bulldozer. The elbowed boom of an excavator. A sprawling, belt-fed crushing machine.

Vince cut across, toward their destination, jostling over deep washboards in the cold, hardpacked dirt. Their load shimmied behind them, harnessed snug under bungee cords.

They arrived at a steel shed surrounded by bins and barrels. Worth saw the fat smokestack protruding from the roof of the shed and felt a salty twinge at the back of his throat.

Inside the shed, more bins. More barrels. In their midst loomed an iron stove the size of Worth's pickup truck.

It took about ten minutes. Vince fired up the incinerator, jerked the hatch open with a rusty screech, and wheeled a short steel trough to the lip. They unloaded Russell James and fed him to the furnace, carpet shroud and all.

After him, Worth swung in three garbage bags, all stuffed full of clothes, bedding, the sections of mattress he'd cut away, other odds and ends from Gwen's apartment. The lamp would have to go somewhere else. He assumed there was a compactor around here somewhere.

Vince wheeled the trough back against the far wall. He returned wearing a tattered, soot-caked oven mitt. He used his mitted hand to slam the incinerator door and set the handle with a hard downward yank.

They stood side by side then, neither speaking of what they'd just done, listening to the walls of the furnace begin to creak and ping.

After a while, Vince said, "Grocery patrol, huh?"

Worth hadn't made a whole background of it. "Long story."

"*That's* a long story." Vince chuckled but didn't seem amused. "Who else knows?"

"Who else knows what?"

"Whatever you and this girl have going."

"It's not like that," Worth said.

"No?"

"No."

Vince let it go. After another minute, he nodded toward the furnace. "What about him?"

"He did a job on her."

"You told me."

"Poor kid's still in the hospital," Worth said. "Doctor said she'll be lucky if she doesn't lose a kidney."

"You told me that, too." Vince leaned down and checked the door handle even though he'd already clamped it tight. The air had begun to carry the faint, acrid scent of burning wool. "I'm asking what you know about the guy."

"Mom and sister in Texas," Worth said. "No family in town. Minor-league record, mostly kid stuff. But he carries a four-hundred-dollar scanner and a snub thirty-eight."

"So?"

"So he's into something."

"Maybe he's into guns and listening to car races."

Worth didn't argue the point. "According to the victim's statement, he'd been drinking heavily over an extended period. When he fell asleep, she escaped the dwelling. The suspect was gone on arrival."

"Simple, huh?"

There was still the mattress back at Gwen's apartment. Worth had cut out as much blood-soaked fabric and stuffing as he could, then flipped the mattress. It would pass for the moment, but he'd need to find a way to do better soon.

The car needed to disappear. But Vince could make the car disappear. He could spread it bolt by bolt all over the bluffs if it came to that. Once it was gone, it was gone.

That left only whatever remained in the incinerator tomorrow morning, and then there would be nothing.

Worth said, "That's the idea."

"And the first time this girl slips up?" Vince spoke like they were standing on the side of a road somewhere, a hood up, talking engine repair. "One person from that store remembers seeing you two making googly eyes at each other."

"I'm telling you it's not like that," Worth said. "There's nothing between me and the girl except my name on the reports."

For the first time since they'd unloaded the GTO, Vince looked at him. "So explain again why you decided to make it your fuckin' problem, Matty. Right? Because I'm seriously not getting it."

Worth didn't have an answer that sounded any good. So he said, "I just did."

He didn't even realize Vince had moved. One minute they were standing there, feeling the heat emanating from the furnace; the next something heavy landed against his head. A cotton thud rocked him off balance, jarring his brain against the walls of his skull. Light flashed, and his left ear went quiet.

Worth stuttered back a step, still reacting.

Vince lowered his hand. Still wearing the oven mitt.

"That's for making it my problem."

"Jesus." Worth covered his numb ear. The side of his face felt as though it were expanding; a buzzy hum echoed in the cup of his palm. He didn't know whether to chop the asshole in the neck or sit down and cry. "Feel better?"

Vince rolled his shoulders. He seemed to give it some thought.

"Little," he finally said. "Been so long since I hit a cop, I forgot how good it felt."

They met eyes, and in the soap-opera pause that followed, the entire situation seemed utterly ridiculous. Looking at Vince Junior—wild and woolly, standing there in his coveralls and oven mitt with the furnace knocking along behind him—Worth felt a tug around the corner of his mouth. A maddening, involuntary twitch.

It was the stress, Worth knew. Just the stress of the past twenty hours, looking for a valve. Still. They'd just put a twenty-five-year-old kid in a garbage incinerator, and he couldn't think of one funny thing about it.

Neither could Vince. A grin wriggled in his beard; he

coughed and ground it out with a knuckle. They looked away from each other, breaking the connection, neither of them saying a word.

Eventually, Vince sighed heavily, put his hands on his hips, and shook his head. A guy standing over a mutt dog tangled up in its own leash.

"Let me guess," he said. "You need a ride home, too."

There wasn't much more to it.

Back in the machine shed, Worth stashed the Judge under canvas while Vince finished mounting the snow-plow on the truck. The shop radio said the storm meant business. It was wading across the river now, gathering power.

But it hadn't reached them yet. They struck off in the big diesel quad cab, smoke still rising from the valley behind them, a gray column against the cold black sky.

# 11

"Hey, Sarge. How many years you been holding here?"

Sergeant Levon Williams leaned over the assembly room table, taking his time browsing the big box of Halloween cookies a lady from the Benson Citizens Coalition had dropped off for the B and C crews.

"Fifteen in January," he said, finally picking a smiley pumpkin with orange and black frosting. "Why?"

"You ever ride with Kelly Worth?"

"I was his training officer."

"No kidding?"

"No kidding. What made you ask?"

Tony Briggs shrugged and lied his ass off. "Some of the B guys were talking about him in the locker room. Guess it happened around this time of year?"

"November seven," Williams said. The sarge was pushing fifty but was still built hard; when he worked the heavy bag in the weight room, you could hear it all the way down in the showers. Briggs didn't know him well yet, but he didn't have any special plans to push the guy any farther than he had to.

Somebody said, "There's the anniversary memorial two weeks from Friday."

"Everybody should try and make that," Williams said. "Some of you knew him, and if you didn't, Kel Worth was good police."

Nods and murmers all around.

Briggs nodded along, thinking *Yeah, but not good enough, though.* The guy was a hero, okay, shit, nothing against him. As far as Tony Briggs was concerned, "hero" was a word you used at a dead cop's funeral.

Across the table, Ray Salcedo bit the head off a smiley ghost with white and black frosting. "Doesn't his brother roll with the Southeast?"

Briggs shrugged like he had no idea. Down the table, Carla Billup nodded. "Yeah, Matt, I think. Maybe it's Mike."

"I heard he was a screwup," Lyle Franklin said. "Yo, Briggs. Pass me one a them Frankensteins."

The chatter started then, everybody throwing in, telling what they'd heard or what they hadn't heard.

Tony Briggs still couldn't get over it. They'd run the plates on the Ranger this afternoon and come up with the name: Worth. Their very own hero cop's kid brother.

"Okay," Sergeant Williams said. He brushed cookie crumbs off the ends of his fingers and squared his shoulders. "Listen up. Streets are slick out there already, so first off, be rolling extra safe."

Around the table, everybody was decked out for the weather: long sleeves, tac sweaters, thermal unders, winter boots.

Tony felt like a little kid getting ready to go outside and build a snowman. He and Ray had worked the last four post periods undercover with the narco unit out of Central. Twenty-four months out of uniform. Right about now, he was wishing they were still kicking back in one of the low-rents on Park Ave., playing Xbox, instead of getting ready to roll out in this shit.

Williams said a bunch of stuff Briggs didn't hear, finally finishing up with "So stay on the radios and be keeping track of each other out there."

And that was that. They all filed out, everybody bullshitting. Tony and Ray stopped by the gear lockup for Tasers, DV bags, and a shotgun.

Salcedo had something to say. Tony could tell. He waited until they were outside, in the car, doors shut, before he said, "What's your deal?"

"You might like this."

Briggs clipped his cell phone to the visor and said, "Lay it on me."

"Ran that other address while you were in the john."

"Yeah?"

"Yep."

They'd followed the babe in the Land Rover all the way out past 156th Street, to an upscale house in shady Pepperwood that made their boy Worth's place look like a cardboard box.

The tags on the Land Rover went to a Sondra Worth. Five known addresses ago, her name had been Sondra Miller. Before roll call, they'd checked the first previous address on the list against the county assessor's database online.

Sure as hell. Matthew and Sondra Worth.

"So are you gonna tell me who owns the place, or do I have to give you my cookie?" Briggs had grabbed a smiley witch on the way out. Purple and black frosting. He'd already nibbled a little off the hat.

"According to Douglas County, it belongs to a Mark Vargas," Ray said.

Briggs knew the name, but he couldn't think why. He sat with it for a minute, and all at once it popped.

He looked over at Salcedo, who sat in the bucket seat, grinning. "You're shitting me."

Ray put his hand on his heart.

"There's gotta be twenty in the phone book."

"Checked it," Salcedo said. "Just found the one."

A gust of wind came around the back side of the Northeast Assembly building, rocking the unit on its suspension, throwing a handful of sleet against Ray's window.

Briggs started the car and turned on the defrost. The Mark Vargas they knew worked Homicide out of CIB. They'd run across him a couple times, most recently around the Orlando Heights shootings last year. A real hotshot.

"He's unlisted," Briggs said. "Couldn't be him."

Salcedo shrugged and said, "Few different ways we could find out." He held up a thumb to Billup and Franklin, who came out the back of the building and climbed into unit 237 beside them.

Briggs finished his cookie while they waited for the engine to warm up. In a minute, the air grew warm enough to clear the windshield without one of them having to get out and scrape. This was such bullshit. It wasn't even November yet.

"It just is not possible," Tony said, "that the cleanup

guy's wife is banging a homicide detective." He looked at Ray. "Is that even possible?"

Ray just chuckled. He keyed the radio and called them into service.

Briggs shook his head.

He licked a smear of frosting off his thumb, checked the mirrors, and put the unit in gear.

---

A little after nine o'clock, a woman named Patty came by the room. She smiled and said she was from Chapel Care.

"We've been so busy today," she said. "I'm sorry it took me so long to come see you."

"Oh," Gwen said. "I . . . that's okay."

It was quiet. The night nurse had just left, and visiting hours were over an hour ago. The television was muted. She felt loopy with painkillers.

Patty from Chapel Care wore a long-sleeved blouse with a floral print. She looked at one of her sticky notes. "Your name is Gwen?"

Gwen nodded, thinking: *God knows.* One of His people already had her name on a sticky note.

"My daughter's name is Gwen," Patty said. "I've always thought it was a beautiful name."

"Oh. Thank you."

"How are you feeling?"

The truth?

When it came to hitting, Russell had always known what he was doing. A few times had been worse than the others. Once, last year, it had been pretty bad. Bad enough that he'd actually begged forgiveness afterward. But it hadn't ever been like this.

"A little sore," Gwen said.

Patty offered a wince of empathy, nodding her head. "I accidentally overheard two of the nurses talking about your chart. I hope you don't mind."

"That's okay."

"Is there anything I can do for you?"

"Um . . . thanks," Gwen said. Feeling self-conscious now. Awkward. "But I guess I'm not really very religious."

Patty from Chapel Care smiled. "Don't worry, I'm not here to preach. We just like to stop by, let people know we're available. I'm a pretty good listener, if you need one."

Even with the painkillers, it still hurt to breathe. She'd told her story to police and doctors what seemed like a hundred times. The last thing she felt like doing was telling it again.

The fact was, she didn't remember much.

She remembered gathering up the courage to tell him she was leaving. She remembered when the beating stopped.

At some point, Russell had left the apartment. She remembered thinking now was her chance to get out of there, but not being able to get up from the bed. She remembered him coming back. Throwing her clothes into a suitcase.

*I'm taking a shower,* he'd said. *Get dressed. You're coming with me.*

He'd been convinced—again—that she was cheating on him. If she was leaving him, there must be somebody else. This time he knew for a fact that it was that cop from the store; he'd seen the way they'd looked at each other. She couldn't lie to him.

He had to go to Chicago for work. She was crazy if she thought he was leaving her alone this time.

She remembered how he smelled, fresh from the shower, when he'd lain down beside her on the bed. She remembered the last thing he'd said:

*Baby, I'm sorry. You know I can't live without you. I don't know what I'd do if you left.*

The next thing she remembered was walking into the bright light of the SaveMore.

The rest was a black spot. A twenty-four-hour hole in her mind.

It wasn't the first one.

She said, "How old is your daughter?"

Patty from Chapel Care smiled. "She'll be twelve next month. She's a pretty girl. Just like you."

Gwen shifted in the bed.

From the bed came a motorized hum, the feeling of movement beneath her. They were brand-new, one of the nurses had told her. Designed to automatically conform to your shape. Relieve the pressure points, provide the best long-term support for you, personally. Gwen thought she could stay right here forever.

"My mom's third husband started coming into my room when I was twelve," Gwen said. "She was sixteen when she had me. His name was Gary."

Patty from Chapel Care put fingers to her lips. She sighed and came closer to the bed. "Oh, honey."

"Know what my mom did when I finally told her?"

"What did she do?"

Gwen smiled. "She looked at me the same way you looked at me just now."

Patty from Chapel Care closed her mouth.

"Then she said it was my fault for walking around with my tail in the air."

"Oh, my word." Patty took a step back. "Honey, I didn't . . ."

"Thanks for the talk."

The woman hadn't deserved any of that. She was only trying to do her job. Gwen shifted positions and looked away.

The hospital bed hummed, shifting beneath her, stopping the moment it had her all figured out.

# 12

In the dream, everybody stood around in the kitchen of the little house on Martha Street. His grandparents were still alive. Mom was still alive. Kelly was alive, but nobody could find him.

Red light seeped in through the windows, tinting everything. Worth peeked around the edge of a curtain, squinting his eyes, and saw that somebody had built a SaveMore out back on the spot where the garage had been. The glow from the big sign flooded the yard.

For some reason, he knew Kelly was out there. He tried to speak up but couldn't.

Nobody noticed when he slipped away. He hurried across the lawn, ground soft under his feet, a thick damp carpet of grass that ended at the front entrance to the store.

The doors slid open for him. He went in.

The store was an empty echo inside. Bright hard light; soaring space. Up front, every check stand stood dark except one.

Gwen worked her way through a pile of groceries that

rose to the rafters in crooked joints, scanner beeping like a pulse in the towering silence. She saw him come in and gave him one of her smiles. For a minute Worth forgot what he was doing there.

Then she pointed toward the back and returned to work.

Somehow, he already knew his destination, but he didn't want to go there. He didn't want to go any farther into the store.

Somehow, he hadn't noticed that Gwen was almost absurdly pregnant; her belly was enormous, ten sizes too big for her body. Every time she scanned an item, she seemed to teeter in place like a grazed bowling pin.

He wanted to stay back and help her. Gwen no longer seemed to notice him.

Worth stood aside and watched himself from a distance. He watched himself follow the wide middle aisle, all the way to the meat department at the back of the store. He watched himself stop at the heavy door to the walk-in cooler. He watched himself grasp the handle and pull.

The door made a sucking sound. There came a rush of cold air, then a reeling sensation, and he returned to his body again.

Cloudy fluorescent tubes flickered on overhead as he pushed into the cooler, through the heavy plastic strips hanging beyond the door.

Shelves. Stacks of boxes. Piles of meat vaccuumed in blood-cushioned plastic.

A dark human shape occupied a grubby mattress in the far corner.

As Worth approached, Kelly propped himself up on an elbow, his face rising into the light.

*Matty.* He cracked a grin. *Hey.*

Cold as it was in there, Kelly wore only boxers and his summer duty shirt. His bare feet were caked with dried mud. The fluorescent light tinged his face blue.

*Been hoping I'd see you.*

Worth wanted to say something. He wanted to ask Kelly what the hell he was doing out here; he wanted to tell him everybody was worried. He just stood there, trying to find his voice.

A tube above his head sizzled, popped, went dark.

Kelly winked. *Can I show you something?*

Before Worth could stop him, Kelly rolled to the edge of the mattress and stood to his feet, moving strangely. His badge flopped facedown against his ribs, hanging from a torn flap of fabric by the pin.

He turned his back and began unbuttoning his shirt. He let the shirt fall.

Worth's heart sagged.

His brother's back was a boiling thunderhead. The worst of the bruises practically seeped blood. Matthew wanted to ask what had happened. He still couldn't make himself talk.

That was when Kelly looked back over his shoulder, eyes dull and milky, and Worth realized he wasn't looking at bruises.

It was livor mortis. Kelly was dead, and he'd been out here long enough for lividity to set in. All his blood had settled.

Kelly shook his head, still grinning. *Isn't that fucked up?*

Worth sat bolt upright in bed, disoriented, swimming in panic and relief, jolted from the dream by a roar and a crash and the sound of breaking glass.

# 2

# BAD GOAT

# 13

At some point Sunday morning, the local weather guys had all agreed to stop saying "blizzard" and start saying "hundred-year storm."

Tony Briggs hadn't lived a hundred years, so he had no opinion on that front. But it was a shitload of snow, no question.

Fifteen inches in midtown overnight. It had come down wet and heavy, settling like a soggy quilt over layers of sleet and ice. According to the weather guys, the teeth of the system had already reached Lake Michigan by the time it dragged its tail out of town a little before dawn, leaving splintered trees and half the city dark in its path.

From his apartment balcony, Tony could hear the buzz of chain saws up and down the street. Below, the pool area was a snow field.

The cold sun came off the white like a klieg light. Orange city snowplows had appeared, crawling around.

Tony went back inside. He stomped his cross-trainers

on the edge of the carpet and dialed Ray's apartment one floor up.

"You ready?"

Ray said, "Gimme ten."

Tony changed out of the warm-ups he'd worn down to the treadmill in the exercise room. He showered, then put on a pair of old jeans, dry wool socks, Eastlands, a Henley, and a heavy flannel shirt.

When Ray knocked, Tony opened up, looked his partner over, and shook his head.

"Jesus," he said. "You kill me."

"What'd I do?"

Slick shoes, pressed khakis, and a turtleneck sweater under a brown leather coat Tony hadn't seen before. Lambskin gloves.

"Nice scarf," Tony said.

"Thanks." Ray zipped up the coat. "Didn't I see you on a bottle of pancake syrup?"

"Man, all I'm gonna say is, we get stuck in a snowbank, I ain't the only one getting out to dig."

They rolled out in Ray's Expedition, following a plow all the way to 60th Street. They picked their way along after that, taking plowed streets where they could, avoiding the deep drifts where they couldn't.

"Christ," Tony said, surveying the damage all around.

Ray nodded up ahead. "Check that out."

A guy in a toboggan hat stood thigh-deep in snow. He was looking at his house, which sat half buried beneath an avalanche of jagged, leafy limbs. The big tree in the front yard looked like a fat wrist with broken fingers, nothing but a broad gap of blue where its canopy had been.

"That right there," Tony said. "See that? That right there is why you rent."

It was the same all over the place. Broken branches everywhere: sticking out of roofs, blockading streets. They'd had a dry summer, the news guy had said, and most of the trees still hadn't lost their leaves; the added weight of the ice and snow had snapped limbs big around as Tony's waist like they were pencils. The remains of stately old trees jutted up from the snow like compound fractures, splintered ends poking at the sky.

"I mean, Jesus," Tony said. He'd figured it was bad to make CNN already, but this was nuts. "It's like an F-5 went through here."

"Too bad we couldn't just call your uncle on the phone," Ray said. He braked to a halt in the middle of Dodge Street; the truck rattled as the antilock brakes grabbed at a slick patch. They idled, waiting for three college guys in down vests to push out a blonde in a high-centered Grand Am. "I mean, that wouldn't make sense."

"Yeah, but then you wouldn't get to wear that stylin' scarf."

"Good point."

They moved on. Between the plows and stuck cars, the creeping traffic, the OPPD crews out working downed power lines, and the general mess, it was after ten by the time they made it all the way down to Eddie's store.

In the empty front lot, four pickups with blades and tire chains worked on pushing snow into heaps. They'd built a tall ridge around the perimeter and were making a big mountain in the middle.

"Head around back," Tony said.

Ray hit the service drive. They found Eddie's

Hummer parked in the warehouse docks, where the delivery lanes had already been cleared.

Ray parked the Expedition alongside and said, "So."

"So?"

"So what are we telling him?"

Tony had been thinking about that all morning. "Maybe we're not telling him anything yet."

Salcedo nodded, waiting to hear more.

---

John woke up in the chair to the snarl of a snowblower digging in outside.

The power was still out; he hadn't brought his wristwatch out to the chair with him, but morning sun had brightened the living room.

He blinked and yawned, stretched a kink in his neck. No mistaking the noise, *bap-bap-bap,* but it sounded too close. Like it could have been coming from the front porch.

John craned sideways, grabbed a crutch, and moved the curtain.

Great billows of snow churned up from his own driveway. He caught glimpses of red through the cloud. When the cloud parted briefly, he saw Matt Worth in a stocking hat and ski goggles working a big blower uphill toward the house. White geysers blasted from the chute, high and long, sparkling in the sun and sifting away.

John lowered the crutch and sat the recliner upright, thinking *How about that?* He eased the footrest down and prepared to get up.

Then he sat there a minute, choking up without warning. It just happened that way. Right out of the blue, no reason at all.

John cleared his throat hard, annoyed with himself. He swore he didn't know what the hell was the matter with him anymore. He'd never cried over much of anything, even as a boy; all of a sudden, lately, he'd tear up like a baby at the least little goddamned thing. TV commercials, even. The doc had warned him it happened that way sometimes.

On the bright side, the leg didn't seem to be feeling so bad this morning. A good way to start the day.

John folded the quilts back and worked his way up slowly, getting the crutches under him, being careful not to overbalance or give himself a rush. It was pure dumb luck, last time, that he'd fallen straight back into the chair.

As close as he could guess, the electricity had gone out somewhere between two and four this morning—right about the time the trees began creaking and groaning all over the neighborhood. The house had grown plenty cold by now. In the kitchen, he set the gas oven to 400 degrees and left the door open. He could keep at least one room warm until the power company sorted things out.

He headed back through the living room, hauled the front door open, and crutched out into the cold. The porch was about the only place he could see that wasn't buried in snow. He stopped at the edge and waved; Matt Worth cut the engine and waved back.

"Nice weather," John called. His voice sounded loud in the sudden quiet.

Matt came around to the bottom of the sidewalk, trudging through the deep stuff, pushing the snow-crusted goggles up on his head. "You getting along okay over here?"

"Power's out, but fine. Just fine. Listen, I sure appreciate the help, but you got your own place to worry about."

"It's no trouble."

"I'll call a service," John said. "Or pay some kid to shovel. Hell, I'm not going anywhere."

"John, really, it's nothing." Matt grinned and gestured toward the snowblower with one fat glove. "Paid enough for that thing, I might as well use it."

John chuckled, feeling a little embarrassed. Past winters, he'd have been the one across the street, clearing Helen's driveway for her. Now here he was, humping around like an invalid, not even able to scoop his own walk. Just standing out here, his leg was starting to talk to him.

"Guess you ended up with a mess," he said.

"Little bit."

They both stood a minute and looked at the sprawling tangle of branches over at Matthew's place. The biggest of the limbs had rammed right through the big picture window in the front of the house, littering the snow-covered bushes with shards of glass. Smaller limbs covered the ground all the way to the street.

The sight of it broke John's heart. Everybody liked that tree: a big old sugar maple that stood fifty feet, spread out thirty, and had shaded that corner as long as anybody around here had lived in the neighborhood. Always turned a pretty, fiery red this time of year.

This morning Helen's old tree stood decimated. It looked forlorn, like a crippled giant that had dropped an armload of firewood. The whole view over there seemed naked and wrong.

Matt Worth gave a weary smile. "Guess that's what insurance is for. Hate to lose that tree, though."

"Maybe it'll pull through yet." The longer John looked, the more he doubted it. His leg gave a twinge, and he realized he didn't like looking at the splintered ends of the limbs. "Old trees like that, they can take a beating."

"Maybe so. Listen, do you need anything?"

"Nah. I'll be fine. I'm sure Liz'll be up soon as they get dug out down there. Or Rodney. No need to worry."

"Well, I've got a two-hundred-foot cord. I'll run it over from the garage and you can plug in."

The power grid ran down the middle of the street. It happened occasionally, one side staying up while the other side went down, but John couldn't remember it happening during weather this bad. Up and down the block, he could see heavy-duty power extensions snaking from one side to the other, orange and yellow lines against the snow.

"I appreciate that, but I wouldn't want to . . . "

"At least keep the fridge going," Matt Worth said. "Watch a little TV."

John sighed and gave in. He needed to get back inside and find the Vicodin anyway. "You're a good neighbor."

"Just returning the favor, John."

While they were talking, a red Chevy Blazer stopped at the corner and turned right. The truck idled bumper-deep in the street a moment, exhaust rolling from the tailpipes, runner panels cloudy with salt. Probably looking at Matt Worth's new woodpile, the same as they'd been standing there doing just now.

Instead of moving on, the Blazer turned into Helen's driveway.

John nodded. "Looks like you've got company."

Chain saw jockeys, he figured, out driving around, looking for cleanup work. While they watched, the back end of the Blazer fishtailed to the right, then back to the left. Then the tires spun, polishing the snow into two slick tracks.

"Huh," Matt said.

"Guess they need a push."

"Mind if I leave this thing sitting in your driveway?"

"Not a bit," John said.

Matt Worth turned and tromped his way back to the path he'd cleared so far. Over his shoulder, he called, "You know where I am. Holler if you need anything."

*Hell of a good neighbor,* John thought.

*And cold as brass tits out here.*

He hobbled his feeble butt back inside.

---

"Hey, Eddie," Ray said, leaning on his cue stick. "Tell me something."

"Shoot," Eddie said, hanging up the phone.

On the word *shoot,* Tony Briggs missed the seven in the corner and cursed under his breath. They'd started a game of nine ball on the pool table in his uncle's office.

"You're sending the kid to Chicago. He's supposed to deliver stuff. Bring stuff back."

"That's right."

"Both ways, it's . . . sensitive. Right?"

"I'd say that 'sensitive' sounds accurate."

Ray looked mystified. "Why let the kid drive a car like that? Out of curiosity."

"Yeah," Tony said. He'd wondered that himself. "A Camry. Minivan. Something a little less . . ."

"Conspicuous?" Eddie said.

Ray touched a finger to his nose. "There you go. Conspicuous."

Eddie nodded, like it was a reasonable question. He

leaned back in the tall chair behind his fancy walnut desk. "Let me ask you something back."

"Sure."

"If you were out on patrol and you saw a car like that, how would you respond?"

Ray shrugged. "Depends where I saw it."

"Suppose you saw it in a questionable part of town."

"Questionable?"

"You know what I mean."

"Like Regency," Tony offered. "Or Country Club. You know, questionable."

Ray chuckled. "I'd notice it."

Now Eddie touched a finger to his own nose, mimicking Ray. "You'd notice it. Now, say the car was, I don't know. Speeding, going too slow, swerving across lanes . . . I don't know, Ray. Hell. Say it was doing something wrong. Would you notice it more or less than you'd notice a Camry? Or a minivan?"

"Something less conspicuous," Tony said.

Ray said, "I'd notice any infraction of the law."

Tony laughed. Asshole.

Uncle Eddie grinned. "And I feel personally safer knowing you're out there. But seriously."

"I'd notice more."

"You'd notice more," Eddie said. "Of course you would. Let's face it, a car like that is a cop magnet. Tony? Am I wrong?"

"A cop magnet," Tony said. "Sure."

"Yeah, Eddie," Ray said. "That was kind of my point."

"Okay, say you're not you. Say you're the guy driving the cop magnet. And you've got, I don't know. Hypothetically."

Eddie raised his hands. "Say you've got a dead hooker in the trunk."

"A dead hooker."

"Hypothetically," Tony said.

"It doesn't matter what it is," Eddie said. "Something illegal. You're driving a conspicuous hot rod and you're carrying something illegal. How would you feel?"

"Like a dumb asshole," Ray said. He leaned over and dropped the seven ball with a stiff crack. "But I see where you're going."

"You'd feel like a sitting duck, right?" Eddie made a finger gun and pointed it at his own head. "And if you had half a brain—which I *thought* the kid did, up until now—you'd drive that hot rod like it was exam day at the DMV." He lowered the gun and started counting off points on the same fingers. "You wouldn't let your guard down, the way you might if you were driving a Camry. You'd wear your seat belt, you wouldn't speed, you wouldn't scratch the tires. You'd make sure you didn't have so much as a broken taillight, so that a state trooper, or a fine city officer like yourself, would have absolutely no reason to pull you over. If you had half a brain."

"Which you thought the kid did," Tony said. He couldn't help it.

Uncle Eddie sighed. "Which I thought the kid did."

Tony looked at Ray. Ray shrugged and considered his shot selection.

"The point is, the kid never got where he was supposed to be going," Eddie said. "I want to know why. More importantly, our friends in Chicago want to know why."

"Sure," Ray said.

"You know what? I don't even give a shit why," Eddie said. "I just want to find the stupid son of a bitch."

Tony said, "Well, at least you can look on the bright side."

"There's a bright side?"

"Easier to track down a BadGoat than a Camry."

Looking tired now, Eddie sighed and touched his nose again. Somebody knocked on the office door.

"It's open."

A pair of young guys slouched in. Both white, eighteen or twenty. The first kid looked like a bulldog: baggy jeans, FUBU sweatshirt, stocking hat pulled low over his eyes. The second kid looked like a heroin addict or a wannabe rock star, not necessarily one or the other: slight build, stud in his nose, no coat. Tats up and down his arms like sleeves.

The FUBU kid looked toward Tony and Ray at the pool table. No expression. A real tough guy. He said to Eddie, "We can come back."

"It's okay," Eddie said. "Troy Mather, Derek Price, this is my nephew Tony. That's Ray."

"Hey," the skinny kid said. He broke away, flopped into the couch in the other corner, and turned on the television.

"Shit, hey," the FUBU kid said. "You guys are the cops, right?"

Tony leaned against the edge of the table and didn't say anything. Ray chuckled and kissed the eight ball into the side pocket.

"Troy," Eddie said, "what did you need?"

"We found some shit out," Troy Mather said. "Thought you might want to hear."

Everybody stood around, waiting. Eddie finally said, "Well?"

"She's in the hospital," Troy said. "This chick she's friends with told us."

"Who's in the hospital?"

"Gwen. Russ's girl."

"Who told you?"

"This chick she's friends with. LaTonya," Troy said. "Me and Derek ran into her at this party last night? She sees us and straps on this attitude. Gets all up in our grill about how our friend beat up her friend again and put her in the hospital this time."

Eddie grabbed a pen. "Which hospital?"

"She wouldn't say. But there's that big place right up the street from the store where she works, right? So we called and asked if they had a Gwen Mullen there."

Eddie scribbled something on a notepad. "And did they have a Gwen Mullen there?"

"Fuckin'-A did," Troy said. "Still do."

Tony looked at Ray, raised his eyebrows. Ray listened to Mather. The kid was pleased with himself; he was a genius. It wasn't bad thinking, Tony Briggs gave him that. For a grunt.

His uncle crossed his arms and sat. In a minute, he looked toward the pool table. "Think you guys could check it out?"

"Hey, Eddie, me and Derek can do it."

Eddie didn't respond. He was waiting for an answer from Tony. Tony looked at Ray again. Ray leaned on his stick and said nothing.

Eddie had his answer. He sighed and said, "You're probably right."

"Seriously," Troy Mather said. "We got it covered, boss. No problem."

Somebody else knocked on the door then. Eddie closed his eyes, rubbed his temples, and said, "Yes?"

Darla, the office manager, stuck her head in. Darla was maybe thirty-eight, dirty blond, kind of sexy in a tapped-out single-mom sort of way. Tony was pretty sure his uncle was doing her. Aunt Joan would sauté his balls.

"Your chain saws are here," she said.

Eddie nodded. "Thanks."

As Darla disappeared, Tony said, "Chain saws?"

Eddie grabbed a sheet of paper and held it out. "Taping the TV spot in an hour."

Tony had wondered why Eddie was decked out in a holiday sweater with reindeer hopping around on it. He stepped over, took the page, and gave it a look.

It was copy of a full-page print ad for the newspaper. Across the top, in shivery blue letters, the ad announced: *Hundred-Year Storm Sale!*

Tice Is Nice Quality Used and Discount Furniture was slashing prices all across the board. You didn't want to miss it; you couldn't even begin to imagine the deals. And if the best prices in town weren't enough, for a limited time, you'd take home a free fourteen-inch Homelite Bandit with the purchase of any bedroom set or plasma screen television.

"Gotta hand it to you, Uncle Eddie." Tony handed the sheet over for Ray to see. "Always one step ahead."

"Twenty-four seven," Eddie Tice said, leaning forward and grinding his knuckles into his eyes.

# 14

Worth trudged down John Pospisil's driveway, back through the narrow corridor he'd cut across the unplowed street. Curtis Modell climbed out from the passenger side of the Blazer.

"Hey, there's a tree in your house."

"And a couple guys stuck in my driveway."

"Man, I told him not to punch it." Curtis wore surplus army pants, a Property of UNO Wrestling hoodie, and a wool cap with ear flaps that made him look a little bit like a World War II tail-gunner. "Guy doesn't know how to drive in snow."

Worth heard Ricky's voice, muffled inside the truck. It sounded like *Eat me.*

"What are you guys up to?"

"Just cruising around," Curtis said. "Dug out our mom's."

"Good boys."

"That's us." Curtis planted his gloves on his hips and surveyed the street like a polar explorer. "Can you believe this shit? We passed, like, three big National Guard trucks coming down Dodge."

Worth wasn't surprised. Given the extent of the damage he'd seen so far, he'd bet money the governor would declare a state of emergency before the day was out.

All around, it was as if the normal sounds of the city had been muffled under mattresses of snow, overridden by a buzzing chorus of chain saws and snowblowers. You could hear the growl of the city plows, the occasional ambulance or rescue truck in the distance. All punctuated by random, meaningless blasts from one of the municipal air sirens downtown. Half the city was out of power, and trees stood in ruins up and down the street. It was like they'd been bombed.

"Anyway, we went by Sorensen's place, helped him scoop," Curtis said. "He said you got creamed."

"Yeah, he called earlier." Sorensen had wanted to know if anybody had arrested Russell James yet.

"Figured we'd swing by." Curtis shrugged.

"I appreciate that, guys."

"No prob."

"How did you know where I live?"

"Sorensen."

"Ah."

For some reason, Ricky decided it was time to give it another go. He gunned the engine; the Blazer rocked in place, wet clumps of snow hitting Worth in the legs.

He thought about leaning in and pushing, but there wasn't much footing, and he didn't think they were going anywhere anyway. Before heading across to John's, he'd cleared an area from the garage to a point about three feet beyond Ricky's front bumper. But there was a deep pothole that ran along the edge of the street, about the same width as the mouth of the driveway, and they'd dug themselves pretty well into it.

Curtis pounded on the side window and yelled. "Dude, you're just making it worse."

When Ricky finally gave up, Worth patted the back fender. "Hang tight. I'll get the truck and a chain."

---

Vince got good and drunk before taking the snowmobile to check the incinerator.

It was only 6:45 in the morning, but Rita was in Phoenix, and he didn't know what kind of job he'd find waiting for him. No matter what, it wasn't a job he planned on doing sober.

There were bones, just like he'd suspected. About six feet of them, resting there on the ash grate like parts laid out for assembly. Some of them had buckled, but they hadn't burned.

Vince shoveled the pieces into an old canvas freight sack, trying not to look. He tried to pretend they were animal bones. A coyote or a deer.

He was doing fine until the girl-beater's skull rolled off the end of the shovel and broke apart on the blackened grate. Vince saw a scatter of teeth in a smooth gray bowl and about lost his stomach.

No mistaking that shit for a deer.

He stepped out of the shed and took some air. Some air and a long pull from the flask. The sun hung bright in the sky, throwing white glare off the snow, forcing him to squint his eyes. His breath puffed out in a cloud. The whiskers around his mouth began to freeze.

Rita would be home tomorrow. She'd probably call to say good morning soon.

Vince hit the flask again.

In another minute, he went back inside and got back to it, shovel blade scraping against iron, loud and ugly in the quiet cold.

---

It took an hour just to clear a path to the tree limb that had punched in through the front window.

Worth thanked the Modells for the offer of help, which he actually did appreciate, and tried to send them on their way. It was his last day off, and he wanted to spend it alone. He wasn't in the mood for company.

But by late morning, he'd grown thankful for the extra manpower. Ricky volunteered to go finish John's driveway while Curtis and Worth went to work on the debris, dragging the manageable branches away from the house, sawing the bigger ones down. The Modells had brought a chain saw of their own, and between the two of them, Worth and Curtis kept a steady stream of wood chips flying.

It felt good to work. It felt good to clear his mind, smell the sawdust and bar oil, to physically overwhelm the disarray a little at a time.

By the time Ricky came back with the snowblower, having cleared the walks along both boulevards all the way to the stop signs on either corner, Worth and Curtis had reduced the rubble of downed branches to three big piles.

They all went to work on the main offender then, Worth running the saw, Curtis and Ricky stabilizing the limb. They finally heaved together, pulling the leafy end from the demolished window with a screech of metal and the clatter of falling glass. They stood in the bushes and looked into the house through the opening.

"Damn," Curtis said.

Worth couldn't think of much to add.

The living room was a mess: a carpet of twigs and leaves, scatters of broken glass, puddles of melted snow. The lamp from the table at the end of the couch lay on the floor, shade mangled, bulb shattered, cord pulled out from the wall.

A chain saw ripped to life behind them, tearing through the silence.

Worth and Curtis both jumped and spun at the same time. Worth actually felt his hand move for the service weapon he wasn't wearing.

Ricky had returned to the middle of the yard, where they'd tossed the cut sections of the big limb from the window. He stood there in his snow bibs and lug boots, safety glasses on, the saw belching blue smoke as he adjusted the throttle.

"Jesus H, dude," Curtis yelled.

Ricky nodded at Worth, then toward the chimney of the house. Over the idling saw, he yelled back, "How big is your fireplace?"

Worth took a deep breath, allowed his pulse to settle a bit, and held up his palms about eighteen inches apart. Firewood dimensions. Ricky nodded, turned his back, and goosed the saw into a high whine.

As wood began to spray and the tang of fresh sawdust filled the air, Worth leaned over to Curtis and said, "Is your brother okay?"

Curtis sighed. "Man, don't worry about him. He's been on the rag all weekend."

"Something wrong?"

"Just a moody sonofabitch, that's all that's wrong with him." A shrug. "Probably still stewing about what happened to Gwen."

"I was thinking he didn't seem like himself."

Curtis waved it off. "Let him mess some shit up with the chain saw. He'll be fine."

---

It was ten in the morning before Vince made it back up to the house. He was hungry as a bear, but the smell of ham and eggs cooking in the skillet made his stomach turn. He ended up tossing the food off the back porch for the stray dog who came around.

Eight or nine o'clock in Phoenix. He could never keep it straight. Was it Mountain or Pacific in Arizona this time of year?

Either way, Reet hadn't called. Probably out walking with her mom. He took a chance, got her voice mail, and left a message. *Hey babe. Everything's fine. Probably be out on the plow all day.*

He brewed enough coffee to fill a gallon thermos jug, got on the tractor, and opened the driveway down to the road. For the next two hours, Vince sat in the heated cab and pushed snow into piles, thinking things through.

The impact crusher had reduced what was left of the girl-beater to a pound or two of fine calcium sand. Later—tonight after dark—he'd drive it away on the snowmobile and sprinkle it in the woods somewhere.

As soon as the temperature broke above freezing, he'd hose out the crusher, grind a few hundred pounds of limestone, and use it for concrete in spring.

He'd dumped the clodded mass of greasy ash from the incinerator's waste bin into the load scheduled for the county landfill. Before he hosed out the crusher, he'd scrub the bin, the interior of the furnace, and the stack pipe with acid solution. Then he'd burn a whole shitload of stuff on top of that.

He'd stop watching those forensics shows on the Discovery Channel. Starting now, that shit was information he didn't need.

Which left only the car.

Vince made it into the shop by one o'clock and cracked open a new bottle of Beam. No need for a hangover in the middle of the day.

It was almost a relief to get started. Fenders and chrome, seats and doors. A steering wheel. An engine block. Vince knew how to handle these things.

He'd sandblast the exterior to bare metal and spark up the cutting torch. With no need to be careful, and no interruptions, he guessed he'd be able to chop the car to its axles in ten or twelve hours.

It took him nearly thirty minutes to figure out what the hell was wrong with the trunk.

---

By midafternoon, everything worth cutting into firewood or kindling had been cut, hauled around back, and stacked against the east side of the garage. It would need to cure for a year, maybe two, but it was good solid maple and would burn warm and slow. They tossed the remaining brush into a single pile in the corner of the yard. Worth could take it away later in the truck.

He had a sheet of plywood in the garage and a spare

bundle of fiberglass insulation in the attic. They nailed the plywood over the exterior of the broken window and laid a few panels of insulation against the inside.

He also had some leftover window film in the basement. The three of them managed to tape a clingy, ungainly sheet of it over the interior window frame. That had been Ricky's idea. Worth had his doubts that it would do much good, but he shrank the film tight with the hair dryer, sandwiching the insulation in between. By the time he finished, the living room already felt ten degrees warmer than it had before.

The plows had been by twice while they worked. While the Modells cleaned up at the house, Worth ran out to pick up a couple pizzas and a twelve-pack of Budweiser from the HyVee on Center Street.

It felt good to go somewhere besides the SaveMore for a change.

He was on his way back home with supper for himself and the guys when his cell phone buzzed. Worth took a look at the ID screen and answered the call.

"Got a problem here," his brother said.

# 15

The county road up into the bluffs was passable, thanks to the thick barrier of oaks and elms along either side. Worth only had to stop twice: once to dig through a drift, once to wait for a small herd of whitetail deer.

At 5:15 in the afternoon, he rolled up the long driveway to Junk Monkey Scrap and Salvage for the second time in two days.

Vince met him at the side door of the machine shed holding a pistol-grip shotgun alongside his leg.

"Jesus," Worth said. "You expecting somebody else?"

"Hell if I know," Vince said. His eyes were glassy, but not incoherent. Even in the cold, his breath reeked of booze.

"What's going on?"

Vince turned without speaking and went into the shop.

Worth followed him to where the GTO sat, uncovered, lift chains attached. The trunk lid was open. A section of carpet liner sat on the concrete, off to the side of the car.

Inside the trunk, Worth saw a smaller lid in the bottom. Also open.

"Trigger button under the dashboard," Vince said. "Electric locks, hidden hinges. Took me half an hour to find it."

The space beneath the false panel ran the width of the trunk, about six inches deep. Worth stood there a minute, just looking.

He'd seen plenty of false compartments in plenty of vehicles, but this one appeared to be a good cut above standard construction. His thoughts began to race, going nowhere.

"Said you figured he was into something." Vince produced a flask and unscrewed the cap. "Guess you pegged that one, huh?"

Worth reached into the trunk. He picked up a rectangular brick wrapped in black plastic, secured with packaging tape.

He tore one end of the plastic away, revealing a bundle of wrinkled bills in mixed denominations: hundreds, fifties, twenties, tens. The entire trunk bottom was lined with bundles just like it.

"Trick or treat," Vince said, pouring the last of the flask into a hole in his beard.

---

"So he's a fuckup," Tony Briggs said. "This we know."

"This we hear," said Ray.

"Dude's rolling nights at a grocery store." Tony looked at his partner. "A goddamn SaveMore, man."

Ray chuckled.

"Store isn't even in his precinct. You know?"

"Point taken."

"Ex is banging another cop. Homicide, yet."

"At least he popped the guy one."

"And gets busted to fitness eval for it?" Tony shook his head. "Forget it. Dude's own commander thinks he's ten ninety-six. Besides that, guy at Central I talked to said Vargas handed his ass to him."

"So life sucks."

"Sucks hard. But then our boy gets it on with the checkout girl."

"Whose boyfriend works for your uncle."

"And knocks her around," Tony said. "No secret, everybody knows."

"So it goes how?"

"Say she knows boyfriend's business. He's stupid and tells her, or she's smart and figures it out. Either way. She knows his runs."

"And when he's rolling heavy."

"So she lays it out, gets our boy Worth on board. He sees his shot, right? Why not? Life sucks hard. At least this way he's getting laid." The more they talked it out, the more Tony liked it. "They plan the night. Girl knows all boyfriend's buttons. She'd have to, right? But now she *wants* to push 'em. So she gets him going. Takes the beating like a super trooper."

Ray went along. "So there's an alibi. By the time Worth files the report, she's in the hospital. Boyfriend's gone."

"And the lovebirds are up the quarter mil boyfriend was supposed to deliver to Chicago," Tony said. "Meanwhile,

Uncle Eddie's giving away chain saws, wondering where the hell his money went."

Ray sat with it awhile. Tony propped a leg up on Matthew Worth's kitchen table and drank a beer from the crisper drawer of Matthew Worth's fridge. The ski mask was making his head itch, so he took it off. He kept his gloves on.

Ray finally tipped his beer. "What about Eddie?"

"What about him?"

"He's still on the hook with Chicago for two-fifty and some change, based on what he said earlier."

"Boo-hoo for Uncle Eddie," Tony said. "Guy's worth at least a couple million. He can eat a couple hundred thou."

"That's cold."

"Cold?" Tony shook his head. "Nah, man, see, cold is when you give some mule a bigger TV than your own favorite nephew."

Ray chuckled.

"I mean, shit. You know?"

"I guess he's not going to wonder how come his favorite nephew is such a big spender all of a sudden?"

"You think I'm stupid," Tony said. "Is that it?"

"Maybe Grocery Boy won't be such a pushover."

"Now you're insulting both of us."

Ray chuckled again, sipped his beer.

"Grocery Boy won't have shit to say about shit," Tony said. "Eddie'll cover Chicago out of his pocket 'cause that's what he'd do without us anyway. Everybody's back to even, live and learn." He spread his hands. "Briggs and Salcedo have a bountiful Thanksgiving."

"Bountiful, huh?"

"Gobble gobble, brother."

Sure. It would have been nice to find a bag full of Eddie's cash under Grocery Boy's bed, go home early, crack open a six-pack, and play some Madden 360. Quick, clean, done. Back to the soup aisle for Grocery Boy.

But even Tony didn't figure they could ask for it that easy. Had to give credit where credit was due.

"So?"

"So, what?"

"So what do you think?"

Ray shook his head, smiling. "It's your uncle, man."

Tony still had half an urge to toss the place old school, make sure they hadn't missed anything. But at this point, his gut said the loot wasn't here.

Guy drew outlines around the tools hanging in the garage, just so they'd always go back in the right spot. Except for the boarded-up living room, the place was buttoned down and squared away. They hadn't found so much as a porno stash.

Guy like that decided to hide something, he hid it good and deep. Eddie's cash wouldn't be here, Tony was sure of it. And tossing the place would only tip Grocery Boy off that somebody was looking.

No point in spooking him. Yet.

Ray finished his beer, then threw Tony a hard look. *Did you hear that?* At the sound of the back door rattling open, he hopped up from the table, pulling down his mask.

Tony hadn't heard a car pull in. Hadn't seen any headlights hit the windows. He was right behind Ray; they stepped out of the kitchen, into the darkened living room.

Grocery Boy was home.

# 16

"Hello?"

A male voice. Medium deep.

"Anybody home?"

It seemed to Tony like they were spending too much time lately getting caught in the act of breaking and entering. He looked across the doorway toward Ray.

Ray tapped the side of his head with one gloved finger, then pointed the same finger at Tony: *Think fast. It's your play.*

"It's John," the voice called. "I'm letting myself in."

Tony remembered four or five stair steps leading up to the kitchen from a small mud porch inside the back door. They heard the back door close, and the stairs began creaking. Slowly.

There came a rubbery squeak at the top of the steps, followed by a heavy, rhythmic pattern. The sound moved toward them across the kitchen floor.

Ray took a step back, retreating into the shadows.

Tony couldn't put his finger on what he was hearing.

Not like regular footsteps. It was almost a mechanical sound: slow, steady, punctuated by labored, pistonlike breathing.

Crutches. It was the sound of somebody walking with crutches.

On Ray's signal, Tony edged forward and took a peek.

A guy in a flannel coat and sweatpants worked his way toward the phone on the near kitchen wall. White, late middle age. On his good foot, he wore a scruffy work boot. The other leg wore a padded splint and one hell of a steel brace, sweats cut away at the knee.

The guy leaned on his crutches as he dialed a number, still panting from exertion, not looking so hot. Every so often, he pressed another number. Punching through menu options, Tony deduced.

"Yeah, hello," he finally said. "My name is John Pospisil. That's right. P-O-S . . ."

He finished spelling the last name, gave his address. Gave somebody permission to access his account.

Tony mapped the address in his head. It had to be right across the street.

He noticed the dirty puddles of melt collecting beneath the rubber tips of the crutches and understood why they hadn't heard a car pull up the driveway. Mr. Pospisil here had come over from across the street on foot. On one foot, literally.

"Yep," he said. "Yes. Well, my power went out in the storm—yep, sure was. You can say that again. Anyway, I've been laid up at home for several weeks, and I can't really drive anywhere, so I've been running the oven every couple hours for heat. Sorry? Yes, the kitchen stove." He sighed. "I know. Yes, I . . . I understand that you wouldn't recommend it, miss. I'm just explaining the situation."

Tony tried to think. Had he and Ray left the back door unlocked after checking the garage? They weren't that sloppy. The guy must have known where to find a spare key.

"Well, that's the problem," he said. "The whole place smelled like gas before I realized the pilot had gone out." A pause. "Yep, I did that first thing. But I can still hear the gas line hissing." Pause. "Yep. It's an old stove, I figure there must be a bad . . . no, I'm calling from the neighbor's. I was afraid if the power came back on all of a sudden I might wake up on the moon."

More talk. The guy gave some billing information, then confirmed his address.

"Thank you, miss," he finally said. "I'll be watching for 'em. You, too, now. Thanks again."

As Pospisil hung up the phone, Tony ducked back and downshifted, rethinking the situation.

He'd geared himself up, ready to take a run at Worth here and now. It hadn't been the plan, but as long as they were here, now was as good a time as any.

But here was this guy. Cold as it was, and after the effort it had obviously taken him to get over here, you could bet Mr. Gas Leak from across the street wouldn't be going anywhere until the utility truck pulled up at his place.

Tony motioned to Ray. Front door.

He heard something crunch beneath Ray's foot in the darkness.

From the kitchen: "Hello?"

Long silence.

"Is somebody here?"

Tony heard a faint clink of glass and remembered their beer bottles on the kitchen table. One was empty, the other half full, both of them probably still frosty from the fridge.

"I said, is somebody here?"

Thud-step-thud.

*Shit.* Tony scratched his nose, stepping back into the corner.

It wasn't until he'd scratched his nose that he realized he'd misinterpreted his partner's earlier hand gesture. Ray had tapped his head and pointed. But he hadn't been telling Tony to call the play.

He'd been saying: *You forgot to put your mask back on, dumbass.*

And now here came Mr. Gas Leak, hobbling through the doorway, gripping Tony's ski mask against the hand-grip of one crutch. He crossed out of the light from the kitchen, into the dark of the boarded-up living room.

"Who's here?"

Jesus. What next?

No time to think about it. Tony followed his gut.

"Behind you," he said.

As John Pospisil turned, Tony Briggs stepped forward and dropped him with a hard overhand right.

Not too hard. He'd worn a new pair of Subduer G5 winter tacticals: cut-resistant fingers, double-thick palms, eight ounces of powdered lead sewn into the knuckles.

Tony just wanted to neutralize the guy, not put him in a coma. So he pulled back twenty percent. Pospisil gave a low grunt and went down like a bag of sand.

At the same time, to his extreme surprise, Tony felt something hard slam against the side of his head. A flashbulb popped behind his eye, and his vision went dark for a moment. He actually staggered, half stunned. It felt like getting hit with a length of pipe.

"Son of a *bitch*."

The guy's crutch clattered to the floor as he fell. Tony hadn't even seen him swing it.

Goddamn. He heard laughing.

"Up your ass," he said to the dark.

Ray came out of the shadows, pulling his own mask up over his face again. He put his hands on his hips, looked down at the motionless pile on the floor, and said, "Nice shot."

"Fuck off."

"What do you do for an encore? Push a little old lady down some stairs?"

"You're an asshole."

"You're bleeding."

Tony touched his scalp. "Jesus."

"Hey," Ray said. Serious now. "I just thought of something."

"What?"

"That's assaulting a police officer." He looked at Tony. "Should we take him downtown? Or do you just want me to hold him still so you can kick him a couple times?"

Tony sighed and knelt down. He lifted the fallen crutches, tossed them aside, and checked the guy out.

Still breathing. Goose egg in the morning, probably. But he'd be fine.

"Here," Ray said. He found a pillow amid the debris in the living room and tossed it over. "Put that under his leg."

Tony got the guy laid out more or less flat. After

getting the pillow situated, he grabbed his mask and stood up again, feeling a warm trickle of blood behind his ear.

"So now what?" Ray said.

"This guy Worth is starting to piss me off."

"I mean him." Ray nodded toward the unconscious neighbor. "Can't just leave him there."

"What the hell else are we going to do with him?"

"Good point."

Tony had to give the man credit: He'd moved quick for an older guy. In the dark, no less. And with only one good wheel. He touched his scalp again; the fingers of his glove came away slick. Jesus.

He grabbed the last of his beer on the way through the kitchen, draining it on the move. So much for easy.

Behind him, Ray said, "Look out! He's got a heating pad!"

Asshole.

# 17

Four blocks away, Worth could see the red and blue glow of emergency lights rippling on the snow-covered rooftops down the street.

Two blocks away, his chest tightened. At the corner, he felt his head getting light.

For a minute he just sat there in the truck, foot on the brake, both hands gripping the wheel. He forced himself to breathe.

*Jesus.* That had been his first thought. *John had a heart attack.* He counted three radio units and an EMS truck, all crowding the street between his house and John's.

But John's house was still dark.

All the lights in Worth's house were blazing.

And there was an unmarked unit sitting in his driveway.

*Shit.*

While he sat there, across the intersection, idling at the stop sign like some rubbernecker, a uniformed cop emerged from the back door of the house, shining a flashlight around on the ground. From a distance, it looked like Dan Wesson from B crew.

Another cop came out of Worth's garage.

So this was it. Worth found his mind drifting like the plumes of exhaust outside the truck.

He'd eavesdropped on his dad and Kelly once. They'd been downstairs at the kitchen table, beers popping, late on a weeknight. Kelly had been a boot in the Northeast at the time; he'd stopped by the house after coming off shift. Worth had still been a senior at Central High. Instead of coming down, he'd stayed upstairs and listened through the air vent, feeling like a child.

*Kid, you gotta learn how to think like the bad guys,* he'd heard his dad say. Up through the vent came the clink of the Zippo, the long exhale. *The bad guys already know how to think like you.*

Worth had never learned how to think like a bad guy. He'd never really learned how to think like a cop. He'd been a damned English major when Kelly was killed.

Who had he thought he could help?

Another vehicle arrived at the house, a dark green minivan he didn't recognize. The minivan slid to a stop against the bank of plowed snow along the curb.

A woman piled out from behind the wheel. She hurried up the driveway, not quite frantic, but somewhere on the verge. One of the uniforms intercepted her.

Somebody related to Gwen?

Somebody related to Russell James?

Worth put the truck into gear. He didn't know where he was planning to go, or what he'd do when he got there. But he needed to think.

There came a sharp knock on the window by his head. Hard light came in through the window, blinding him.

*Shit.*

Outside the window, a muffled voice said, "Matt?"

The light went away. As the spots swam out of his vision, Worth's chest began pounding. He realized he was holding his breath. He exhaled and ran the window down.

"Hey," a third uniform said. Worth hadn't even seen him approaching the vehicle. "We've been looking for you."

The voice seemed familiar. Worth blinked his eyes.

"Sorry about the light."

"Ken?"

"Good for you I'm not a carjacker," Ken Bailer said. "You okay? How come you're just sitting over here?"

"Trying to figure out how to get to my house," Worth said. "What the hell's going on?"

Ken Bailer shook his head. He holstered his Maglite. "Man, you'd better come with me."

The lead man on site was a guy named Sheppard. Mid-forties, sandy hair, quiet eyes. Sheppard worked out of the South Investigation Unit; Worth remembered him from an apartment burglary at the Livestock Exchange Building two or three years ago.

He didn't get the impression that the memory was mutual, but Sheppard had seemed like an okay guy then, and he seemed like an okay guy now.

"Mr. Pospisil says that he came over to use the phone here after discovering a gas leak inside his home," Sheppard said. "He says he rang the doorbell, but nobody answered."

"It's broken," Worth said. He'd meant to fix it all summer.

"Yeah, we found that." Sheppard looked at his notepad. "So Mr. Pospisil went ahead and let himself inside with a key he says you provided him. I'm assuming you can confirm the house key?"

"Yes," Worth said. "The property was vacant for a few months last year. John looked in on the place for me."

"That's what he said."

"Can you make a point of entry?"

"Same door, most likely," Sheppard said. "No sign of force."

Worth thought about it. He remembered locking the door when he'd left. After leaving the garage unlocked with the GTO inside on Saturday, he'd been doubly careful about that.

The house didn't have a security system. Whoever had been here had known how to bypass a basic dead bolt. No big deal, but it showed more sophistication and stealth than a regular smash job. As far as Sheppard would be concerned, storm looters were out.

"Photographed two different sets of footprints," he said. "Besides Mr. Pospisil's."

If John had needed his key to get in, it meant that they'd locked the door behind them after entering. Which meant they'd planned to be here awhile.

Detective Sheppard grinned. "Here's the part I like."

He led Worth to the doorway into the living room and pointed at the threshold. Worth saw a single droplet of bright red blood on the white kitchen tile. The spatter had already been circled in grease pencil.

"Mr. Pospisil took a swing toward a voice," Sheppard

said. "Since he isn't the one bleeding, I assume he connected."

"What do you mean, he took a swing?"

"Right crutch," Sheppard said. He stood in the doorway and pantomimed the action, swinging an imaginary crutch toward Worth's head. He was still smiling.

"Clank," one of the EMTs said.

In the living room, John sat in the blue chair, leg up on the footstool, holding a gel pack to the left side of his face. The EMT stood by, replacing the batteries in his penlight. His partner rolled up a blood pressure cuff and shoved it in a bag.

The woman from the minivan knelt beside the chair, one hand on John's shoulder. John's daughter, Worth assumed. Elizabeth.

"Didn't see his face," John muttered.

"Jesus, John." Worth went over. He gestured toward the gel pack. "Can I see?"

John peeled the pack away from his face. Worth saw a purple knot the size of a racquetball above his neighbor's left eye.

"Don't think there's a fracture," EMT #1 said.

"But he has a concussion," John's daughter said. "They knocked him completely unconscious. Just completely unconscious."

John sighed and patted her hand. Liz, he always called her. Worth knew that she lived down in Plattsmouth with her husband and kids, but he'd never actually met her before tonight. Worry lines crinkled her brow.

"Guess the guy got me better than I got him."

John said it like a joke, but he was obviously hurting. His complexion was the color of spoiled cheese, and large drops of sweat beaded on his forehead. Worth looked to the med techs and said, "How's his leg?"

"He didn't fall on it," EMT #2 said. "But as far as whether anything twisted on the way down . . ."

"It's fine," John said.

". . . his orthopedist needs to have a look. Right now, he's got some pain."

John grunted. "Nothing new there."

"I've been trying to get him to come stay with us," Elizabeth said. She shook her head and rubbed her father's forearm. "Stubborn."

EMT #1 said, "One burglar in town who won't be back, though. Right, John?"

"Johnny Crutches," said EMT #2. "That's what we call him."

"Don't encourage him," Elizabeth said.

Sheppard caught Worth's eye. Worth put a hand on John's shoulder, then followed the detective back into the kitchen. He took care to step over the blood evidence.

The occasional flashlight beam passed over the windows as cops searched the perimeter outside. It felt as though he were walking through a dream.

"Lab unit should be en route," Sheppard said. "There's been a two-person team working houses around Field Club, maybe . . . maybe something here matches up."

Worth nodded along, not bothering to point out what Sheppard hadn't said. This place wasn't a house around Field Club. It wasn't even close.

Somebody was on to him; it just wasn't the good guys. Not yet. Worth couldn't decide if he was relieved or not.

"What can I do?"

"Well, first thing, take a look around," Sheppard said. "See if anything's missing."

There wouldn't be, Worth knew. Whoever had broken in here had been looking for one thing, and they wouldn't have been able to find it.

"You had some storm damage, I take it?"

"Big limb through the window," Worth said. "Barely started cleaning up in there yet."

"Besides that room, nothing much looks disrupted." Sheppard dropped his voice. "I figure Mr. Pospisil broke up the party, but just to cover all the bases, can you think of any recent collars that stand out? Any BGs making threats on the street?"

BGs. Bad guys.

On the street, the only undisputable good guys were your fellow cops. In this situation, Worth didn't know what that made Sheppard. Let alone what it made him.

"Let me think about that," he said.

# 18

In high school, Gwen Mullen had gone to the senior prom with the quarterback of the football team. He'd had too much to drink at the after-party, and they'd gotten in a car wreck on the way home.

There wasn't much to it. Just them and a light pole, more or less head-on. Keith had tumbled out with a scuff mark on his cheek, a totaled graduation present, and his first DUI. Gwen had spent two days in the hospital: concussion, broken ribs, a punctured lung.

"It feels about like that," she said.

Dr. Mandekar smiled. "Then you must be healing."

"Almost like a new girl."

"I want you to rest in bed for the next several days."

"You'll write me a note for my midterms?"

The doctor raised a finger to show that he meant what he said. "If you experience any of the symptoms we discussed, you must call the nurses."

"Low output, fatigue, fluid retention," Gwen said,

continuing until she'd repeated the entire list by memory. "Got it."

Dr. Mandekar patted her shin through the bedcover. "A good student. I'd like to see you in one week's time."

"Okay."

"We'll repeat the IVP, evaluate the kidney. And then we'll see."

Gwen nodded. She'd observed a couple surgeries during practicals so far this semester, but the idea of going under the knife herself still scared her a little. It must have shown on her face.

"But I'm very optimistic," the doctor said, sensing the question she hadn't asked. "You'll follow my instructions?"

"Cross my heart."

Mandekar nodded and patted her leg again. On the way out the door, he stopped and turned back.

"Miss Mullen?"

"Yes?"

For the first time since he'd come in, the doctor glanced toward Marly Kenna, who sat behind the roll-around table on the other side of the bed. Kenna wore a turtleneck sweater and slacks today, ID badge hanging around her neck.

"Please consider everything Detective Kenna tells you to be an order from your physician."

Up went the serious finger.

Gwen said, "Yes, Doctor."

Dr. Mandekar maintained a stern expression, but he winked. Then he turned and went on his way.

After he was gone, Detective Kenna—Marly—said, "Quarterback of the football team, huh?"

It was like she'd seen through it the whole time. Gwen dropped her eyes, felt herself blush. Not because she was embarrassed.

"Am I that easy to read?"

"I've had a little practice."

"He wasn't a quarterback," she admitted.

"Keith?"

"He was the assistant guidance counselor."

Marly gave a little smile. "The assistant guidance counselor took you to the prom?"

"He took me to a Super 8."

"Classy."

"His wife was out of town. I was stupid."

"Not stupid. Young."

"He lied his butt off," Gwen told her. "But he still ended up losing his job." She didn't mention how everybody had looked at her after that. The other male teachers especially.

"What about the wife? I hope she divorced the scumbag."

"I never heard."

They sat for a minute, comfortable, almost like girlfriends. Then Detective Kenna asked a question Gwen hadn't considered.

"So why turn him into a quarterback?"

"Why what?"

"When you tell the story," Marly said. "Why do you make him the quarterback of the football team?"

"Oh." Gwen rested her head against the pillow. "Sometimes I make him a wrestler I thought was cute."

"Yeah?"

"Or this one kid from band."

"Why make him anything?"

*Because if you let somebody catch you lying about something small, it's that much easier to lie to them about something big.* People always thought they had you figured out.

"I don't know." Gwen shrugged. "The truth seems so . . . trashy, I guess."

"I understand." And it seemed like she honestly did. After a pause, Detective Kenna added, "As long as you understand who the trash is in that story. You know?"

"I know."

"Because it isn't the high school girl."

"Anyway," Gwen said. "I don't tell it very often."

The door opened, and the morning nurse came in. Sharon. She smiled at Gwen on her way to the chart.

"Morning, kiddo. How you feeling?"

"Better," Gwen said. "I guess they're springing me today."

"That's what I hear. Ahh."

Gwen opened her mouth; Sharon popped the thermometer in. Marly Kenna checked the pager on her belt. The thermometer beeped.

"Ninety-eight point four." Sharon snapped the plastic thermometer sleeve into the bio bin. "Now you get your needles out."

"Yay."

"I'm going to disconnect these fluids and remove your lock." Sharon rolled the IV stand so that Gwen could see better. "So what I'll do first is just take and clamp the leader off like this."

She went on that way, automatically describing each step in the process. Gwen had asked so many second-year clinical questions that most of the nurses had simply started talking out loud while they worked.

Most of them didn't seem to mind. A few were grouchy. Gwen listened carefully to everybody, trying to absorb everything she could.

"Okay," Sharon said. "I'll be back in a little while to tell you about your meds."

Marly Kenna waited until she walked out. As the door closed, her demeanor shifted. Back to Detective Kenna.

She held up a cell phone.

"I want you to keep this handy," she said. "All the time. It's programmed so that if you hold down any number, it automatically dials 911."

"Um . . . okay."

"It's not a friends-and-family plan, so don't give out the number to people. But my cell number is in there. And the hotline I told you about."

"Okay."

"I mean it. Carry this with you." She placed the phone on the table.

Gwen nodded. "I will."

Next, Detective Kenna held up a blue folder. "Keep this handy, too."

"What is it?"

"Information," Detective Kenna said. "All the stuff we talked about. There's a sheet with more phone numbers. Like I said, you've got mine, and I promise you that's good anyplace, anytime. But I want you to find an independent advocate, as well." She waggled the folder. "There's a list in here. I circled a few names I like."

"Okay," Gwen said. It didn't sound like enough, so she added, "Thank you."

"I want to be clear. This isn't me passing you off. This is about adding people to the team."

"The team?"

"I'm scaring you, aren't I?"

"Maybe a little." Gwen smiled. It didn't feel genuine, and it didn't feel like an act. Sitting here, going along with all of this, she could almost believe that Russell really was out there somewhere, pissed off that she'd gone to the police. Waiting.

"Don't be scared." Marly Kenna reached over, gave her hand a squeeze. "Scared is over. You've been doing the scary part for a while now."

"I'm sorry." The next smile came a little more naturally. "I guess I'm more nervous about leaving than I thought. Or something."

"You don't have anything to be sorry about." Marly shook her head. *You don't.* "As for the rest of it . . . look on the bright side. Now that you've done the hard part? Leaving? The stats say the risk drops way off after the first forty-eight hours." She grinned. "So you're way ahead of that curve."

Gwen had already decided that she didn't like lying to Marly Kenna. She took a breath, held it a moment, let it out. A deeper breath today than yesterday, she noticed. Every day, it was getting easier to do.

"Okay," she said. "I'm fine."

"Are you sure?"

"Absolutely." Then, just because it felt good to say something honest, she said, "Your hair looks pretty today."

"Oh, Jesus." Detective Kenna made a face, moving a stubborn lock away from her forehead. "Static city."

"No, I mean it. It's always so shiny."

"Well, thank you." Marly smiled. "I'd love to have your eyes."

Gwen didn't know what to say to that, so she didn't say anything. Detective Kenna leaned down and squeezed her hand again.

"Just keep 'em open until we pick up shithead, that's all. You're going to be fine."

---

By Monday morning, Tony Briggs had a throbbing gash on the side of his head that wouldn't stop seeping no matter what he did.

Neighbor guy really had caught him a good one. It was more of a burst than a cut, jagged and star-shaped. Probably infected by now.

Tony had forgotten how much of a pain in the ass a scalp lac could be. It wasn't like you could put a Band-Aid on it, and they bled like all holy hell. This one wasn't clean enough to Super Glue, and the swelling only made it yawn open wider.

He'd ended up wrapping gauze all the way around his head before going to sleep. He woke up looking like the fucking flute player from that Civil War painting. He called Ray.

"Revolutionary War," Ray said.

"Whatever. I need stitches."

"I told you last night you needed stitches. You were a tough guy, remember?"

"Yeah, well. Come down and get me."

"Man, we go on shift at three. I'm asleep."

"Come on. It'll only take an hour."

"You don't know that." Ray yawned into the phone. "Shave a patch and put strips on it."

"Forget that. I ain't shaving shit."

"Drive yourself, then."

"Dude, I have a head injury."

Ray showed up at the door in half an hour, coat over his arm, looking annoyed. His shirt was actually untucked. Tony recognized the coat from last winter. That was some haphazard shit for Ray Salcedo.

"You know they're just going to shave a patch at the ER," Ray told him.

"Bullshit." Tony pulled the door closed and locked the bolt. "They can stitch it like this. I've seen 'em do it."

"Twenty bucks."

"Twenty bucks what?"

"Twenty bucks says it takes three hours, and when we come back, your head looks like a cat's asshole."

"How long you been into cats?"

On the road, Ray went the wrong direction. Tony looked over from the passenger seat, holding a fresh square of gauze over the open cut. "Hit the clinic on Dodge, it's closer."

Ray just shook his head slowly. He kept driving east, toward midtown.

"Where are you going?"

"To a hospital," Ray said. "We've got a legit reason to be at a hospital. So I'm taking you to a hospital."

It didn't happen often. Hardly ever, in fact. But rarely, every once in a great long while, Tony Briggs felt stupid.

The girl. He'd been so preoccupied with all of last night's bullshit that he'd forgotten all about her.

Ray could take a stroll around while he was getting

sewn up. Guy had a touch with nurses anyway. At least one of them was using his head for something besides stopping crutches.

"Score one for Salcedo," Tony said. "If they haven't let her out yet."

"Hey," Ray said. "Heads up."

"What?"

"Two o'clock."

"Where?"

He nodded up the street. "Brick house, front yard."

Tony squinted into the glare and saw a bunch of little kids building a snowman. "What's the problem?"

"That one with the pigtails."

"What about her?"

"She look like trouble to you?"

"Man, what are you talk . . ."

Tony stopped without finishing the sentence. He looked at Ray, clenching his jaw. He checked his gauze pad. Folded it over. Pressed it back against the cut.

"In the Care Bears coat," Ray said. "Seriously."

"Blow me," Tony said. "Seriously."

"Hop out and punch her before she sees our faces."

"Why don't you just fucking drive?"

# 19

In the elevator, a young guy loaded with gift bags got off on the maternity floor. He looked like his whole world had opened up. One floor later, a middle-aged woman got on and pressed the button for the oncology lab. She looked like her world had caved in.

Worth rode along in silence, adding up time in his head. Counting what he'd managed last night, after the crime scene at his house cleared out, he'd slept a total of about eight hours in the past seventy-two.

He felt clear and alert, but he knew it was an illusion. Just his body tricking him with adrenaline. It would be easiest just to push through until his shift tonight.

It would also be a bad idea. He figured he needed at least a couple more hours today, just to keep the tanks from going bone dry. He didn't want to let that happen.

Worth offered a smile to the woman when he stepped off on Gwen's floor. She didn't seem to notice that anyone else was there.

• • •

"Knock knock."

Gwen's face brightened the moment she saw him. "Hey."

"Hey." He smiled back. "How are you feeling?"

"Better," she said. "Lots better."

In the time it took for that, Worth realized that over the past few days he'd stopped thinking about her like a person. Gwen had become a situation.

Seeing her smile, a fresh start in her eyes, he remembered why he'd done what he was doing.

"You look great."

"Yeah, right." She made an attempt to arrange her gown, then waved off the effort. "Do you guys know each other?"

Worth nodded to the detective from the Domestic Violence Squad he'd spoken with early Saturday morning. Kendrick. Kendall?

"Hi," he said. "Didn't mean to interrupt."

"You didn't. We were talking hair."

Kenna. She stood up, shouldered her Softsider, and gathered her coat and scarf. She patted Gwen's toes through the sheet and said, "I'll keep in touch. Call if you need me. Okay?"

"I will."

Detective Kenna caught Worth's eye. She glanced toward the door. Worth looked at Gwen—*back in a minute*—and followed.

Outside the room, Kenna pulled the door closed behind them. "It's Matt, right?"

"Good memory, Marly."

"Not bad yourself."

It wasn't impressive. Back when they'd still been trying, early on, he and Sondra had gotten one false positive from a home pregancy kit; a few days before she'd started her period, almost two weeks late, they'd sat up past midnight picking baby names. Marly had been Sondra's top choice in the Girl column.

He didn't mention it. "I don't mean to step on your toes. I was just in the neighborhood, thought I'd check up."

"Jesus. My toes?" She had a likable laugh. "Step on 'em. It's refeshing."

"Anything happening?"

"They're discharging her today. The warrant on James came through this morning." She glanced over his shoulder, and they both moved out of the way of a nurse pushing an EKG cart. "There's a vacant one-bedroom in a building over near Creighton University."

"Good," he said. "That's good."

In the ten years since Tiffany Pine, the department's DV Squad, the Domestic Violence Coordinating Council, and local shelters had worked together to create a county-funded network of safe apartments across town. Cases the squad deemed high risk were given temporary shelter on an individual basis. This was the news he'd been hoping to hear.

"She made me talk her into it," Kenna said. "But look, I've been doing this awhile, and I'm not seeing a girl who wants to go back to her apartment."

"I don't suppose she does."

"I'll be honest," Marly Kenna said. "I'm not liking this one."

"Anything in particular?"

"Just one of those bad feelings. You know?"

"I know exactly," he said. Thinking: *You have no idea.*

"Basically where we're at is, the girl's barely back on her feet, shithead's in the wind, and I'm up to my tits in casework."

Worth felt his eyes flicker down to the front of Detective Kenna's sweater. It happened before he could stop it. If she noticed, she didn't make it an issue.

"Plus half the town's been cooped up without utilities for the last, what?" She looked at her watch. "Forty-eight hours? And counting?"

"I take it calls are up."

"You'd think it was Christmas."

*Careful, now.* "Anything I can do?"

"Well, as long as you're offering . . . when's your next shift?"

"Tonight," he said. "Just came off two, so I'm on the next four."

"If the radio gets slow, think you could roll by the place, maybe?" Her face clouded as soon as she said it. Apologetic. "But you're not in the field. Sorry, I forgot."

"It's no problem."

"Hey," she said. She touched his arm; Worth sensed that the gesture embarrassed both of them. "Not for nothing, but I've heard of some bullshit details, you know?"

He waved it off. "One of those things."

"Then again, it's probably lucky for Gwen in there that she knew right where to find a cop she felt she could trust."

"Give me the number, I can check in on her," he said.

"Any problems, I'll radio dispatch, have them send a unit over."

"I'd appreciate it," Kenna said. "I'll tell Northeast to be aware of the location, too. But you know how it goes."

"Northeast assholes," another voice said. "They just want to chase bangers. Find guns and whatnot."

The guy walking toward them carried gloves in one hand, a corduroy coat on his arm. Tall, nice clothes. A clean smile.

When Marly Kenna saw him, her eyes flickered, then hardened a little. But only a little.

She smirked. "Spoken like an asshole."

"Marly Kenna. You look great."

"I know."

"Who's on bullshit detail?"

Kenna glanced at Worth. He saw in her expression that she didn't want to embarrass him further, wasn't sure what he'd want her to say. He extended a hand and spared her the awkwardness.

"Matt Worth," he said.

"Hi." The guy had a friendly grip. "Ray Salcedo."

"Good to meet you, Ray."

Salcedo tilted his head. "Worth?"

"That's it."

"Any relation to . . ."

"Kelly," Worth said. "Brothers."

"No kidding." Ray Salcedo gave a nod of respect. "Our sergeant talks about him. Highly."

"Thanks," Worth said. "Nice of you to say. Who's your sergeant?"

"Levon Williams."

Kelly's FTO. A good man. "Tell him I said hello."

Marly Kenna checked her pager, then dug into her bag. "Nobody sick, I hope, Ray?"

"Not like that," he said. "My partner's downstairs getting his head stitched."

"Yeah?"

"We've got a CI with a stab wound up here." Salcedo made a gesture to indicate the floor in general. "Figured I'd check in on him, as long as I was waiting around."

"Same guy?"

"Who?"

"The guy who stabbed your informant," Kenna said. "Same guy who cracked your partner's head?"

Ray Salcedo chuckled. "The CI was stabbed by a girl. Tony just forgot ice was slick."

"Oops."

"He remembers now." Salcedo nodded toward Gwen's door. "Who's yours?"

Marly Kenna gave him the basic rundown on Gwen and the warrant for Russell James. Her voice had gone a little further toward the chilly side, Worth thought.

While she talked, she scribbled an address and a phone number on the back of one of her own business cards. She handed the card to Worth.

"That's the safe unit," she said. "My info's on the other side."

"Got it," Worth said.

"Listen, we're on tonight," Ray Salcedo said. "Give me the place. Maybe we can look in."

Kenna raised an eyebrow to that. Then she shook her head, warming a little, trying not to show it. She scribbled on another card and handed it to Ray.

To Worth, he said, "Baker Thirty-five, if you want to hit us direct. When do you go ten-eight?"

"Eleven o'clock," Worth said.

"Got a make on the hitter's vehicle?"

As Worth described Russell James's one-in-four-hundred GTO, he realized that he didn't particularly like giving Salcedo information.

Maybe he was picking up on Kenna's initial demeanor, adopting it instinctively. Or maybe he suddenly felt more than the general paranoia he'd been carrying around for three days now. Maybe even more than the basic protective urge toward Gwen, in overdrive since the break-in at the house.

This was slightly different. This had begun right around the moment Salcedo showed up. All of a sudden, it was like he'd started feeling . . . territorial.

A nurse carrying a meds tray needed to get into Gwen's room. They parted the way for her. As the door opened, Worth caught a glimpse of Gwen, sitting up in the bed, looking out the window. She saw the nurse and smiled. Even when it was directed toward somebody else, he could feel the smile all the way out in the hall.

By the time the door eased shut, Worth was forced to acknowledge what Vince had known purely out of instinct: He'd fallen for this girl.

*Get it together.* The stakes were too high to be running around with some kid-stuff crush on a college girl with pretty eyes. This would be exactly the sort of bullshit that ended up ruining everything. Worth knew it. Whatever he'd thought he was doing, whatever he'd hoped to accomplish, it would all be for nothing in the end.

The fact was, Ray Salcedo seemed okay. Worth couldn't

be around Gwen all the time, and even if he could, it wouldn't look square.

And Gwen was obviously holding her own so far. Given the situation at this point, frankly, the more cops on board, the better.

"Thanks, guys," Detective Kenna said. "This girl's easy to like. You know? Be nice if it ended up right."

"Agreed," Worth said.

"Absolutely," said Ray.

Kenna said, "Officers."

She headed for the elevators, heels clicking, working her way into her coat as she walked. Ray Salcedo gave Worth a nod and caught up with her.

Before he turned away, Worth saw Salcedo lifting Marly Kenna's coat so that she could get her other arm into the sleeve. He saw Marly Kenna shrug, bat his hand away. Then she slapped him on the arm just for good measure.

But not too hard.

*You said you were going to call me.*

Ray Salcedo held up the business card she'd given him. Worth couldn't hear what he said. But she laughed.

They got on the elevator with a maintenance guy, a nurse pushing an old man in a wheelchair, and a doc in scrubs who looked tired and late.

Worth watched the doors close on all of them.

Then he turned, opened Gwen's door, and went inside.

# 20

The setup for the new TV spot consisted of a span of fifteen-pound sign paper stretched over an aluminum frame six feet square.

The signage was a blowup of the ad Eddie had run in the Sunday newspaper. In the center of the ad was a picture of a Homelite chain saw, made to look like it was coming out of the page, encircled by snowy pine boughs.

The bit with the pine branches had been Darla's idea. She'd also used her computer to make *Hundred-Year Storm Sale!* look like it was carved out of ice. She'd put snow along the tops of the letters, even made the exclamation point look like an icicle. The woman had talent, that was all there was to it. Eddie sometimes wondered how long he'd be able to keep her happy in the back office of a furniture store.

"Okay," Wade Benson said. "Cue chain saw."

From behind the paper came the sound of a stagehand pulling a starter rope. After a couple of tries, a chain saw whined to life, then settled into an idle growl.

Eddie shrugged his shoulders and ran his lines one last time in his head. He itched all over, and he was sweating like a sonofabitch.

Wade did the *three, two, one* thing with his fingers. He pointed to the cameraman.

Rolling.

Wade pointed to the voice guy.

*"Don't get caught in the cold,"* the voice guy said. He sat under a boom mike in the corner, but he was just there for timing; Wade said they'd dub the voice-over later, in the editing room, so you wouldn't hear the chain saw racket in the background before it was time. *"Come on down to the Hundred-Year Storm Sale at Tice Is Nice Quality Used and Discount Furniture, where the prices are . . ."*

The chain saw revved and came tearing through the center of the paper, cutting off the voice guy in mid spiel. The actor kicked his way through the slit and brandished the saw over his head. He had the coveralls, the hockey mask. The whole nine yards.

Wade pointed to Eddie.

"Raaaarrr," Eddie Tice said.

He lumbered into the camera frame, spreading his abominable claws high and wide. It was the same exact snow beast costume the actor now playing the chain saw maniac had worn for the initial Hundred-Year Storm spot yesterday morning. The inside of the suit was still damp with day-old stranger sweat when Eddie pulled it on.

After chasing the chain saw maniac out of the picture, Eddie lifted off the shaggy white head. He tossed the head aside, pointed to the camera, and said:

"Forget the cold! Don't let early winter ruin *your* Halloween. Come down to Tice Is Nice tomorrow night for our one-day-only Spooktacular! We'll slash our Storm Sale prices to positively ghoulish new lows."

Here was where the spot would cut to the new graphics Darla had done up. Bats and skeletons and megadeals.

"And don't forget to bring the kids! Safe, warm, indoor trick-or-treating begins right here at six P.M. We'll stay open 'til the witching hour. Shake off the ice at Tice Is Nice!"

"Cut!" Wade Benson said. He gave a satisfied nod. "Way to go, Eddie. I think we got it that time."

"Thank Christ. I'm broiling in this fucking thing."

Wade gave the voice guy a thumbs-up. "Great job, Otis."

The voice guy hung an unlit cigarette between his lips and performed a little bow.

"Hey, Wade?" The chain saw maniac pulled off his mask. "I just thought of something."

"Sure," Wade Benson said.

"Shouldn't it be the other way?"

"Shouldn't what be the other way?"

"Well . . ." the young actor said. "The script says don't let winter ruin Halloween. Right?"

"That's right."

"So shouldn't the chain saw maniac chase off the snow monster?"

"I'm not sure I'm following."

The actor put the chain saw down and blocked out the movement of the commercial with his hands. "Like, if the snow monster chases off the chain saw maniac . . . you know? Halloween loses."

"I see what you're saying." Wade glanced over his shoulder at Eddie and rolled his eyes. "But it's not a real snow monster, right? It's Eddie in a snow monster costume. Costume, Halloween, there you go."

"So it's like . . . Halloween against Halloween?"

"I think you're overanalyzing it," Wade said. "People will get the idea."

"Okay." The actor shrugged. "So, is that a wrap? I got a thing across town at three."

"We're done. Thanks, Andy. Nice work."

Andy the chain saw maniac tipped a salute, left the hockey mask and the saw behind, and hustled toward the dressing room.

Eddie went straight to the water cooler. Wade met him there, chuckling.

"Jesus," he said.

"Where do you find these fucking dipshits?" Eddie filled a paper cup and knocked it back. "I swear."

"Actually, the kid does sort of have a point. It doesn't really make a whole lot of sense."

"It's fine."

"Good enough for a town this size." Wade paused. "Hey, Ed. You okay?"

"I'm fine." Eddie gulped more water. "Why?"

"Because you look like shit."

"Thanks."

"I thought you looked like shit yesterday, but I didn't mention it. Today you look like dogshit."

"I'm wearing a goddamn ape suit, Wade. Give a guy a break."

"Yeah, that's kinda what I mean," Wade said. "Two spots in two days, Eddie?"

"Ahhh," Eddie said. "Okay."

Wade Benson was an old college buddy; he did all of

Eddie's production work in exchange for an at-cost discount at the store and the occasional eightball of blow.

"Say no more. I'll pay for the time if it's a problem."

"Don't be an asshole," Wade said. "I'm just asking. Why the sudden frenzy?"

"I have brain cancer," Eddie said. "The doctor says I'll be dead by Christmas. Happy?"

"Very funny," Wade said. "Shouldn't make jokes like that, my friend."

What was Eddie supposed to tell the guy? That he'd rather keep busy than sit around thinking about how he was two days away from eating a quarter million bucks? Ten times that, counting next year's business, if his friends in Chicago decided he couldn't handle their traffic, after all.

There was no future in furniture. Not in this town. Not with the Furniture Mart mafia running the city and Rod fucking Kush vaccuming up business down the street. Asshole had the same idea as Eddie for *his* storm sale, only instead of fourteen-inch goddamned Homelites, he was giving away sixteen-inch Stihls.

The fact was, Eddie Tice could film TV commercials until his dick fell off, and it still wouldn't change a thing.

Somewhere, Russ was out there. Laughing. The little puke. A twenty-five-year-old kid with no long view, counting his stupid trunk full of short dough. Thinking about it made Eddie want to go pick up the piece-of-shit chain saw over there on the floor and . . .

"I'm fine," he said. "Okay? I appreciate the concern. Now please go finish my Halloween commercial before Thanksgiving, huh?"

Wade shrugged and headed for the back of the

studio. Over his shoulder, he said, "You should give yourself a day off."

As if on cue, Eddie's cell phone buzzed inside the suit.

Jesus. He found the hidden zipper and dug around for the phone. Wade joined the voice guy and the camera guy. They all disappeared together into the editing suite.

Andy, the chain saw maniac, reappeared in street clothes. He slung a duffel bag over his shoulder and hurried out the back exit.

That left Eddie Tice standing alone, still wearing the ridiculous snow monster getup, sweat pouring down his face, cell phone buzzing in his big furry hand.

The caller ID screen didn't show a number. Just the corresponding name from the internal phone book. *Chicago.*

Just then, it hit him.

*They're both right,* he realized. *This stupid commercial doesn't make one fucking bit of sense.*

He didn't answer the phone.

---

The apartment was small but clean: a couple of rooms and a kitchenette, a few basic pieces of furniture. There was a color television and a cordless telephone and a spider plant hanging in the glass door to the balcony. Lydia House had supplied a few items of clothing and a plastic Walgreens sack filled with toiletries.

"Home sweet home," Gwen said.

Worth checked the place over, knowing it was a pointless activity. The volunteers from the YWCA had a checklist; the officer from the Victim Assistance unit who brought Gwen from the hospital would have made sure things were square.

In fact, there wasn't really any good reason for him to be here at all. Worth knew that. He had to be at assembly for roll call in forty minutes; he should have gone straight to work.

"Are you settled in?"

"Settled as I'll probably get." She gave a self-conscious smile. "But it's nice."

"Hopefully it won't be long." The building was secured through the telephone system. He picked up the phone, made sure there was a dial tone. "Has anybody been by to check on you?"

"Just the lady from the shelter," Gwen said. "She even brought my homework from the apartment."

"Okay."

Ray Salcedo and his partner, Tony Briggs, were rolling C-shift. Worth told her she might see them at some point.

She nodded and tucked a fallen strand of hair behind her ear. She was more or less dressed for bed: a snug cotton T-shirt that stopped at her belly button, flannel lounge bottoms that rested low on her hips. Worth tried not to look at her.

Gwen dropped her eyes, folding her slender arms over her waist. "Are you mad at me?"

"Of course not," he said. "Why would I be mad at you?"

"You're acting different," she said.

"I don't mean to."

"But you are."

"I just want to make sure everything is secure."

"Why?" she said. "Who would be coming?"

In her voice, Worth heard what she left unspoken, but he didn't know what to say.

He hadn't told her about the money he'd found in the trunk of her dead boyfriend's car. He hadn't told her that whoever the money belonged to had already come around looking for it.

He hadn't told her because he needed Gwen Mullen to keep doing exactly what she'd been doing so far. Until he had more information to work with, no good would come from leaving her alone here in a state of alarm.

Earlier, she'd told him that two of Russell's buddies had come to harass her at the hospital on Sunday afternoon. A kid named Troy Mather and a kid named Derek Price. They worked with Russell in the warehouse at a local furniture store.

Confronted with a prickly female OPD detective on her way back from the coffee machine, Mather and Price had claimed not to know Russell's whereabouts. Worth wondered—no doubt for altogether different reasons from Detective Kenna—whether these two had been lying or telling the truth.

Either way, Gwen would be safe here for now. He'd know more soon.

"You're looking at me different," she said quietly.

"I don't mean to, Gwen."

"You're not actually looking at me at all."

He finally did, and her face nearly broke his heart. It wasn't the face he'd seen earlier today in her hospital room; it was closer to the face he'd seen three days ago, in Sorensen's office above the store.

"Please don't start looking at me different." Her eyes glistened. "Please."

Some force moved him toward her. He didn't get there under his own power. It wasn't his doing, moving to hold her.

He just went numb for moment. Two seconds, tops.

The next he knew, she'd somehow folded into his arms.

"I know what I did," she said into his neck. "I don't know how. I hardly even remember doing it now. It's like a big red blur."

"Gwen. Shhh."

"I was too scared to leave but I couldn't let him hit me anymore." She pressed her face against his. Her hot tears seemed to burn his cheek. "I meant to turn myself in. When I came to the store. I did."

"I know."

"Please believe that I did."

"I believe you," Worth said.

"I'm screwed up, Matthew. You don't have any idea. But please don't look at me differently."

He opened his mouth to tell her he wouldn't, but somehow her lips ended up on his. She clawed her hands into the back of his jacket, but her mouth was soft as warm silk.

He wanted to push her away but he couldn't. All of a sudden, he became aware of the length of her body pressed against him. Through thin cotton and flannel he felt her breasts, her stomach, her hips. Her mouth parted, and he felt the wet velvet flick of her tongue.

His mind flashed to Sondra's kiss in the kitchen on Saturday. It hadn't been like this. This reminded him that he hadn't really touched a woman in over a year.

It wasn't what this was supposed to be about. Gwen hadn't even healed from her injuries.

Yet she sighed in his mouth and he was hard as a rock. Angry at himself for letting this happen, swept up in it at the same time.

"Thank you," she murmured. She touched his face. "Thank you."

He drew Gwen closer, telling himself over and over to step away.

---

Tony Briggs hit the john on the way to roll call. He looked at the side of his head in the mirror while he washed his hands at the sink.

They'd shaved a patch at the hospital.

It had taken the doc eleven stitches to cinch the wound up. The job had left a puckered spot the size of a quarter in the fresh bald spot on his scalp.

Leaving the hospital, Tony said, "Get it over with." Ray had just smiled to himself. He hadn't said a word.

Tony dried his hands on a paper towel and made his way down to the muster room. Everybody was there already, sitting around the table, shooting the shit. They all stopped talking when he walked in.

He looked around. "What?"

"Meow."

Tony couldn't tell who said it.

Carla Billup started making a purring sound. She pretended to lick the back of one hand, smoothed it over her ear.

Pretty soon everybody joined in.

"Meeeow."

"Reeow."

"Mrrrowwww."

Down at the end of the table, Ray Salcedo had a big, shit-eating grin on his face. Tony glared at him. Ray just shrugged: *Don't look at me.* Even Sergeant Williams was smiling.

Pathetic. It sounded like a bunch of goddamned back-alley strays in there.

"Hey, I get it," Tony Briggs said. "You guys are a bunch of pussies."

Carla Billup made a claw and swiped at the air. "Fffft."

The whole crew broke up over that.

Hilarious.

# 21

The woman pulled out her debit card and laughed. "I thought Halloween was tomorrow."

When Worth made eye contact, her grin faltered and slowly collapsed. He watched her eyes flicker to his shield, down to his gun, widening slightly with the recognition that neither was a costume prop. It didn't seem to matter that he was smiling. That he'd spoken to her in a friendly tone of voice.

"Oh. Gosh," she said, evading his eyes now. "Um, plastic, please?"

What did people think? Worth remembered his father coming home with plates of food from people in the neighborhoods. Was it like this back then, too? Reach out to the average law-abiding citizen and half the time they acted like you were there to shoot them or put them in jail.

Worth tossed eighty bucks' worth of shampoo and vitamins into a one-ply sack. He handed the sack to the woman and said, "Watch your ass."

The woman inhaled sharply.

Then she tucked her chin and scuttled out of there.

Watching her go, Worth could feel LaTonya looking at him. He looked back at her. "What?"

LaTonya just held up her palms. "Baby, I ain't said a word."

All night long, the minutes seemed to crawl. Worth saw an old man with ashy skin lift two packages of D-cell batteries. Instead of busting him, Worth handed him a ten-dollar bill. The man said, "Lord bless you, brother," and walked out without paying for the batteries.

At 2 A.M., he normally walked the outside perimeter. Tonight, Worth went to the break room for coffee instead. Ricky and Curtis were there, eating Snickers bars and reading the newspaper.

"Hey, Supercop." Curtis threw him a nod. "What's shakin'?"

"Guys." Worth poured coffee into a Styrofoam cup. "Thanks again for all the help yesterday. I owe you."

Curtis waved it off. "You bought the beer. Hey, we went by to see Gwennie today. They let her out, huh?"

"This afternoon."

"When you think she's coming back to work?"

"Few days, maybe." Worth shrugged. "She's still pretty banged up."

"You guys find jerk-off yet?"

Worth sipped his coffee without answering.

Curtis nodded. "Sooner or later, right?"

Worth said, "I expect."

Ricky got up from the table. He tossed his candy

wrapper in the trash, tied his apron strings around front, and went over to the time clock on the wall. He punched back in, gave Worth a nod, and went back to work.

Since his second or third week in exile at the SaveMore, rare was the occasion when Ricky failed to flip him some type of good-natured shit. The kid's recent demeanor was beginning to nibble around the edges of Worth's thoughts.

He was about revisit the subject with Curtis when his cell phone buzzed on his belt.

Worth didn't know the number on the ID screen. He stepped out of the break room and answered.

"Matthew?"

The safe unit. Worth felt his pulse kick up. "Are you okay?"

"I . . . yeah," Gwen said. "Not really. I don't know."

"Tell me what's wrong."

"Can you come over?"

"I'm not sure that's a good—"

"Please come over," Gwen said.

She answered the phone after three or four rings and buzzed him into the building.

Ray Salcedo opened the apartment door.

It was 2:35 in the morning. Salcedo and his partner should have gone off duty over two hours ago, but Ray was still dressed in patrol gear: long sleeves, turtleneck, comset on his shoulder, trouser legs bloused into the tops of his boots. He must have arrived at the apartment just ahead of Worth. He still hadn't taken off his gloves.

"What happened?"

"Eight-eight," Salcedo said.

Situation secure. Worth had been on channel 2 all night; he hadn't heard this address go over the radio. "I thought you guys went off at midnight?"

"Covering sick-outs," Salcedo said. He held the door and stood aside; Worth entered the apartment, feeling a tingle in his gut.

Another cop appeared from the hallway to the bedroom. Salcedo's partner, Tony Briggs. Worth could see the stitches in the guy's head from across the room.

"Goddamn," he said, adjusting his belt. He wore gloves just like Ray. "That bitch knows how to suck dick."

Worth wasn't sure he'd actually heard what he'd heard.

But there wasn't any mistaking the sound of the apartment door closing behind his back. He looked over his shoulder, saw Salcedo giving the bolt a twist. *Click.*

All his senses went hot. He suddenly became hyperaware of the size of the space, the layout of the room, his position between Salcedo and Briggs.

Briggs walked straight toward him. "Matt Worth in the house."

Worth stepped back and angled himself so that he could see Briggs and Salcedo both. Briggs kept walking. Salcedo leaned against the door.

Worth moved his right hand to his radio. "Where's Gwen?"

"Gargling, my guess." Briggs laughed. "Swear to God, Ray? My balls feel lighter."

Worth felt something flare in his head. Like powder burning out of a priming pan. Down the hall, the door to the bathroom was closed. Light glowed along the bottom edge.

"Hey, man, you gotta tell me something." Briggs stepped close, tapping him on the chest with the back of one glove. "She ever let you—"

Worth hit his hand away.

Briggs grinned and slapped him.

Worth saw it coming from his blind side, reacted a split second too late. Leather smacked his cheek. The blow landed much heavier than he'd expected, throwing off his response.

The room shimmered, then dimmed.

He wasn't sure how things happened from there. One minute he was stepping in tight, coming up under Briggs's jaw with a short left. Then a grenade went off in his solar plexus and he was on his knees, unable to breathe.

Worth fell to his hands and time stopped for a little while. He tried to inhale and couldn't. The carpet went out of focus, and his nerve system began sounding alarms. Worth forced himself not to panic, knowing it would just make him pass out that much quicker.

At last he managed to drag in a small sip of air. Then another. Worth finally crouched back onto his heels and looked up, into the muzzle of Tony Briggs's nine-millimeter service weapon.

"Welcome back," Briggs said. "Stand up."

Worth discovered that his own Glock had already been removed from its holster. He had a lockback knife in a belt pouch, but he knew he couldn't do much with it at this point except make things worse.

He'd never been a good fighter. He didn't have the natural instincts, and he'd known it coming out of academy. On the street, he'd always relied on superior training and bigger brains. When a scenario had to go hands-on, he'd learned through hard experience how to gain advantage where he could. How to know where he couldn't.

But in almost ten years on the job—as many wrong moves as he'd made, even counting the fights he'd out-and-out lost—he'd never been caught dead-bang until now.

"Up."

Worth stood to his feet.

"Lose the gear and take two steps toward me."

He unstrapped his handset, unbuckled his belt, and dropped it all in a heavy pile on the carpet.

*Never give up your weapon.* It was like a Bible verse. *No matter what happens. No matter what. Never, ever, not ever do you let the other guy end up with your gun.*

Tony Briggs pointed his own at Worth's face, slipping his finger inside the trigger guard. Worth finally noticed the sap gloves he wore. Prohibited old-school gear, no doubt purchased through the mail or over the Internet. Steel or lead in the knuckles—nothing you'd probably notice unless you'd ever worn or been hit by a pair.

He was thinking of the knot above John Pospisil's eye. The stitches in Briggs's head.

Slipped on ice, Ray Salcedo had said.

Standing there, staring into the round black hole of Briggs's gun barrel, Worth could see the whole thing: John coming through the doorway to the living room, Briggs waiting in the darkness at his left. He could choreograph the exchange of blows on wound location alone.

"Come on out," Briggs said over his shoulder. "Everybody's friends."

The bathroom door opened and Gwen appeared, hands cuffed in front of her. Her gray eyes blazed, nearly green in appearance. "I didn't touch him."

Tony Briggs chuckled. "That's sweet."

"Matthew, I didn't."

"He knows you didn't, sweetie." Briggs looked at Worth and holstered his weapon, just to show he didn't need it. "He also knows who the alpha dog is. Right, brother?"

Worth turned his back, stooped, and picked up his gear belt. He took his time strapping it back on. Briggs stood by, watching, seeming amused.

"So you're Tony?"

"That's me."

"I heard you got your head cracked open by a one-legged guy," Worth said. "Is that really true?"

Behind him, Ray Salcedo chuckled.

Tony Briggs smiled, nodding along. "That's good. Hey, where's your gun, funny man?"

"What do you want?"

Briggs shook his head. "Don't even play."

Worth walked over to Gwen. He used his own key to undo her cuffs. He tossed the bracelets to the carpet and rubbed her wrists between his hands.

She stepped in close, but her body stayed rigid. If there had been any time in the past three days when he'd made her feel safe, he didn't make her feel that way anymore.

"He said if I didn't go along he'd shoot you in the head when you walked in," she said. "He showed me the gun he was going to use. He had it in a paper bag."

Worth saw the wrinkled lunch sack sitting on the table off the kitchenette. He wondered how often Tony Briggs dropped a piece to make a story work out his way.

"Let's skip the bullshit," Briggs said. "We know all

about what you two tricksters have been up to. So you don't need to knock yourself out, pretending you don't know why we're here."

Ray Salcedo came away from the door, shoulders square, thumbs hooked in his belt. He offered Worth a companionable shrug. *Sorry, guy.*

"Here's what I'm wondering." Briggs walked over and picked up the phone. "Say I had a line on a homicide case potentially involving one of our own. If I called right now? You think Detective Vargas would pull his dick out of your wife long enough to answer the phone this time of night?"

Worth felt his face get hot. He ignored it this time.

"I wouldn't," Salcedo said.

"Dude, me either," said Briggs. "I was Detective Vargas, I'd need two dicks."

"So for you that would be what?" Gwen said. "A two-hundred-percent increase?"

Worth looked at her, surprised.

Ray Salcedo laughed out loud. "Snap."

Tony Briggs gave her a long, slow grin that started in his eyes. "You're a handful, aren't you?"

"You wish."

"I'll bet it was you who did old Russ," Briggs said. His radio crackled; he reached to his hip, listened to the chatter a moment, then turned it down. "Isn't that right? Lover Boy here doesn't have the sack for it. I can see that. But you got a little freak back there, don't you, baby?"

If Gwen's eyes had been laser beams, Tony Briggs would be a smolding black scorch mark in the carpet. It was like she'd shifted into a gear Worth hadn't known she had.

He turned his attention back to Briggs and Salcedo. Somehow they knew Russell James was dead. They thought he and Gwen had planned it together. Worth wondered what else they knew.

"Hey, whatever," Briggs said. "The stiff is your business. We're not judging."

"Wouldn't be our place," said Ray.

"Hell, any guy hits his girl the way that guy hit on you? My book? Baby, I don't care who he works for. That's a guy who got what he deserved." Briggs shrugged. "As soon as you two adjust your thinking, accept the fact that you don't get to keep what isn't yours? I don't see where the four of us have a problem."

There it was.

Of course they knew about the money. Because it was *their* money. Briggs and Salcedo. Russell James must have been working for them somehow. And they were working for somebody else. Somebody higher up the ladder.

Gwen looked at Worth. He could see the question in her eyes. *What is he talking about?*

He looked at Briggs and Salcedo, again wondering how far ahead they really were.

They were up on Sondra. They'd been inside his house. It wouldn't take much for them to figure Junk Monkey Scrap and Salvage into the equation, if they hadn't done that already. Worth thought of the effortless manner in which Ray Salcedo had procured the information he needed from Detective Kenna.

He put his arm around Gwen's waist like they were Bonnie and Clyde. "I guess you win."

Tony Briggs smiled.

# 22

Rita missed her connection in Denver and didn't get home until late Monday night.

Vince waited up for her at the kitchen table, reading the paper and sipping Jim Beam. She came up the back stairs with her suitcase and a long sigh that said she was happy to be home.

"Brrr."

Vince didn't turn. "Told you to pack a coat."

"You don't need coats in the desert."

She left the suitcase at the top of the steps. Twice a year she visited her mother, two weeks at a time, and she'd never packed more than the one small suitcase. A few changes of clothes and a sketch pad or two. *I'm coming right back,* she always said.

She came up behind his shoulder, burrowed a hand into his hair, and scratched the back of his head like a puppy. "Hey, babe."

Vince scraped his chair back and swatted her rear.

"Let's get you warmed up," he said.

• • •

Rita had gone gray early. She had a wild springy mass of hair, and by her forty-third birthday, every strand of it had gone the color of stone. But where Vince had put on sixty pounds over the years, at fifty-one, Reet still had the body of a thirty-year-old marathon runner. Slim and sinewy.

She took care of herself first, making the same sighing sound as she'd made walking in the door. *Home sweet home.*

Just as Vince was about to let himself go, she stopped at the very top. The last possible inch. She held herself there, grabbed two tight handfuls of his chest hair, and pinched her knees up under his ribs.

"I thought you weren't going to drink while I was gone."

"Jesus," he said. "Come on."

"Well?"

He coughed out a breath. "I got lonesome."

She screwed up her mouth in the moonlight and gave a sharp tug with her fists. It hurt about as much as she'd wanted it to. Then she slid down slowly, rocking her hips, squeezing gently as she lowered herself.

That was all it took.

It always had been. Twelve years ago, Rita had waited for Vince under a blooming crabapple tree in the parking lot of the state penitentiary. She'd smiled when they let him go at the gate, snuggled in close as they'd walked back to the car. Just before they got in, she'd kissed him on the cheek and whispered, *This is the last time.*

That was the day he'd stopped all the bullshit and

embraced the lucky truth: Rita could do him in whenever she decided it was time.

They lay around together in the bed for a while. Eventually, she propped up on an elbow. "Mom says hi."

He chuckled. "Someone says hello to you, too."

"Uh-huh." She reached under the covers, gave him a squeeze.

"Guess again."

"I'm too sleepy." She yawned and stretched. "Who'd you see?"

"Matty."

She leaned back. "Your brother?"

"Day before yesterday," he said.

"You went back?"

"Didn't go anywhere. He came out here."

"I'll be darned." She seemed pleased by the news. "It's about time you two started keeping in touch. How is he?"

"Same as us," Vince said.

"Happy?" She grinned. "Broke?"

"Older."

"Speak for yourself."

Vince put a hand behind his head. He probably should have taken a shower before she'd gotten home. "Sondra's pregnant."

*"Really."*

"Isn't his."

Rita slapped his chest. "That's not funny."

"Didn't say it was."

"Poor Matthew." Rita stayed quiet a moment, then said, "You know, at your mother's funeral, he was the only one in your family who came over and talked with us."

Vince knew. It wasn't the first time she'd brought it

up. Next she'd remind him that Matty also had been the only other person standing with her under the crabapple tree that day at the pen.

The stupid shit.

Rita seemed to get an idea. Her voice grew concerned. "Is it your dad?"

"What about him?"

"Oh. Good." She planted her elbow in the pillow and rested her head on her hand. "I was just thinking, for Matthew to come all the way out here . . ."

"Nah," Vince said. "Old bastard's still alive far as I know."

"So what was the occasion?"

Vince shrugged. "Brought me a stolen car with a dead guy in the trunk. We took the body down to the burn shed. Spent today getting rid of the car. I was gonna chop it yesterday, but then we found a whole shitload of cash hidden inside."

He waited through another yawn.

"My," Rita said. She reached across him, grabbed her little granny-style bifocals from the nightstand, and perched them on her nose. "Sounds like you two had a nice time. I'm going to make tea."

Vince watched her pad across the cold floor, barefoot and naked, scrubbing her hair with her fingers as she moved. Soon he heard clattering in the kitchen. Cupboard doors, the pot rack. The sound of the faucet at the sink.

Of course she hadn't believed him. Who the hell would?

He lay there and looked at the shadows on ceiling, wondering how he was going to bring himself to do it.

How he would go to the closet, pull out the old ratty duffel bag he hadn't used in years, and show her the money he'd stowed there.

Two hundred and sixty-four thousand dollars. They'd counted it out together, him and Matt, sorting the soft wrinkled bills into loose stacks. It was street money, on its way to be laundered somewhere. Drugs, guns, skin, bets, fake IDs for all they knew.

As soon as they'd finished, Matty had told him to burn it. Same as everything else. The guy had disappeared; his money had to disappear with him. No leftovers.

Standing there, half tanked, looking at all that grubby dough in one big pile, Vince had agreed. They'd scooped the bills into a Hefty bag and drove it all down to the burn shed together.

He'd sobered up on the way.

Because disappearing some dead asshole was one thing. Butchering the car was another. Both had made Vince sick to his stomach, but for some goddamned reason, for Matthew, he'd been able to do it.

Ash-canning two hundred and sixty-four thousand dollars in green money? That was something else.

They lived in the goddamned hills, him and Rita. Between the yard business and what Reet brought in every so often on a public art comission, or selling her crazy scrap-metal lawn ornaments, they could pay everything they owed and live on the leftovers when they got old.

He'd gotten behind on the trash while she'd been gone. Thing was, down in the shed, there was a whole pile of Hefty sacks waiting to be burned. Every one of them looked more or less the same.

Matty's head had been back in Omaha, working

through all the things the money might mean to the situation he'd created for himself. He hadn't seen Vince make the switch.

Vince listened to Rita in the kitchen. Pretty soon the teapot began to whistle, slowly building until it rattled and shrieked on the stove.

---

Worth added it up.

Even with the lowball offer they'd already accepted, he and Sondra would turn a decent profit on the house. If he took his share of the gain, cashed in his savings and investments, withdrew the limit on his Visa card, and sold the Ranger off, he could probably scrape together a little less than half the amount he and Vince had found in the GTO.

If he raided the escrow account that paid for Dad's care, he could probably almost get there. Close.

He'd rattled off something he'd seen in some movie. Told Briggs and Salcedo he'd stashed the money in a storage unit. Six hours away.

*Then go get it,* Tony Briggs had said. *We'll give you a day.*

In the meantime, Briggs and Salcedo would check in at random using a cell phone Briggs had shaken off a dope slinger in North O. If Gwen missed a call at the safe unit, they'd arrest the slinger, log his phone as evidence, and call a lab unit to the apartment Russell and Gwen had shared.

Worth could see where they were going. The slinger's phone records would show a clog of calls to the safe house, where Gwen was supposed to be hiding. That would give Briggs and Salcedo enough probable cause to search the apartment where Russell James had been killed. Worth had done the best he could to neutralize the crime scene, but appearances were one thing. Apart from any evidence Briggs and Salcedo decided to plant there themselves, a lab workup would produce red flags.

It wouldn't take much before somebody began adding up all the connections just beneath the surface.

In the meantime, Briggs and Salcedo held all the cards. They were in position to shape the facts however they wanted.

*You'll hear where to make the drop.*

Worth walked over to the television, retrieving his service weapon from where Salcedo had placed it on the way out. He took it back and holstered it.

Gwen stood a few steps away, eyes gone distant, her arms drawn in around her waist. She still hadn't looked at him.

"I'm sorry," he said.

She flinched at his voice.

Worth couldn't remember feeling lower than this. Not when Sondra had told him she was leaving. Not when the guy she'd left him for had punched his lights out in front of half of CIB. Maybe not even bearing Kelly's casket toward a hole in the ground.

This was different. Dirty.

He looked at his watch; he'd been away from his post for thirty-five minutes.

Gwen said, "How much money is it?"

"Enough."

"How much?"

"It's not important, Gwen."

Now she looked up, eyes flaring. "Don't tell me that."

Worth didn't know what else to say. He didn't know

how to tell her that there was no money. Not anymore. He'd watched Vince fire up the incinerator and toss in the sack.

Twenty-four hours.

"It's going to be okay," he said.

"How?"

An excellent question.

"I'll take care of it," he heard himself say.

# 23

By Tuesday morning, the temperature had risen above freezing, even with a foot and a half of snow on the ground. By afternoon, the streets coursed with runoff, and the storm drains babbled like happy brooks.

*Don't like the weather? Just wait five minutes.* People around here loved saying corny bullshit like that. Eddie Tice couldn't get a break.

"Don't worry," Darla told him. "It'll pick up tonight."

But it didn't. Business was slow for any Tuesday, let alone a one-day-only Spooktacular.

Eddie sent Troy Mather and Derek Price to Rod Kush's Furniture on a reconnaissance run. When they returned, Troy said, "Don't worry, boss. It's even deader'n this over there." But Eddie could tell by looking at Derek that it was a flat-out goddamned lie.

Around nine o'clock, a bunch of high school kids came in and sat in the recliners, fiddled with stereo knobs, and ate about a hundred pounds of candy. Eventually,

Eddie ran them all out. Half the little shitbags weren't even dressed up as anything.

By then it was official. Halloween night was a royal bust at Tice Is Nice Quality Used and Discount Furniture.

What else was new? At ten-thirty, Eddie closed the store early and sent all the employees home. When nobody was looking, Darla rubbed his back through the stupid Dracula cape he'd worn and said, "It's okay. This just leaves more time."

Eddie couldn't help but grin a little, despite his black mood. Looking at her did it to him. "Snow White, huh?"

Darla took a step back and curtseyed. She'd chosen the costume because her daughters were into the DVD. "Not for much longer."

Eddie didn't deserve the woman. That was all there was to it. She'd worked all morning to get the place decorated: black and orange crepe paper, jack-o'-lanterns sitting around in beds of loose straw, ghosts and bats hanging from the ceiling tiles. It seemed like a shame.

After everybody was gone, he locked the doors and shut down the lights. He used the cape to wipe the stage blood from the corners of his mouth, then wadded the whole thing into a ball and tossed it in the trash.

In the office, he pulled the bourbon from the middle drawer of his desk and filled a glass all the way to the rim.

Eddie had half a buzz working by the time he realized he wasn't alone.

"Holy Christ," he said. He sat up too quickly in the chair, sloshing fine Kentucky whiskey over the back of his hand. He reached out to the lamp on the desk and pulled the chain.

The man from Chicago rose from the Queen Anne

replica chair in the corner. He came out of the shadows, into the dim yellow light.

Eddie said, "When did you get here?"

"Earlier," the man said.

"You're staying downtown? I told Plaski I'd send somebody."

"That's not a concern."

"Jesus." Eddie offered a welcoming smile. "You almost gave me a heart attack."

"Apologies," the man from Chicago said.

---

Worth must have counted two dozen Spider-Men.

You couldn't look in any direction without seeing a Harry Potter or an Incredible. Ballerinas appeared to be making a comeback, while angels and pirates seemed thin on the ground. Up and down the street, light-sabers bobbed along like disembodied stalks of neon in the silvery dark.

He sat at the curb and watched the parade of trick-or-treaters until long after dusk. They moved in chattering coveys, bundled up under their costumes, paced by adults on foot or in creeping SUVs. He saw firemen and surgeons, carpenters and ball players, even a cowgirl. So far, he hadn't seen a single kid dressed up like a police officer.

By seven-thirty, the temperature had dipped enough to scatter the festivities to the indoor shopping malls at Westroads and Oak View. Soon homeowners began to emerge, huddle down their walks, and douse the paper-sack luminaries that glowed orange around the neighborhood.

*You can't just sit here.* It was a wonder some vigilant

soul hadn't already called him in. Worth knew he was being foolish, but he couldn't seem to get off the dime.

With everything else that had been happening, he'd actually forgotten that tonight was Halloween. Somehow he found himself transfixed by the innocent clockwork of it all.

Later, bored teenagers would show up in gore-splattered packs to festoon what was left of the trees with toilet paper. In other parts of town, buildings would get tagged. Shots would be fired, tires slashed. Property would end up listed on insurance claims.

But for now, it was still about little kids playing make-believe, dressing like their heroes, filled up with faith in a system that wouldn't trick you if you played by the rules.

Worth didn't realize he'd nodded off until he was jerked awake by somebody pounding on the window. When he saw who it was, he got a bad taste in his mouth.

"I thought we were done with this," Mark Vargas said.

The street ahead had emptied, and the cab of the Ranger was cold. Worth moved his watch into the light of the streetlamp: 9:15.

This was crazy. He shouldn't have driven out here. But he had, and here he sat. He took a breath, twisted the ignition to the accessory position, and ran the window down.

Vargas hadn't put on a coat to come outside. He stood there in jeans and a sweater, breath coming out like steam. Just the sight of his face put a knot in Worth's gut.

"She's in there scared." Vargas nodded across the street, to the house with all the landscaping and the big detached garage. "Does that make you happy?"

"No," Worth said. "I'm not—"

"Sitting outside my house?" Vargas looked like he was ready for anything. "Seriously? We're not done with this yet?"

Hearing it like that didn't sound fair. All of that had ended months ago. "I'm not—"

"I told her it was a mistake to talk to you."

"Look, this isn't—"

"Put your hands where I can see them."

Jesus. The guy actually thought he was here to hurt somebody.

Worth put his hands on the steering wheel and said, "I came to talk to you."

"We talked already."

"This isn't about that."

"Then what the hell are you doing here?"

Up the street, a guy straight out of an Eddie Bauer catalog stood up straight and looked their way. Vargas raised a hand to him. *Don't worry. Everything's under control.* The guy gave the Ranger a long sideways look and went back to snuffing his luminaries.

Worth realized he was gripping the steering wheel.

He made himself stop, looked at Mark Vargas, and swallowed every last ounce of his pride.

"I need your help," he said.

---

It was painful, no question about that. But it didn't hurt as much as he'd expected it would.

Eddie finished counting three hundred grand from the office safe, laying it into the plain brown case on the desk. Crisp new bundles, all twenties.

Honestly, the message from Chicago hurt more than the money. Eddie could be trusted; there was no reason to send a collector all the way here. But Mr. Plaski had insisted. Fucking Polacks.

"How about this weather?" he said.

The man from Chicago didn't seem interested in chatting about the weather or anything else. He just wanted his boss's money. The money Russell was supposed to have transported days ago. He stood on the other side of the desk with a long wool coat draped over his arm: expensive suit, dark turtleneck sweater, a classy-looking watch on his wrist.

Eddie was surprised the Poles had sent a black guy. For some reason he'd thought the old-country types were prejudiced.

"I hope Mr. Plaski understands that this isn't the way Eddie Tice normally does business."

He turned the case, lid open, and nudged it across the desk. It was at least 40K more than Russell had stolen, but Eddie wanted to express his contrition over the whole goddamned sorry bullshit situation.

Tony had advised him against it. *You don't volunteer to pay somebody more than you owe, Uncle Eddie. It sends all the wrong signals.*

But Tony wasn't a businessman. And Eddie wasn't trying to get some broad in the sack. He was making a good-faith investment in a business partnership. A partnership between reasonable men.

The man from Chicago stepped forward. He closed the case with one hand, snapping the latches one at a time.

"I'm sorry you had to make the trip," Eddie said. "This is a one-time adjustment, believe me. I've addressed the problem, I can promise you."

The man nodded. "You've addressed the problem?"

"Mr. Plaski can be assured of that."

"What is the problem, in your view?"

"Well, obviously there was . . ."

"How have you addressed it?"

Eddie closed his mouth.

"Mr. Plaski has concerns," the man said.

"I can understand that." Eddie nodded to show that he understood completely. "Whatever I can do to reassure . . ."

While Eddie was talking, the man from Chicago put his hand beneath his overcoat and casually produced an automatic pistol. Eddie was so busy planning what he was going to say next that he didn't even notice at first.

All at once, everything changed. It was as if the office began to hum all around him. Eddie took one look at the gun pointed at his stomach and felt his scrotum shrink.

"Hey, no, look. Listen."

"Which?"

"Jesus," Eddie said. "Which what?"

"Do you want me to look? Or do you want me to listen?"

"I just . . . Jesus, wait."

"Wait? You're being indecisive, Mr. Tice."

The gun had a long, fat cylinder attached to the barrel. Eddie had seen that shit in the movies. Professional killers used it when they wanted to shoot you so nobody could hear.

"Just wait." Eddie held up his palms. "I think I can . . ."

He heard a quick splurt of air, and something burst in his leg. For a split second, it felt like he'd been hit in the knee with a hammer. His whole leg went numb.

Then there was pain.

A whole big world of pain.

Eddie didn't realize he'd buckled until he found himself sitting in his chair. He heard screaming. For a moment, based on the roar in his head, he assumed the screams were his.

Then he saw Darla. She stood in the doorway, holding a feather duster, eyes wide and swimming with fear. Her hands flew to her mouth; the feather duster fell to the floor.

*No.*

What was she *doing* here? They'd agreed to meet at the hotel. She'd left an hour ago, with the other employees.

But now here she was, back again. She'd transformed from Snow White into a slutty, sexy maid. Garters, stockings, cleavage and lace, a frilly apron the size of a handkerchief.

Eddie whispered, "Please don't."

The man from Chicago had already turned. Eddie heard the same sound a second time—just a little puff of air. Like a whisper.

A small hole appeared in the bridge of Darla's nose. Something splattered the door frame behind her head. Her eyes went dull, and she stood there a moment, half naked, seeming confused.

Then she sagged.

*Oh, no.*

*No, no, no.*

Eddie's hands were slick. His pants leg was slippery with blood. What was happening? What had happened here?

"Please," he said. He looked at the man from

Chicago. What more did he *want*? It was all in the case, the whole wad. With interest. "Tell me what I—Jesus, why are you doing this?"

The man from Chicago put on his coat. He took the case from the desk. Case in one hand, gun in the other, he looked at Eddie.

He said, "'Put a bullet in his knee. If he spits in your face and tells you to fuck yourself, put him on the phone and I'll speak with him further.' Those were Mr. Plaski's words."

How could this be happening? Eddie wished he could start over. Do something different. He couldn't find any words to say.

"'If he begs or tries to bargain, just blow his stupid brains out and come home.'" The man from Chicago shrugged. "Mr. Plaski's words. Not mine."

It felt as though his knee were being crushed in a vice. The pain crawled up his ribs; cold sweat trickled down his spine.

He looked into the man's eyes. "But *why*?"

"This was a mess." The man from Chicago looked at his watch. "A small mess, all in all. But even a small mess creates a trust issue. Trust issues create liabilities. Mr. Plaski doesn't believe in liabilities. I'm sorry about your maid."

Eddie looked at Darla on the floor. She'd fallen on her knees, facedown on the carpet, arms bent beneath her, bare rump exposed. Just for him, she'd dressed that way. For fun. It wasn't really Darla's personality at all.

"Please," he whispered. "Please, just let me . . ."

The man from Chicago said, "You're still doing it."

Eddie saw the little puff from the hole in the cylinder, but this time he didn't hear the sound.

# 3

# PROTECT AND SERVE

# 24

Vargas had an office on the main floor. Dark walls and deep pile carpet, golf clubs in the corner and a humidor on the desk. He had some black leather furniture and a television. Even with the tension and hostility, there was enough room left over for a putting carpet, a speed bag, and an elliptical machine.

"Nothing was stolen," Worth said.

Vargas sat with his arms folded, listening.

"Television, stereo, nothing touched. Four hundred cash in a bank envelope, still in the top drawer of the nightstand."

"Nothing stolen," Vargas said. "Your neighbor interrupted, took a knot on the head. I get it."

Worth pulled a Ziploc bag from the brown kraft envelope he'd brought inside from the truck. He handed the bag to Vargas.

A stroke of genius. Or the stone dumbest thing he'd ever done. Either way, he'd done it. There was no undoing it now.

He said, "I found that under my bed this morning."

Vargas held up the bag and looked at Russell James's wallet through the clear plastic.

Originally, Worth had been thinking of using the credit cards to create a trail; in a few days, he'd book a motel room somewhere. Nobody would show up for the reservation, but the activity would be there just the same. At least enough to help solidify Gwen's story. Their story.

"Last Friday, I took a battery call on a store employee," he said. "Suspect, boyfriend, was code four at the apartment. Girl spent the weekend at Clarkson, released to a DVCC safe house near Creighton University yesterday afternoon. Boyfriend hasn't been located."

"What's one thing got to do with the other?"

"That wallet," Worth said.

He reached back into the envelope and pulled out a latex glove. Vargas humored him. He put on the glove and broke open the bag. He opened the wallet by the edges and looked at the driver's license. "Russell T. James."

"Warrant went out yesterday morning."

"This is the boyfriend?"

"That's him."

Vargas allowed a smirk. "So dumbass broke into your house, attacked your neighbor, and left his wallet behind." He dropped the wallet back into the bag. He put the bag down on the magazine table. "Who's working it?"

"Roger Sheppard out of South."

"Why aren't you talking to him?"

"I will," Worth said. "But I need to talk to you first."

"Look, no offense, right, but given the shit . . ."

Vargas dropped his voice. They both knew Sondra was out there, listening. She'd looked about as stressed as

Worth had ever seen her when he'd followed her new fiancé in the front door.

"Given the personal situation, I'm not seeing your point in being here."

"It's not exactly comfortable for me, either."

"Well?"

Worth took out a second bag and put it on the table next to the first. Hard plastic clunked against glass.

"I called in this morning and took an annual day," he said. "Spent the day turning my house over. I found that in my dresser drawer, tucked in a sock. Way in back. Never seen it before today."

Russell's phone. He'd intended to check the voice mail all weekend, but the phone had been as dead as its owner on discovery. One thing after another had diverted his attention since then. The storm. The trips to Vince's. The crime scene at his house. Gwen.

First thing this morning, after the surprise meet-up with Briggs and Salcedo at the safe unit, Worth had paid cash for a Radio Shack battery charger and found Russell's mailbox choked to capacity. Almost every one of the new messages had come in from the same number: Tice Is Nice Furniture on L Street, where Russell James had worked. Worth had deleted every message dated prior to Friday night, leaving the rest for Vargas.

"Back up," Vargas said. "Somebody breaks into your house. You find a wallet. Instead of reporting it to the primary, you go and toss your own place? That's your first instinct?"

"There's more," Worth said.

"Wouldn't there have to be?"

It was difficult to pinpoint the sensation. Sitting here

in Mark Vargas's den. Handling the contents of the envelope, laying them out in plain view.

Nauseating. Reckless. Supercharged. Like attempting to dismantle a bomb in the dark.

Worth dried his palms and took his time.

---

It was a quarter past two in the morning when Tony and Ray arrived at the furniture store. They parked Ray's Expedition around back, between the Dumpsters and the building, out of view of the street.

Troy Mather met them at the service door. He looked like he'd stumbled out of a car accident.

Tony grabbed him by the throat, shoved him inside, and slammed him hard against the wall.

"You don't ever fucking call me," he said. "Not ever. Nod if you understand."

Mather's eyes went wide. He tried to nod.

Tony eased his grip enough to give the kid a breath. Ray checked outside and pulled the service door closed behind them.

"The fuck you doing with Eddie's phone in the first place?"

"I . . . shit," Mather croaked. "Let me talk."

Tony let go of his throat, grabbed Mather by the sweatshirt, and shoved him a few feet down the dark hall. "Talk."

Mather caught his balance and straightened up. He rubbed his throat, caught his breath. All Mr. Thug Life, the last time Tony had seen him. Right now he looked like he wanted to cry.

"Man, I . . . you guys . . ."

"Take it easy," Ray said. "Just chill out."

"I didn't know how to get you," Mather said. He was practically whining. "I found 'Tony' on your uncle's phone, man." He dug the phone out of a deep pocket in his pants and held it out like a baby bird he'd accidentally squeezed too hard. "Sorry. Shit. I . . . yo, I didn't know *what* the fuck else to do. Me and Derek—"

"Shut up," Tony said. He stepped forward and swiped the phone out of Mather's hand. Mather flinched. "Now take a breath and quit acting like a bitch."

Troy Mather looked at Ray. He looked at Tony. He shook his head, took that breath, and chuckled like he'd heard something terrible.

"Fuck, man," he said. "This shit ain't right."

Tony Briggs began to get a bad feeling. He looked at Ray.

"Hey, Troy," Ray said. "Get a grip. It's okay."

"Fuck, man."

"Tell us what happened."

"Man, you guys need to come with me."

---

"These guys had done their homework on me," Worth said. "And they knew about . . . our situation."

"Whose situation?"

"You and me. Sondra."

For the first time in several minutes, Mark Vargas looked up from his notepad. "What does that mean?"

"I don't know if it means anything. That's what I'm saying."

"Are you saying they used her name?"

"To punk me," Worth said. "Let me know they had my number."

"Tell me exactly what they said. Word for word."

"Briggs picked up the phone like he could call you at home. He asked me if I thought you'd answer." Worth held up his hands. "Look, I'm not going to say it word for word. The two of them went back and forth on what they figured you guys would be doing that time of night. That was the gist of it."

Vargas leaned back in the chair.

"Like I said, they were trying to work me over." Worth shrugged, as though that had been the extent of it. "Look, you know half the force has heard some version or other. I walk into a room full of cops, half of them grin."

"I don't give a shit about half the force."

"Me, either," Worth said. On this point he was being a hundred-percent straight. "That's why I'm talking to you first."

Vargas sat with that. Worth let him sit. Sitting there, they both heard a faint sound, soft, like a dust cloth on wood.

Without saying anything, Vargas got up, crossed the room, and opened the door. Sondra jumped back. She stood there in a robe and shaggy slippers, looking up at Vargas, backlit in the doorway. Half defiant, half sheepish.

Vargas touched her shoulder and stepped out with her. He pulled the door after him but held the knob with one hand, not quite closing it completely.

Worth didn't particularly feel like overhearing their conversation. While they spoke in low voices, he got up and wandered.

It seemed like a nice house. Comfortable. Based on

the layout of the office, the way things were set up in here, Worth would have bet anything that the black leather furniture had all been out in the living room before Sondra had moved in.

He wondered if, one day, he'd be able to see any humor in the fact that he'd decided to take a poke at a guy with a speedbag and a pair of training gloves hanging in his den.

On the desk he saw the new issue of the police union newsletter, a SigArms catalog, and a Grisham novel. He picked up the newsletter, scanned the front page absently, dropped it back where he'd found it.

He overshot by an inch. The newsletter jostled the computer mouse, and the monitor screen seared to life. Worth saw the last thing Vargas had been looking at on the Internet.

Sports? News? Hard-core porn?

Baby cribs.

It was a shopping site, bright and pastel, cued up to a section containing cribs of all different kinds.

Worth wanted to hate the miserable prick more than ever. But he couldn't seem to feel it. Standing there, looking at the computer screen, it was like he just couldn't muster the voltage anymore. He thought again of how happy Sondra had seemed on Saturday.

If anything, he felt like he'd walked into a stranger's home with shit on his shoes.

Over by the door: *Yes, I promise. Okay?*

Worth wandered back to his spot as Vargas stepped back into the office and closed the door. They reconnoitered at the magazine table.

"She okay?"

"A little freaked."

"I'm sorry," Worth said.

Vargas looked at him squarely. Back to business. "There's a lot about this that doesn't make sense."

"I agree," Worth said. "But I know John Pospisil put a lick on whoever attacked him at my place. And Tony Briggs has a fresh set of stitches in his head. I'd bet money the blood at the scene puts him inside the house."

Vargas didn't comment on that. He went over to a shelf and turned on a base model signal scanner. The buttons lit up and chatter came crackling.

"You know them, don't you? Briggs and Salcedo. I could tell you recognized the names."

"We crossed paths a few times last year." Vargas tapped a button and found the digital traffic for the Northeast District. "They worked undercover at Orlando Heights."

"Vice?"

"Narco."

Worth felt a flush of triumph. Like he'd gambled, snipped an unmarked wire, and hadn't blown his head off. "Briggs and Salcedo worked Narcotics?"

Vargas tweaked the gain knob on the scanner, his silence conveying the affirmative.

"Okay," Worth said. "That explains a couple things."

"Maybe," Vargas said. "Maybe not."

He returned and sat back down in his chair. Worth did the same. Vargas picked up his notepad and tapped it a few times with his pen. They listened to the radio for a minute or two.

Somebody was on foot, chasing a tagger northbound on 50th toward Military Ave. An Adam unit took a Signal 6 from central dispatch. Two Baker Four and Two Adam Sixty were eight-zero at California Taco downtown.

"Here's my question," Vargas said.

Worth waited. *Tick tick tick.*

"Last night, you say this girl called you from the safe house?"

"That's right."

"You give everybody on the street your personal mobile number?" Vargas looked him in the eye. "Or is that only for special circumstances?"

Red wire.

Worth steadied himself. He needed to carefully separate this wire from the rest of the snarl in front of him.

He reached out. Took hold.

"I guess you would have to say there are circumstances."

*Snip.*

# 25

*Sweet Jesus.* That was Tony's first thought. *Aunt Joan smoked Uncle Eddie.*

Poor bare-assed Darla, too.

They both looked humiliated to be dead. Sprays of blood and brain matter coated the doorway. The wall behind the desk looked like a slaughterhouse floor.

Tony had run through the names of a few good defense attorneys before he saw the cabinet behind Eddie's chair. The door of the enclosed safe hung open.

"Out."

Mather and Price stood there like a couple of retards.

"Guys," Ray said.

Troy Mather blinked. "Is this fucked up? I mean, is this fucked up or what?"

"Step out for a minute."

Price, the skinny one with all the tattoos, bit off a hangnail and headed out the door. Mather looked from Ray to Tony, then edged around Darla's corpse like he didn't want to startle her.

When they were gone, Ray said, "Shit, man. I'm sorry."

Tony didn't have a goddamned thing to say. He couldn't believe this. Poor fucking Uncle Eddie.

"Thoughts?"

"Tonight was his meet-up." Tony rubbed his forehead. "He said he had it handled."

"You think he tried to short 'em?"

Jesus. The opposite, if anything. Eddie had been talking about how he was going to smooth the whole thing over. Actually considering giving the people in Chicago more than he owed.

Goddammit, Tony knew he and Ray should have been here, but no, Uncle Eddie had it covered. *I changed your diapers, kid.* That was exactly what he'd said.

"Not to push," Ray said. "But this could be a problem."

"I'm aware." Tony looked at his watch: 2:37 A.M. "Hey!"

After a couple of seconds, Mather poked his head back in. He tried not to look at Darla on the floor but he couldn't help it.

"Get back in here. Bring your buddy."

Ray looked at the splatter on the door frame, traced it with a finger to about where Tony was standing. The back of Darla's head was a ragged mess. The look on Eddie's face was tough to take.

Price and Mather came back in. Tony said, "Does he hold anything here?"

Mather blinked.

"Shithead! Does Eddie hold anything here?"

Price stepped up. "Nah, man. Stuff always goes to the off-site."

The storage unit in Florence. Tony had helped his uncle set it up with a fake name.

This was bullshit. Eddie was a born snake-oiler. He wore too much Tommy Bahama, and he obviously wasn't smart enough to know when he was in over his ears. But he was mostly a good guy. Mom's favorite brother.

The doer had kneecapped him first.

"Hey." Ray spoke in a calm voice. *Go easy. We need to think.*

A bunch of other cops looking into Uncle Eddie's affairs wasn't going to work. Who knew where the guy had gotten careless? Once they started hitting red flags, it wouldn't take much for some CIB asshole to look up and notice that one of the victims in his Halloween double homicide, a prominent local businessman, happened to have a drug cop for a nephew.

Tony spoke to Price instead of Mather. "Do you know the security schedule?"

Price shook his head.

"Ain't one," Troy Mather said. "Eddie used to have like these Wackenhut dudes overnight, but—"

"Who the fuck asked you anything?"

Mather shut his mouth.

Ray looked all the way around the perimeter of the ceiling. But Eddie didn't use cameras in the back office. Tony stood in place and turned; the doer would have been standing on this side of the desk when Darla walked in. Bang.

Had Eddie been dead already? Or had the doer made him watch?

"Darla have any other boyfriends?" Tony addressed

them both together. "What about the ex-husband? Either of you guys know anything?"

Price shrugged.

Mather said, "So I can talk now?"

"Careful," Ray counseled.

"Her ex lives in Ralston. She and Eddie hook up whenever the kids go down there to stay."

Tony could read the look on Ray's face. *Slow down, Serpico. We're not going to orphan any kids.*

But Ray was just going to have to get realistic. The setup was perfect, and they didn't need much. Just enough to put the ex at the scene. Maybe a smear or two of Eddie's blood inside a vehicle. It would be a slam-dunk picture, right down to the guy's denials. No deep digging.

"You two," he said. "Stay here."

"Stay where, man?"

"You with the tats. Price. What's your first name?"

"Derek."

"Okay, Derek, I want you on point. Go to wherever the cleaning crew keeps their shit and find some kind of gloves. Then go to the camera banks and take all the tapes out of the machines. You following?"

Price shrugged. "Gloves, tapes. Yeah."

"Stuff that shit in a sack or something and stay put. You. FUBU." Tony pointed at Mather. "Don't touch anything else."

The punk had shown the sense to call them—okay, he earned a couple points there. But Troy Mather still got under Tony's skin. He had a big mouth, a stupid face, and thought he was a tough guy. Bad combination all the way around.

"You guys are leaving?"

"We'll be back."

"Hey, fuck that, man." Mather raised his hands. "I ain't *even* staying around here."

"Listen up, assface. You do what I tell you, when I tell you, and keep your mouth shut. Understand?"

"Nah, man. You can kiss my balls. I did my part. I'm Gandhi."

Tony reached around his back and pulled the small-frame Colt from the lumbar holster under his jacket. Far from department-issue. He thumbed back the hammer and leveled on Mather.

"This is where you stop and think," he said.

Mather's eyes went wide. He held out his palms and shook his head. "Hey, shit. I mean, hey."

Even while the kid stood there, still running his mouth, flashes started going off in Tony's head. He thought about the scene. Thought about where he was standing. Thought about the odds of this mutt Mather keeping his shit together for more than a day.

He squeezed the trigger and shot him, high and right, one ring wide of center mass.

The range was too close, even for the low-grain rounds Tony carried. The bullet passed through Mather on a short rope of blood, spidering the one-way plate-glass security window looking out on the darkened store. The sound of the discharge in the space of the office was enough to make Tony's ears ring.

Troy Mather flailed to his right and stumbled back two or three steps. His face had gone dull with shock.

"Mother*fuck*." His features contorted and he gripped his shoulder. Within moments his sweatshirt had soaked through. "You shot me, man."

"Yeah," Tony said. He must have nicked the brachial artery, the way the kid was pumping out. "Why you standing around?"

"I . . ."

"You're getting blood all over the place," Tony said. "I'd be hauling ass out of here. That's me personally."

Mather didn't look well at all. He looked at Tony like he'd been betrayed by a brother.

It took a lot to get a reaction out of Derek Price. He stood there, leaning back just a little on his heels, his expression somewhere between surprise and amusement.

All at once Troy coughed, turned, and staggered out of the office, trailing blood the whole way.

"Derek," Tony said. "How'd you like a lifetime get-out-of-shit-free card?"

It took a couple beats before Price said, "Cool."

"Drive him to the ER," Tony said. "Take the long way. Make sure he's out of mud before you get there. Get what I'm saying?"

"Yeah," Derek said. He paused. "What do *I* say?"

Tony thought about it. "He have a cell phone on him?"

"I guess so. Yeah."

"After he's done, get his phone and call yourself. So there's a record. At the hospital, say he called you from here and told you to come pick him up. Understand?"

"He called me from here."

"You my guy?"

Derek Price shrugged. "Sure."

"Get going."

Price hustled out, following his buddy, being careful not to step in the blood trail. Tony thought, *Attaboy.*

He watched Derek disappear into the shadows leading

out to the showroom floor. Then he went around the desk and pressed the .45 into Uncle Eddie's cool dead hand.

He raised his uncle's arm and fired two more shots, both in the vicinity of where Troy Mather had been standing a minute ago. They'd need blowback on Eddie's hand for the lab. He lowered Eddie's arm so that it hung the way it had been. He let the gun drop to the carpet.

Just before he turned away, Tony had another thought. He opened the whiskey drawer.

Yep.

He removed Eddie's .38 and put it around his back, into the empty holster. He left the drawer open.

Ray was looking at him.

"What?"

"All finished?"

"About." Tony straightened, looked things over. "What do you think?"

"I think we should be going," Ray said.

# 26

*Nine out of ten women murdered are killed by men,* the fact sheet said.

She'd found it in the blue folder Detective Kenna had given her. Gwen had seen the sheet before. It was a flyer published by a local coalition titled "The Truth About Domestic Violence." One of her professors had used it as a handout in her social welfare seminar last semester.

*Of those women, half are slain by their husbands or partners.*

In fact, she'd seen the flyer even before then. A couple of times a year, somebody from the YWCA would go around the student union and distribute copies to all the tables and bulletin boards.

The first time she'd looked at this stupid piece of paper, she'd been at school. Sitting in the auditorium with a hundred other girls, a handful of amusingly uncomfortable-looking guys.

Now here she was, reading the same numbers in a

victim's hideaway provided by the same group that had published the flyer.

"Gwen, are you listening?"

She closed the folder and looked at Matthew across the small table off the kitchenette. It was six o'clock in the morning, still dark outside. She'd kept every light on in the apartment overnight.

"Do you understand what we need to say?"

"We've been sleeping together," she said. "For about three weeks."

"Since early October." He seemed so tired. "Russell found out about a week ago, and that's why he . . . that's why it was so much worse this time."

Something about seeing Matthew in street clothes instead of his uniform reminded her of what she'd found so sweet and appealing about him. It had grown harder and harder to remember, these past few days.

"I guess I don't understand," she admitted.

"We need to say that he came to the store to confront you, and I intervened. That's what set him off." Matthew closed his eyes and rubbed them with the backs of his fingers. "The parking lot cameras will back that up."

She hadn't told him how close to the truth that part of the story actually came.

"I mean, I don't understand why you want to say we've been sleeping together," she said. "It makes it sound . . . it makes you sound involved."

"That's what it needs to sound like now."

Because they needed a way to explain, Gwen realized. To other people. They needed a plausible explanation for why Tony Briggs and Ray Salcedo were coming after both of them, and not just her.

It made no sense otherwise. Why would Briggs and Salcedo think Matthew had known anything about the money Russell had been carrying? He was just the police officer who had driven her to the hospital and filed the reports.

Unless the two of them had been having an affair. That made things different.

"But we're changing our story," Gwen said.

He nodded. "It actually helps. It looks like we tried to hide something small."

*If you let somebody catch you lying about something small, it's that much easier to lie to them about something big.*

He was a cop; he would know how it needed to look. Gwen imagined he'd probably run across every kind of liar in the world.

Still . . .

"All the pieces are there," he said. "We just need to put them in the right light. And we need to do it first."

"Nobody will be suspicious?"

"Everybody will be suspicious," he said. "But there's more evidence to support our story than theirs."

"As far as you know."

He didn't have an answer for that.

They sat in silence for a minute.

Gwen said, "Can I ask you something?"

"Of course."

"What happened between you and your wife?"

He looked at her like he didn't understand the question. "How do you mean?"

"I mean, why did you get divorced?"

Silence.

"She wasn't happy," he said.

"Why wasn't she happy?"

"Probably because I wasn't happy."

"Why weren't you happy?"

He sighed. "I don't know."

"Did you ever hit her?"

"Jesus." Matthew got a look on his face like she'd asked him if he had some kind of a thing for little kids. He leaned back in his chair. "No."

"Really?"

"Of course not," he said. "Why did you ask that?"

"I just keep thinking," she said. "Sitting here in this apartment, it's like I can't stop thinking. Even when I try."

"Gwen . . ."

"And I just can't figure it out." She paused, not sure how to say what she wanted to say. "I mean, I'm thinking, maybe this guy accidentally slapped his wife once, and now he's trying to make up for it?"

"Look, let's just—"

"Or if this story we're telling now was true? If we really were screwing each other's brains out? Maybe I could see it. But I can't. . . ."

Matthew leaned forward, finally looking at her for the first time in minutes.

"I believe you did what you had to do," he said. "That's all."

"But you don't even know me."

"I know enough."

*You didn't do this for me.* That was her thought, but she couldn't say it. What did it matter anyway?

So she said, "They haven't called since midnight."

Matthew said nothing.

"One or the other of them has been calling every

two or three hours," she said. "Now all of a sudden it's been six."

"It's okay."

"What do you think that means?"

He shrugged. "They're feeling like they've got us conditioned. At this point, not calling keeps you on-line as well as calling every two or three hours. Maybe even better."

*An individual uses a pattern of abusive behavior—phsyical, psychological, even economic—to establish power over his or her partner.* She'd practically memorized the "truth" by now. According to the flyer.

But Matthew was right. She'd been awake all night, waiting for the phone to ring. In fact, she'd been listening for it all this time they'd been sitting here.

*The abuser maintains control through fear and intimidation.*

If Matthew was right about that, maybe he was right about everything. Maybe he really could fix it, if she trusted him.

Didn't he deserve that much?

Why hadn't he told her about the money?

Did she trust him?

Just then, as though she'd summoned it, the telephone rang.

It seemed loud as an alarm bell in the quiet apartment. Gwen jumped half out of her skin. Matthew calmly reached out, touched her arm. *It's okay.*

She took a breath, picked up the cordless receiver by her hand, and answered.

"Hello."

"Kenna," a cool voice said. "I'm downstairs at the door."

Gwen closed her eyes, exhaled. Marly.

"I'll buzz you in," she said.

After she hung up, Matthew came around, bent down, and kissed the top of her head.

"Don't worry," he said. "You'll be fine."

"You're leaving?"

"I need to go hold up my end." He touched her arm with the back of his hand. "It's almost over."

"Tell me again."

"Tell you what?"

"That it's going to be okay."

Matthew took her face in both hands and looked down into her eyes. "It's going to be okay."

He was such a bad liar. How could this work?

Why did she need him to tell her anything?

A knock sounded at the door. Matthew went over, undid the locks, and pulled the door open.

Marly Kenna stood there, bag on her shoulder, coat open, cheeks lightly flushed. There must have been a breeze outside. Her hair looked like feathers.

She smirked at Matthew, shaking her head slowly. "Officer Worth."

"Detective Kenna," he said. "It's nice to see you again."

She blew that off, came into the apartment, and pointed a finger in Gwen's direction.

"I've got a bone to pick with you, girl."

---

Tony and Ray made it down to the riverfront two and a half hours before dawn.

Sunday morning, after the snow, Uncle Eddie had pissed and moaned about his boat. He hadn't winterized it yet. Who the hell expected a foot of snow before Halloween?

They parked Ray's Expedition on Eighth Street and hiked down to the boardwalk on foot. There were three other boats still moored at the marina: two runabouts and Eddie's forty-foot cruiser. *Joan's Arc.*

The smaller boats dipped low in their slips, covers laden with unmelted snow. It hadn't felt cold in the city, but the air on the river froze the hairs in your nose. Out beyond the landing, the three-quarter moon danced in place, rippling on the wide, slow current.

They boarded Eddie's boat and used their feet to push all the snow off the aft deck. Clumps and soggy clods splashed the dark water. Tony used the spare key from Eddie's desk and searched the cabin; Ray checked the helm and all the storage wells.

After an hour of looking, they agreed.

Except for a personal stash—two or three grams of flake in a small ivory box, tucked up into the upholstery in the sleeping berth—there was nothing on board. No product, no ordnance, no emergency cash. No address books written in funky code. Nothing that would cause anybody to look past the scene they'd set at the furniture store.

Back on the landing, Tony took the sack of demolished VHS security cassettes and upended it over the railing. Shards of plastic and ribbons of tape floated down to the water.

The water swept the pieces downriver. The current was faster than it looked.

They stayed awhile, slowly getting cold, passing a pint of Bushmills back and forth between them. The river flowing past created the sensation that it was the platform that was moving, not the river itself.

Little by little, the sky began to lighten over the tops of the trees along the opposite bank. They should have been long gone by then, but Ray said nothing. He just took his share of the whiskey and hung.

Tony killed the last of it. When the booze was gone, he screwed on the cap, drew his arm back, and hurled the empty bottle as far out as he could. The bottle hit the water with a faint slap, disappeared, then buoyed back to the surface a few feet downstream.

They stood there in the twilight, watching the bottle bob and weave among chunks of ice, riding the floe. Pretty soon they couldn't see it anymore.

Ray said, "Ready to roll?"

In another minute, Tony nodded.

They walked back to the car.

# 27

It was a five-minute drive from the safe apartment to Central Station on Howard Street.

Worth arrived a few minutes before 7 A.M. Traffic was still thin, and frost skimmed the streets. Downtown seemed to glow with early light.

He used his key chip to enter the parking facility, left his personal weapon with lockup on the way in. He felt an urge to explain himself: *I don't normally carry off-duty.* But the clerk barely looked up.

Worth went on inside.

Mark Vargas waited for him at the elevators on the fourth floor. He had a stack of folders under one arm and a paper cup of coffee in the other hand. Badge on his belt.

"Come on back," he said.

It seemed strangely quiet on the floor; no chirping phones, no squawking fax machines, no watercooler chatter. A momentary seam between night and day.

Worth unzipped his coat and fell in step. They passed cubes and offices, open desks, drawing occasional glances along the way. Across the bullpen, he saw one detective standing at a printer, tracking them.

The guy looked familiar, but Worth couldn't remember his name. Mid-forties, balding. He wore an empty shoulder holster and half a grin. When Worth made eye contact, the guy put up his dukes.

Another guy at a nearby desk covered his mouth with his knuckles. He didn't look up from whatever he was doing.

Vargas kept his eyes forward and walked on, ignoring everybody. Worth couldn't decide which was worse: the asshole by the printer, or the fact that Mark Vargas kept turning out to be basically an okay guy.

It had been about this time of day, their now-famous exchange. Middle of July. The nights had been hot and sticky and it had been the end of a long bad shift; Worth had been hand-delivering an LD-512 he'd forgotten to write up on an agg burglary two weeks before.

Vargas had been walking to his desk, reading a print-out and eating a Crane Curl.

Worth didn't remember thinking about it. He still didn't remember making a fist. But he'd seen Vargas coming a good three seconds before Vargas had looked up and seen him.

He'd never thrown a punch that came more naturally. It had been almost like watching somebody else do it. *Pop.*

He remembered the cinnamon twist flying. The bite of his knuckles hitting teeth. When he'd told the story to the Modells in the stockroom, Vargas had ended up on his ass, wondering what had hit him.

But that wasn't quite the way it had happened. Vargas

had stumbled back a step; that was about all. Worth never saw the counterpunch.

Later, somebody else had claimed they'd seen him touch leather after Vargas put him down. His service weapon had been locked up downstairs; his holster would have been an empty hole in his belt. But somebody had claimed the motion had been there.

It was bullshit. Worth remembered catching his own blood in his hands and not being able to see.

They'd recorded the comment at the review out of formality, but nobody else had been able to back up the claim. Not even Vargas, who'd been standing directly over him at the time.

Because it was bullshit. Even if his head had been screwed on crooked for a while there, Worth knew it in his heart: No way had he gone for his gun.

It just wasn't like anything he'd do.

Vargas dropped the folders at his desk and they walked on, past a uni heading the other direction and a clump of detectives milling around another desk. The meeting room was tucked back in the northeast corner between the coffee station and the cold case library.

Quite a group waited for them inside.

Worth's heart did a little back flip as he followed Vargas into the room. He saw familiar faces, all seated along the same side of the table, all of them facing the door:

His lieutenant. His union rep. Regina Torres, Vargas's captain. Roger Sheppard from the South Unit. Briggs and Salcedo's sergeant, Levon Williams from the Northeast.

At one end of the table sat the Deputy Chief of

Criminal Investigations. The Deputy Chief of Uniform Patrol.

There were other faces he didn't recognize.

Vargas pulled the door closed behind them. "Okay, I don't know who knows who, so . . ."

"Let's just get started," Deputy Chief Riley said. He nodded to Vargas. "We'll meet each other as we go."

D.C. Pullman sat next to Riley. Pullman had headed the Uniform Patrol Bureau the past five years, and Worth hadn't had much contact with him before now. Mid-forties, salt-and-pepper hair, a smoker's voice. He motioned across the table to one of the empty chairs.

"Have a seat, Officer."

Gina Torres had captain's bars on her collar now.

She and Worth had graduated academy together. They'd always been able to crack each other up. They'd fallen out of touch, but he'd caught lots of good talk about her over the years. It always made him happy to hear.

Last year, she'd made the newspapers. Youngest captain in the department. He'd meant to send her a card, but he never did. Now didn't seem like the appropriate time to offer his congratulations.

She said, "And when did you meet Miss Mullen?"

"In August," Worth repeated. "When I started my provisional. We didn't start . . . seeing each other until recently."

Gina—Captain Torres—nodded along. "Five, six weeks ago, you said?"

"About three," Worth said. "Early October."

"What was your reason for omitting that information before now?"

The bearded guy in the denim shirt beside her was Narcotics. The guy wearing the necktie was Internal Affairs. Neither of them had said much yet.

"In retrospect, I wish I'd followed my first instinct and radioed the call to another unit," Worth said. "I let my emotional involvement interfere with my judgment."

"I didn't ask what you wish you'd done in retrospect, Officer." Torres raised her chin. *You're not going to get any breaks here, Matt.* "I asked why you chose not to inform your shift commander of your personal involvement with Miss Mullen and the subject."

Worth glanced at his lieutenant and received an interested gaze in return. He looked across the table. Many faces, few expressions.

"I'm on provisional duty pending clearance," he told them. The sigh he gave was genuine. It just never stopped sounding pathetic. "I guess it didn't seem like the kind of thing that would help my case."

He very nearly added more. Something about the family's good name in the department, the upcoming memorial. Casting a shadow on his brother's remembrance.

But he stopped himself. Of all the lines he'd crossed these past days—lines he'd never have considered himself capable of approaching—exploiting Kelly's death to help save his own bacon wasn't going to be one of them. Worth decided that then and there.

Mark Vargas unclipped his pager and looked at the screen. He glanced at Captain Torres.

"Excuse me," he said.

After he'd stepped out of the room, Roger Sheppard

said, "For the record, after the break-in at Officer Worth's residence Sunday night, I did ask if he could think of any possibles. Mr. James was named at that time."

Deputy Chief Riley said, "Let's focus on Officer Worth's account for now. We'll compare and contrast as things get more formal."

The meaning in that bit of guidance was clear enough. *Keep what you know on this side of the table.* The same basics Worth had been taught to apply in the field applied to him now.

Nine liars out of ten will hang themselves if you just get out of their way and let them.

The bearded guy from Narcotics had introduced himself as Detective Neil Granger. Granger glanced at D.C. Riley, eyebrows raised. Riley nodded him clear.

"With all due respect to the, um, love triangle aspect," Granger said, "how much is the drop?"

"I don't know," Worth said.

"How is that?"

He'd told them that Briggs and Salcedo seemed to believe that he and Gwen were in possession of cash. Cash that Russell James had, apparently, either owed them or been meant to deliver to somebody else.

He'd told them that Russell James had, apparently, come to a bad end. He assumed this because Briggs and Salcedo had threatened to frame him and Gwen for the murder if they didn't hand over the dough. Dough that neither Worth nor Gwen Mullen knew anything about.

"They never verbalized an amount." He left the rest unspoken. *Since I personally have no knowledge of any stolen money, I would have no way of knowing the amount myself.*

"Where and when?"

"I don't know that, either. They said we'd hear."

"Hear when?"

"Before now." Worth glanced at the clock on the wall for effect. "It's past the twenty-four-hour mark."

"Tell me something." Detective Granger leaned back and folded his arms. "Who does the talking? Tony or Ray?"

"Mostly Briggs," Worth said. "Salcedo stays pretty quiet."

"But you say Salcedo engineered the apartment address."

"That's right."

"Who makes the calls to the apartment?"

"Either or, Gwen says. I've never been there for a call."

At this point, the IAD investigator finally spoke up. "Twenty-four hours?"

Worth hadn't gotten his name. His tie had a stripe pattern. He couldn't have been thirty years old.

Worth nodded. "That was the clock Briggs set."

"Right," IAD said. "And that clock started when your shift ended yesterday morning."

"That's what I said."

"You approached Detective Vargas at nine o'clock last evening?" IAD leaned forward. "Setting aside the deviation from anything resembling your chain of command, tell me. In your own words, Officer Worth, what took you fourteen hours?"

All this talk of clocks had started the invisible bomb in Worth's head ticking loudly again.

"Subtracting the eight hours I spent tearing my house

apart?" He looked IAD in the eye. "I guess it took me half a day to decide how to end my career."

"Do you feel the need for sarcasm, Officer?"

"Not at all," Worth said. "Son."

In his peripheral vision, he saw Gina look down at the table. Roger Sheppard looked toward a wall.

The guy was only a handful of years his junior. It was an easy point to score. There wasn't a cop in the room, brass or otherwise, who'd come up with a good taste for Internal Affairs. Especially the young guys who came indoors early. It felt a little cheap, using that; Worth knew what it felt like to be looked down on by fellow cops, and this kid was just doing his job. But he needed all the points he could get.

Before Granger asked his next question, the door opened again. Vargas poked his head back into the room. "Captain?"

Torres looked past Worth's shoulder. Then she pushed back from the table. "You all keep going. I'll be back."

Over his shoulder, Worth caught an accidental glance from Vargas. Something was happening.

A moment later, Captain Torres reappeared. More silent communication among the command branch in the room. The Deputies Chief and Worth's lieutenant all stood and followed her.

Detective Granger watched them go.

He looked around the table, decided the action was obviously elsewhere at the moment, and followed them.

IAD almost beat him to the door.

Nothing else happened for a few seconds.

Finally, over at the far end of the table, Sergeant

Williams sighed. He stood slowly, stretched his back, and went to see what was going on.

On his way to the door, he put a hand on Worth's shoulder. "Hey there, Matty."

"Hey, Sarge. Long time no see."

Sergeant Williams wore dark blue warm-ups and clean white cross-trainers. Worth hadn't seen him in a couple of years, but Williams still had a chest like a barrel and looked like he could punch through bricks. The sergeant should have made a command post years ago, but Worth knew it was nothing political. Levon Williams hadn't been passed over or shut out. Levon Williams was happy doing exactly what he did. That was all.

"How's your pops?" he said.

"Dad's okay." Worth shrugged. "About the same."

The doctors had assumed for years that the cirrhosis would get him before the Alzheimer's, but the stubborn son of a bitch continued to buck the odds. He patrolled the halls of Elmwood Manor in his wheelchair, terrorizing the nurses, mixed up as a bag of nuts. Half the time, he thought the nurses were Mom, and that Matthew was Kelly, and that his roommate wanted him dead.

"You get by to see him?"

Worth nodded. "Usually once a week. At least once every couple."

"Good boy."

Williams gave Worth's shoulder a squeeze.

Then he left the room with everybody else. That left Worth and his union rep sitting there alone, looking across the table at each other.

"You could have called," his union rep said.

*"Dad."*

John blinked. "What was that, hon?"

"I asked if you wanted more toast." Liz frowned, wiped her hands, and came over. "You're on cloud nine this morning. Are you feeling okay?"

"I feel fine," he said. "Just reading."

She checked his forehead anyway.

You'd think he'd had a damned heart transplant, the way she mother-henned. Hell, you'd think he was eighty years old. John sat there and let her treat him like a convalescent anyway. It was easier than arguing.

She looked over his shoulder at the newspaper he'd spread out. "What's so engrossing?"

He hadn't been reading so much as staring at a photo. "Just this thing. Tell it to you when I'm done."

"So did you want more toast?"

"Not for me." John hadn't eaten this well this many days in a row since Jean had divorced him fifteen years ago.

Too many more days and he'd start getting used to it. He watched Liz go around the table, picking up the girls' empty cereal bowls. She poured all the leftover milk together, stacked the bowls three high, and piled the spoons on top. Off toward the dishwasher without missing a step.

Above his head, he could hear the morning ministampede. Didn't seem to matter what time anybody got up, there was always the last mad rush to get ready for school.

First couple days here, he'd been nervous as a cat. It was like staying in a guest room at the zoo. If that wasn't enough, Liz counted all his pills and wouldn't let him drink more than one beer a day. Made him keep the goddamned walker by the bed.

But John was starting to feel a rhythm to the chaos by now. He'd even gotten to enjoy it a bit.

Liz's husband, Bill, worked as a lineman for the power company; since the storm, he'd been pulling fourteen-hour days, leaving the house by 5 A.M., coming home to a plate of supper wrapped up in the fridge. But he always had enough energy left to help the girls with homework or spend some time horsing around.

John had always liked his son-in-law well enough; these past couple days, his affection had deepened a good bit. Part of him knew he'd think better of himself if he'd been more like Bill when he'd been Bill's age.

Liz took the girls to school in the morning and worked part time at the city clerk's. Since John had been there, she'd been to a school board meeting, gone to choir practice at the church, passed out Halloween candy for four and a half hours, and clipped about nine hundred coupons out of the Wednesday supplement.

The girls were thirteen, eleven, and eight now. The same tornado hit the bathroom twice a day.

And John had slept better the past couple nights than he had in the past ten weeks. The fact was, even sitting here now, his damned ruined leg didn't seem to hurt quite so bad.

He could still use more than one lousy beer a day. But overall, John was starting to feel as though a hazy curtain had parted. A screen between him and the real world he hadn't even noticed.

Maybe that sucker-punching shitbag had done him a favor. Maybe he'd gotten a bit off track, crutching around home all alone. Maybe sitting around feeling sorry for himself was part of the reason he'd been hurting so goddamned bad all this time.

The stampede descended and moved toward the kitchen. In the girls came, one by one: Natalie, the oldest, Emma, the middle, and Zoe, the baby of the bunch.

"See ya, Gramps."

"Bye, Grampa."

"Bye, Grampa."

Three kisses, three hugs, single file.

"I'll be back this afternoon," Liz said, passing out lunch cards and herding everybody toward the coat room. "Call if you need anything, okay?"

John waved. "Drive careful, hon. You girls learn something."

"'kay."

"'kay."

"Yeah, right."

Pretty soon they were on their way.

After the garage door came down and the sound of the minivan disappeared down the street, silence settled down over everything.

Monday morning, he'd been so relieved he could hardly stand it. Tuesday, the peace and quiet had still been just fine with John. Today, he already found himself looking forward to the end of the schoolday.

Hell. John felt lonely in the house by himself.

He hauled himself up and cruised around the table to the counter by the sink. He topped off his coffee, put the full mug on the table, and slid it back around to his chair a couple steps at a time.

When he finally got settled, he went back to the section he'd spread out in front of him. Liz and Bill took the Omaha paper as well as the *Plattsmouth Journal*; John stuck to the *World-Herald* with his coffee, just like he did at home.

He liked checking the Crime Watch column on the City page. They'd been running it for the past couple years, ever since the new chief took over. They'd give information about suspects in this case or that, print phone numbers for the tip lines, that sort of thing.

All week he'd been checking to see if they'd run anything about the break-in over at Matthew's place. Nothing yet.

But today they'd run another bit that caught his eye.

Some kid being sought on a domestic violence warrant. They'd printed a picture of the kid and a picture of his car side by side. The kid looked like a cocky punk to John, but it wasn't the kid's face that bugged him.

It was the car.

He was almost positive he'd seen it before. And recently, too. Black GTO, '71. Big spoiler on the back, *BadGoat* on the tags. There was something distinctive about the look of it, and those plates rang a bell.

All morning, he'd been trying to think. Between the way he'd been sleeping and getting his lights knocked out, the past two or three weeks had turned into a muddled gray soup.

BadGoat.

Except for trips to the doctor's and across the street Sunday night, he hadn't been anywhere but his living room in weeks.

But he'd seen that car somewhere. The more John thought about it, the more certain about it he was.

They had the tip line right there, printed in bold. He'd do his part and call in for once, if he could figure out where the hell he'd seen those plates. He sipped his coffee and thought about it. *BadGoat.* It had been nibbling at him before; now it was starting to gnaw.

What the hell.

It was only a quarter to eight in the morning; nobody would be back until four. He wasn't going anywhere. It certainly was quiet enough around here.

John guessed he had time to keep working on it.

# 28

Tony Briggs wanted breakfast.

By the time they made the short haul back to Ray's Expedition from the vacant river walk, he was so hungry he wanted to punch somebody. They stopped at Manley's on Military and took the corner booth in back.

Connelle's section. None better in the place. Connie had an ass like a basketball and biceps like a pair of well-fed snakes. She never wrote down an order, gave shit as good as she got, and could throw coffee into your cup from ten feet away.

There had been a few empty tables when they got there, but the bell on the front door kept jingling, and little by little the place packed in. Tony ordered the Manley Man Combo: waffles, eggs, bacon, link sausage, and a greasy pile of hash browns big enough to smother a fourth grader.

Ray had a glass of tomato juice and a plate of fruit.

A plate of fruit.

Jesus Christ. Tony hadn't even known they even had fruit here.

They sat and ate, not saying much, sunrise climbing in through the open blinds. Beneath the general din of voices and silverware and clattering plates, Ray's personal handheld unit crackled softly beside the napkin dispenser, tuned to the department all-channels frequency.

They caught the call at 7:35.

Southeast to dispatch, dispatch to Central, snow cone times two. Officers on scene, support units requested.

Tony washed down a mouthful of eggs with hot black coffee. He knew it was Uncle Eddie before hearing the address.

Two snow cones meant two bodies. The call could have indicated stringbeans or dresser drawers and it would have meant the same thing. Department radio protocol hadn't changed, but a lot of cops on the street had stopped using the handbook code for homicide; it was the latest informal attempt to keep civilian scanner rats from showing up before the police, looking for action, contaminating scenes. Forget about the media.

The force had switched over to digital trunking systems three years back. Private gear like Ray's on the table cost four times the old analog gear everybody owned.

Little by little, though, the civvie wannabes had caught up with technology. It wouldn't be much longer before they caught on to the talk. It always happened eventually.

For now, nonsense still meant murder. Support units meant Henry detectives. Lab vans. A meat wagon.

Ray said, "You okay?"

"All secure." Tony messed up a sausage link and chased it with OJ. "You didn't finish your cantaloupe."

Ray looked at his plate.

Connie came by with the coffee. "How you doin', five-O?"

"Perfect," Tony said.

She filled his mug to the top. "Whatcha do to your head?"

"He slipped on some ice."

"You gotta be more careful, baby." She winked. "Them bald spots might stop growing back."

"Yeah," Tony said. "But I'd still look good."

"Shit." She laughed and moved on.

For the next couple minutes, Ray sat quietly on his side of the table, leaning forward on his elbows, listening to the radio.

Nothing worth hearing now. Tony finally reached over and snapped it off. "Wonder who caught it?"

Half a smile. "Vargas, probably."

"Jesus." Tony shook some Cholula on his hash browns. "That'd be about the way it would go. Wouldn't it?"

Ray chuckled softly at the idea, but not like he really thought it was funny.

"Hey," Tony said. "You hear the Polack mafia's been at it in Chicago again?"

"Huh?"

"It's true." Tony nodded. He folded the last strip of bacon into his mouth and chewed it down. "Two more victims were found with their heads tied together. Shot through the hands."

Ray just sat there like he didn't get it. After a second, he shook his head.

"Eddie always told that joke." Tony picked up his fork and got back to breakfast. "Every time I'd say something, try and give a little advice? He'd peel that off like a twenty-dollar bill." He dug into the last of the hash browns. "Guy thought that shit was hilarious."

"Sounds like Eddie."

"Yeah. Guess he wouldn't think it was all that funny now, huh?"

"Probably not," Ray said.

"I don't want some asshole hauling Aunt Joan down to ID the body." Tony slugged some coffee, wiped his mouth. He pushed his plate to the side. "You know?"

Ray sighed. "Yeah."

"Need to figure out how to show up down there without raising any flags."

"We'll just go," Ray said. "Whenever you're ready."

"Like we heard they had a good price on dinettes, right? Thought we'd come down and check it out?"

"Like we were getting breakfast," Ray said. "Caught the call on my hobby box."

Tony grinned. "That's us, baby. No such thing as off duty."

"Hey." Ray said it low. The tone in his voice was new.

Tony put down his fork. He picked up his freshened coffee, blew away the steam. He had a sip and looked at his partner.

They'd kicked in doors. They'd chased shitheads with unknown weapons into dark alleys. They'd worked crowd control, written tickets for littering, and gone before shooting inquiries. One time, just last year, they'd come within half a breath of losing two years of cover in a small room full of fierce young guys with guns.

In all of that, it had been a rare thing, seeing Ray Salcedo look concerned.

"I really am sorry about your uncle," he said.

"Thanks, man." Tony nodded. "Me, too."

Ray moved his eyes to the table. He gave it a beat before he looked up again.

"But this changes things. You know that, right?"

"Obviously."

Ray had more to say, but Connelle picked then to come back around. She hit Tony's mug again, scooped up all their plates, and balanced the whole stack in one hand.

"So how you doing, Connie?" Tony said. "Kids okay?"

She chuckled. "Their daddy still won't pay."

"Yeah? Which one?"

"Parnell."

"No shit?" Tony took another sip of his coffee. "He still flop at the Towers?"

"Far as *I* know."

He nodded across the table. "Me and Ray, maybe we'll stop by."

*Because that's what we do,* he said without saying it. *We take care of our own.*

"Yeah? Stop by and what?"

"Have a visit," Tony said. "You know, friendly. Remind him of his court-ordered responsibilities. How'd that be?"

"Shit." Connie dropped them both a grin and kept moving. Over her shoulder she said, "Long as you still plan on leaving a tip."

---

Worth didn't know how much time had passed. He hadn't worn his watch, and there wasn't a clock on the wall. Twenty minutes, maybe half an hour.

While he sat there, he overheard muffled snippets of information on passing voices, chattering radios.

Captain Torres was the first person to return to the meeting room. She came in, looked all around, and said, "Where's your rep?"

"He went to the bathroom," Worth said. That had been fifteen minutes ago. Worth hadn't minded the time alone.

Captain Torres stepped out, scanned the floor, stepped back in and sighed. "Come with me."

He rose from his chair and followed her out.

Gina headed around the far side of the bullpen, angling toward the interview rooms tucked back in the corner on the other side. On the way, Worth saw Vargas sitting at his desk, working the phone. Two other detectives shrugged into their sport coats and headed for the elevators. One of them was the guy Worth had seen standing over by the printer before.

She kept walking. Worth followed along.

In the room, she pointed to a chair and said, "Sit tight."

It was like any other interview room he'd ever been in, except it had new carpeting and a long window looking out over downtown. The blinds were open; beams of morning sunlight made stripes on the table.

In one corner, on a wheeled cart, sat a polygraph machine. He knew it wasn't for him; they'd schedule something formal through his rep and whoever he ended up hiring for a lawyer. But lie detectors didn't normally sit around idle in interview rooms. He was meant to see it.

Worth pulled the chair out, but he didn't sit.

He said, "Am I in custody?"

Another sigh. "For now? If you don't ask that question, we won't have to get into answering it. Just sit tight. Okay?"

Worth sat down.

As Captain Torres turned to leave, he said, "Gina."

She stopped, looked back.

"Come on," he said. "You know me."

"Do I?"

"What do you think?"

Captain Regina Torres looked him square in the face. Worth could tell by looking at her that she hadn't decided the answer to that question yet.

But she stepped back into the room. Lowered her voice.

"What are you *doing* here, Matt? I mean, Jesus Christ. What happened to you?"

Worth didn't know how to respond. He said, "I heard the chatter out there. You caught a double?"

"If you heard, then you already know."

Two bodies, somewhere in the city. He couldn't help but think back to what Gwen had said before: *One or the other of them has been calling every two or three hours. Now all of a sudden it's been six.*

*What do you think that means?*

"It isn't them," he said. "Is it?"

"Who?

"Briggs and Salcedo."

She gave him a look. "Why would you ask that?"

"Because we haven't heard from them. Two plus two, okay?" He pointed at his wrist where his watch would have been. "That's all."

"No," she said. "It isn't them."

Worth said, "What's going on?"

Captain Torres pulled the door closed until it clicked.

"Look," she said. "Narco's had Tony Briggs and Ray Salcedo under investigation since they rotated back out to patrol. Okay? I'm choosing to believe you really didn't know that already. For now."

"I didn't, Gina."

It was all he could do to keep his face neutral. Every step he took, something new clicked into place. It was like he had St. Michael running interference strictly on his behalf.

"I swear."

"Save it," she said. She looked at her pager. "I can't tell you anything more now. I shouldn't be telling you anything at all."

"I appreciate it."

"You'd better not be wrapped up in this, Matt. Swear to God. You know?"

She turned and opened the door to walk out. Worth's union rep stood there on the other side, raising his hand to knock.

Gina didn't miss a beat. "We're in here."

She stood a full inch taller than the rep. The rep tiptoed, craning for a look past her shoulder, finding Worth sitting in the chair.

He said, "What is this?"

"You were in the bathroom," she said. "I needed to shuffle up."

"This is an interview room," the rep said.

"Well observed."

"Has Officer Worth been placed in custody?"

Captain Torres looked at the ceiling and walked out without answering.

The rep had to step aside to let her by. After she was gone, he just stood there in the doorway, smelling like cigarette smoke, apparently vexed.

"We're not supposed to ask that question," Worth said.

---

"Theoretically," Tony said. "Say you needed to disappear somebody. And their little Goat, too. How would you do it?"

Ray triggered the utility compartment in the console above the rearview mirror and took out his sunglasses. He put them on, waited for a gap in traffic, and pulled into the westbound lane. "It's never come up."

"Dude, you're not even trying."

"I'm driving."

"Okay, forget it," Tony said. "Ask me how I'd do it."

Ray checked his mirrors. "How would you do it."

"Who, me? Easy." Tony pointed over his shoulder, behind them. East toward the river. "I'd take 'em both sixty, seventy miles across the state line, where my brother owns this junkyard out in the middle of nowhere. He's got all this demolition-type shit, right? A bunch of land. Nice and secluded."

The department Web site had a whole corner dedicated to the twenty-odd cops who'd died in the line of duty in the past hundred-odd years. The front page contained the same names as the ones carved into the marble monument that stood out front of Central Station. Except here you could click on the photos of all the dead officers and get a couple paragraphs of extra info. Career history, the nutshell story on how they'd gone down. Quotes from cops who had known them. Survived-by information.

They'd looked up Kelly Worth on Ray's computer even before the storm hit Saturday. But they hadn't been looking for anything in particular then. Just brushing up on basics.

"Sounds perfect," Ray said. His voice seemed flat.

"Tell me about it," Tony said. "I mean, here's this kid riding around on a shitload of dirty cash. Right? I mean, he's into something with somebody. But if he disappears? It's not like they're calling the cops."

"He's got a mom somewhere."

"Maybe. How do I know?"

"He's got somebody somewhere."

"So?"

"So somebody wants to know where he is. And the cops are already looking out."

"Yeah, but how much time has passed by now? I got time to arrange things. Order a new mattress for my girlfriend's apartment, for starters. Clean up all the little odds and ends."

"You'd miss a couple," Ray said. "They'd come up sooner or later."

"And then?"

"And then some smart cop would ask his partner, hey, if you needed to get rid of a car, how would you do it?" Ray hit his blinker, slowed for the car beside him, and merged left. "And the partner would say, hey, you know what? This guy has a brother who junks cars for a living."

Tony smiled. "Shit. Nobody's looking at *me,* man. I'm a cop, too."

Ray shook his head.

"Besides, by then, these smart cops have talked to enough people to get the picture. This guy who went missing? He was into something with somebody. Maybe he's hiding out somewhere. Hell, maybe . . ."

Tony made a gun with his finger. He put it to his head, pulled the trigger, and collapsed in the seat.

He sat up again. "Either way, I'm not sweating."

"You sound overconfident."

"Nah. There's no body, no car. I got all kinds of reports to cover why I was in the guy's apartment in the first place. Nobody's going to the D.A. on me, man. Shit moves on, time goes by. It's one for the cold case unit."

"Uh-huh." Ray turned left and headed south on 72nd. "Only one problem."

"What's that?"

"You don't have a brother."

"Oh, yeah." Tony nodded. He let a beat go by, then said, "Shithead has one, though."

"Did have one," Ray said.

"You're forgetting somebody. Never make detective that way."

Tony made a *tsk* sound. Yesterday, he'd done some extra digging on his own.

"The older brother? Vince? Lives sixty, seventy miles over the state line."

"Let me guess. Owns a junkyard."

"He does now," Tony said. "Know what he did before that?"

"Not a clue."

"State time." Tony chuckled. "I pulled him up. Whole family of cops, right? And this guy's got a sheet going back thirty years. Regular black sheep and shit."

Ray said nothing.

"In and out of county, this and that. Two in the pen for robbery." Tony chuckled. "Then five of ten for *armed* robbery, reduced to felony larceny."

Blinkers again. Ray merged right.

"Day's drive away, my ass," Tony said. "Big brother handled this. And he's been holding the loot this whole time. Bet you my share on it. Just goes to show you . . ."

Without a word, Ray slowed down and pulled off the street, into the empty parking lot of an abandoned video store. He pushed toward the center of the white-bound lot, tires kicking up unplowed snow. He braked to a stop and sat there.

"The hell you doing?" Tony said.

"Shut up," Ray said. "Okay?"

Tony leaned back.

Finally. Here was the big heart-to-heart Ray had been sitting on for the past couple hours. It had taken him long enough.

Tony looked out the passenger-side window. This video store had been Cinemarz until a few months ago. A little private operation, no match for the big chains. Now the front windows had all been soaped over; clumps of weeds poked through the shallow snow around the base of the store. The place made him think of Uncle Eddie, for some reason.

"Tell me something," Ray said.

Tony said, "Sure."

"You and me. When did we get into the murder business?"

"The hell you talking about?"

"That kid wasn't even twenty, man. You know?"

Honestly, it hadn't been until that moment that Tony realized what had crawled up Salcedo's ass. It came as a genuine shock.

"You mean FUBU?" He'd figured Ray had been getting worked up about their exposure. But this? "You're serious?"

"That shit wasn't necessary," Ray said.

"Hey," Tony said. "The kid wanted to be a player, he got to be a player. What, you'd rather have 'em hunting up suspects?"

"Straight-up not necessary."

"Oh, I get it," Tony said. "It's okay if the bangers light each other up over this shit, as long as me and you don't pull any triggers. Is that it?"

"This isn't *even* about that."

"No?"

"No. And you know it."

"Then what? Seriously."

"Listen up," Ray said. "We're brothers, okay, that's solid. You know I have your back."

"Never once crossed my mind to ask."

"But I know you," Ray said. He reached and pressed a finger to Tony's forehead. "I know exactly what you're sitting there thinking in that stitched-up head."

Tony could feel Salcedo's finger on his forehead even after Ray took his hand away. He didn't like it.

He said, "What am I thinking?"

"You're thinking there's no fucking way," Ray said.

"No fucking way you're gonna let this guy Worth get over on you."

"Us," Tony corrected. "Right, partner? I'm thinking there's no fucking way we're going to let this guy get over on *us*."

"*Us* didn't put a bee in that kid for no reason. *Us* doesn't have an uncle with the back of his head blown out."

Tony arranged himself in the seat. "Spit it out, man. I'm listening. Say what you need to say."

"This was a simple shakedown," Ray said. "Nice payday, no complications. Right?"

"Oh, I don't know." Tony thought about it. "Shakedown makes it sound like we're the bad guys."

"Call it what you want, it's not simple anymore," Ray said. "Everything's red hot now. It's going to *be* hot for a while."

"And that's my fault?"

"Not saying that," Ray said. "I'm saying we need to start taking the long view."

He'd lost his nerve. All the years they'd rolled, Tony never thought he'd see it happen. But here it was: Ray Salcedo, folding. This, on top of everything else.

"Aside from all that, man? You've got family down," his partner said. Just making it worse now. "Maybe that's enough for one day."

Tony let what seemed like an appropriate amount of silence go by.

Then he said, "You're worried I'm going to make this personal."

"Man, you were making this shit personal already." Ray pointed. "Ever since you got your bell rung the other night. But now it's blood personal." He softened his voice. "That's why it's time to step back."

"Maybe you're right."

Ray looked him in the eyes. "I need to hear you say it."

"Say what?"

"That you get it. That we're on the same page with this thing."

"I get it," Tony said. "We're on the same page with this thing."

Ray watched him a long time.

"Okay," he finally said.

Tony nodded. "Okay."

They rolled on.

# 29

The day warmed slowly as the sun rose, an amber coin in a turquoise sky.

Vince got back from the landfill around half past noon. In the time he'd been gone, the road back up into the bluffs had turned to sloppy, slushy mush. He followed a set of fresh tire tracks all the way back to Junk Monkey, feeling a little more hopeful with every mile.

Turning into the driveway, his spirits sank.

He'd been hoping those tracks meant Rita had come home. Instead, he met the county sheriff coming down the hill.

The sheriff raised a hand, and they pulled alongside each other. Vince ran his window down. The sheriff lowered his own.

"Morning," Vince said.

Sheriff Myron Poole lifted his chin. "Morning there, Vince. Guess my timing wasn't as bad as I thought."

"What's the news?"

"Got a minute?"

"Sure."

"I'll turn around," Poole said.

All the way up to the house, Vince tracked the sheriff's Bronco in the rearview. He could hear his blood beating in his ears. It was the first time in years he'd felt it: that clench that came with the law on your tail. It came back too easy.

*Pull your head out of your ass.*

This wasn't anything to worry about. They needed him to get out on the rig somewhere, that was all. Vince parked out front and got out of the truck, waited for the sheriff to pull in behind.

Poole climbed out of the Bronco and slammed the door. He strolled over, the cuffs of his pant legs tucked into the tops of rubber four-buckle overshoes.

"Warming up," Vince said.

"Sure is." Poole nodded toward the column of brown exhaust rising up from the incinerator shed in the distance, where Vince had been burning garbage, compost, and roadkill for most of the past two days. "Trash day, huh?"

"Yep. Just got back from the dump."

"Yeah, that's what Rita said. I caught her leaving. Helped her load up her suitcases."

Vince felt a tingle in his gut. She couldn't have timed it better if she'd been watching from a hill with binoculars.

Sunday night, after he'd showed her the money, sat down to tell her everything he'd done and everything he knew, she was dressed and gone before he'd even finished talking.

He knew she'd have to come back at some point, even if it was just for a change of clothes. He'd left her a note on the kitchen table, just in case she came back while he was gone: *Back in an hour. Wait for me, babe. Don't go.*

Sure enough, she'd been here. But she hadn't waited. He hadn't seen her anywhere on the road.

"Come on in," he said.

"Nah," Sheriff Poole said. "Thanks, I can't stay long."

Poole stood a couple inches shorter than Vince, about half as wide. He had a razor-burn complexion and a watchful air. They were about the same age, though the sheriff had three grown daughters. Vince had pulled one of the daughters and her half-rolled Sunfire out of a drainage ditch a few years back. He'd been picking up side work towing for the county ever since.

"Everything okay, Sheriff?"

Poole nodded his head. "I guess there's a little something we ought to talk about."

Vince shoved his hands in the pockets of his coveralls. It was fifty degrees out by now, and he needed to take off about three layers of clothes. Water gurgled in the eaves troughs; way out in the trees, it sounded like rain.

"Got a call this morning from your old neck of the woods," Myron Poole said. "A Captain Torres with the Omaha Police. This was a couple hours ago, I guess."

Vince felt something fold up in his chest. They didn't need him out on the rig. He'd known that. He'd known it the minute he saw Poole's car.

"Fuck."

Sheriff Poole gave him a curious look.

Vince said, "What happened?"

"How do you mean?"

"Matty." Vince had been waiting for something like this. Now he didn't want to hear. "What happened?"

"Oh," Poole said, waving his hand. He looked apologetic, maybe even slightly relieved. "Shoot, Vince, I'm sorry, I wasn't thinking. Your brother's just fine, at least as far as I know. Sorry for the scare."

"Jesus." Vince let out a long breath. *Keep your shit together.* "Yeah, okay."

"Call I got was about you." Poole folded his arms and dipped his head. He might have been thinking, or counting the driveway rocks poking up through the slush. "I guess I probably shouldn't be out here. I'll just tell you I debated awhile." He nodded to himself. "But the fact is, I've always known you to be real reliable, Vince, and I know you do fair business with folks. And I don't know anybody around who doesn't think pretty high of Rita. So I decided I'd rather come on out and have a chat before anything else."

When Poole looked up, Vince studied his eyes. He couldn't read much. He said, "What are we chatting about?"

"Seems like Omaha PD wants me to put in some paper with the county attorney," Poole said. "Search warrant for your grounds here."

"Search warrant? What the hell for?"

"Don't know all the details yet." Poole was lying about that. Vince could tell that much. "But PD seems to think they've got cause to have a look for some stolen property out here."

"What stolen property?"

Poole raised his hands. *Take it easy.* "Listen here. The truth is, something like this happened one other time. I just never told you about it."

Vince looked right at him. "What the hell are you talking about, Myron?"

"This was seven, eight years ago." Sheriff Poole shrugged.

"Didn't ask how long ago it was."

"State patrol over there had picked up a guy, turned out to be one of your old running buddies," Poole said. "You were a few years closer to your parole period back then, remember. Anyway, they called, looking for a truck-load of stolen microwaves."

"Microwaves."

"Don't know if their suspect was trying to give them the runaround, or if you were just the first place they thought to look."

Vince wondered if the sheriff was talking about Buck Lavelle. He remembered Buck going through the occasional appliance phase.

"Point is, they found their merchandise in a warehouse somewhere that same afternoon." Poole smiled. "Called me back, apologized for wasting my time. That was that."

"Jesus," Vince said. Fucking Buck Lavelle. He remembered, now, why he'd stopped running around with that asshole in the old days.

"I told Captain Torres that story this morning," Sheriff Poole said. "Also told her they'd need a little more than they had to get me comfortable. But I get the feeling she knew that already."

The longer Myron Poole spoke, the more Vince understood the purpose of the sheriff's visit. He claimed this had happened before, yet today was the first Vince had ever heard about that.

Because this time was different. Whatever Captain Torres from the Omaha Police Department had told him might not have been enough to sell the sheriff on a warrant, but it was enough to send him out here personally.

"Listen, Vince." Sheriff Poole kept his arms folded, looking at the ground again. "I know you've got some history behind you. I also know you've worked pretty hard to keep your nose clean out here all these years."

"That's goddamned right," Vince said.

Thinking: *Not even a week.* Matty, the college boy, had it all figured out. And they hadn't even made it a goddamned week.

"I also know you two have had it a little tough out here lately." Poole looked off toward the scrap yard. "Money-wise, I mean."

Vince said, "We're getting by."

"I know you are." Poole finally looked at him. "Also know you hooked up a vehicle for me thirteen months ago. My brand-new, twenty-one-year-old deputy, who I ended up firing two months later anyhow, had forgotten fifty-six hundred dollars in cash evidence bagged up in plain view on the dashboard. You had that vehicle in your sole possession for a good hour."

Vince didn't say a word.

"But every dime of that money ended up in my evidence locker," Poole said. "Wouldn't have been too hard for a guy to slip a couple hundred into his pocket, leave it looking like a green rookie miscounted the amount. Especially a kid everybody knew couldn't find his ass with both hands and a GPS."

"Yeah, well." Vince looked off toward the smoke from

the incinerator shed. "That was thirteen months ago, you said."

"Hell," Poole said. "I don't figure people change too much in a year. Not where it counts, anyway. I just wanted to come on out as a friend, let you and Rita know you might be seeing me back later. With some other folks, I'd imagine. If it comes to it."

"Nothing here worth hiding, Sheriff. Come on along."

"That's what I told Captain Torres you'd probably say."

Sheriff Poole clapped him on the arm and headed back toward the Bronco. Over his shoulder, he called, "Tell Rita I hope her mom feels better."

"I'll do that," he said.

Rita's mother was healthier than Vince and Myron Poole put together. Seventy years old and the woman jogged six miles a day.

As Poole climbed back into his Bronco, Vince said, "Sheriff?"

"Yep?"

"Appreciate the hand with the luggage."

"Didn't do much. Like I said, caught her heading out."

Vince tried to put a chuckle in his voice. "Just out of curiosity, how much she take with her this time?"

"Oh, I'd say she's pretty well set." Poole laughed. "Three big suitcases and a couple of those, what do you call 'em? Garment bags. Wasn't sure we'd get the trunk closed."

She never packed more than the one small suitcase. A few changes of clothes and a sketch pad or two. *I'm coming right back,* she always said.

Poole slammed the door and waved through the open window.

Vince raised a hand back. He stood and watched the sheriff turn around, roll down the driveway, and disappear around the bend.

The sun was warm. The sky was blue.

All around, the shape of the land seemed to be changing. Drifts and ridges shifted in place, gradually collapsing on top of themselves. Everything had been white a few days ago. Pretty soon, the last of the snow would soak into the mud.

Vince stood there long after the sheriff had gone, looking out over the scrap yard, watching the smoke rise.

---

Contrary to the vigorous recommendations of his union rep, Worth had no plans to bring in a lawyer. Not yet.

It hadn't gone unnoticed. Vargas poked his head into the room just a few minutes after Worth's rep had left to bring back lunch.

"Hey," Vargas said. "Can you stand in a lineup?"

"That's funny," Worth said.

"Seriously."

"You want me in a lineup?"

"Not like that," Vargas said. "We just need bodies. Shouldn't take long."

Worth looked at him.

They didn't just need bodies.

He'd be an idiot to say yes. If his rep had been here, he would have laughed in Vargas's face for even trying.

Worth wondered who they'd pulled in. A neighbor in Gwen's building? Somebody from the house next door?

The thought came like a kick in the groin, certain and sickening. It was the most basic point of weakness in the whole house of cards. Somebody had seen something.

"Come on," Vargas said. "It's not like you have anything better to do."

He'd be an idiot to say yes.

If he declined, he'd look like he didn't want to fill in some routine lineup.

If he told Vargas to wait for his rep to get back, he might as well have called in a lawyer hours ago. More than anything else, now of all times, he needed his fellow cops to see him as one of their own. He was the one who'd come inside. Not Tony Briggs and Ray Salcedo. His was the honest position. Not theirs.

The minute he held up a right and attempted to shield himself with it, everything he'd done so far today was lost.

Worth took a breath, shrugged, and said, "Sure."

Twenty minutes later, Mark Vargas took him to a different room, closed the door, and said, "Sorry about that."

Worth kept his face neutral. "Sorry about what?"

They were in an audit room now. Small, no windows. A table and a few chairs. There was a multimedia cart with a color monitor, a VHS deck, and a snarl of cords hanging behind.

Vargas walked over and turned on the monitor. A video image of one of the interview rooms wobbled onto the screen.

While they watched the monitor, another detective

escorted a bony kid to the table, sat him down, winked up at the camera, and disappeared from the frame.

"Derek Price," Vargas said. "Southwest patrol picked him up this morning at Bergen Mercy ER. Public defender's office is sending somebody over."

Worth put the kid somewhere between eighteen and twenty-two. He had a stud in one nostril. Both arms were covered in tattoo ink from his T-shirt sleeves down to his wrists. He had straight black hair cut short in back, longer in front, a greasy curtain hanging over his eyes.

"Did you say Price?"

"That's right. Know him?"

"No," Worth said. "But I recognize the name."

"How's that?"

"Gwen said he came to see her in the hospital," Worth said. "Price and another guy. Both friends of Russell James. Detective Kenna talked to them."

"Happen to remember the other guy's name?"

"Mather," Worth said. "First name Troy, I think."

"Dead on arrival at Mercy," Vargas said. "Arrived at oh-five-thirty with a bullet hole in his chest and about eight pints of blood in the passenger side of Price's Le Mans." Vargas looked at Worth. "You're sure you've never seen the kid before?"

"I'd remember the tattoos."

"Yeah." Vargas nodded. "He didn't pick you out, either."

Worth began to grasp the situation.

The lineup had been for Derek Price. Price had been the person on the other side of the glass. Vargas had tried for a connection and hadn't gotten one; Worth had clipped another wire and still hadn't detonated himself.

How much grace had it bought him?

"Price isn't the shooter," he said, testing.

"According to Price, Mather called him after the fact." Vargas reached into a folder and handed Worth a sheet of paper. It was a printout of a digital photo, tagged with an evidence number. A blood-covered cell phone lying on a sidewalk. "Price initially claimed he drove from his apartment to Mather's location and took him to the ER from there."

"Initially," Worth said.

"Something didn't track," Vargas said. "Based on the amount of blood at the location, the amount of blood in the car, the time stamp on the call, the attending doc's assessment of the wound . . . Price either picked Mather up earlier than he stated, or drove him farther. One way or another, his time frame doesn't work."

Worth said, "Huh."

Price had picked Mather up at the corner of 72nd and Q, Vargas said. The blood trail led six blocks in the opposite direction, all the way back to the warehouse/retailer where Price and Mather had been employed: Tice Is Nice Quality Used and Discount Furniture.

"That's where Russell James worked," Worth said. "The voice mails on his phone? Almost all of them came from Eddie Tice."

Vargas nodded. "Also dead. Along with a third employee, Darla Mackler."

"Jesus." Three bodies. "You're kidding."

No wonder the place had gone hot. Three bodies constituted nearly ten percent of the citywide homicide rate for the entire year to date. All in one night.

All around Russell James.

"Eddie Tice had a nephew in the department," Vargas said. "Kind of coincidental."

"Who?"

"Tony Briggs."

It wasn't possible.

Vargas said, "There's one other thing."

Worth didn't know what to say. He actually felt lightheaded.

"Detective Kenna and Gwen Mullen are here."

"Here at Central?"

Vargas nodded and said, "Briggs called the safe unit with instructions for the money drop thirty minutes ago."

# 30

Within a few months after returning to a regular patrol rotation, Tony Briggs and Ray Salcedo had established one of the highest collar rates in the Northeast District. They led the precinct in drug arrests—presumably utilizing the knowledge of markets and players they'd developed over the course of their two-year stint with the Narcotics unit.

But irregularities in their undercover operations—including discrepancies in the amounts of cash and drugs seized during a joint OPD/DEA raid on the Orlando Heights housing projects last year—had attracted internal notice even before they went back into uniform.

"Based on their pattern of arrests, we suspected Ray and Tony were manipulating the street trade in certain areas," Detective Neil Granger said.

He pushed up his sleeves and repositioned the condenser mike he'd taped along Worth's sternum. Worth winced as the tape pulled hair.

"Ten months ago," Granger said, "after ICE hit the Latinos, we started seeing new product filter in."

Operation Community Shield. Last January, U.S. Immigration and Customs Enforcement agents, the department antigang unit, and uniformed officers from the Southeast District—including Worth himself—had arrested and/or deported more than fifty key members of Mara Salvatrucha, Sureños, Lomas, and other South O Street gangs that had come to dominate the distribution of cocaine and methamphetamine in recent years.

The operation had disrupted the Latino traffic for the short term. But in the years since Kelly had been gunned down, the black sets in the Northeast had mostly fallen into disorganiziation, turf warfare, and pointless homicide. A perfect time for a new crew to set up shop.

"In twenty years, I've never seen a serious heroin market," Granger said. "Not in this town. But all of a sudden, we start seeing the crack and amp slingers carrying around dime bags of China White. And it's not coming through the Salvadorans or the Mexicans."

The supply shift Detective Granger described coincided roughly with Briggs and Salcedo's return to the street.

Worth had still been married then, he realized. Not by much, but still. It hardly seemed possible, from then to this, that not even a year had passed.

"How's that?" Granger said.

The audio technician in the other room adjusted his headphones and gave a thumbs-up.

"Before the public defender got here, we explained the particulars of involuntary manslaughter to Derek

Price," Mark Vargas said. "He's been highly voluntary since then."

"According to Price, this money Tony and Ray are looking for was supposed to have been en route to Chicago," Granger said. "Price says that Russell James muled contraband between here and there, transporting product and returning cash."

He motioned for Worth to button his shirt, checking for bulges.

"Price and Mather distributed the product to the dealer level via furniture trucks, inside television boxes and whatnot," Granger said. "Price says they handled collections along the same routes. Ray and Tony handled protection and managed beefs on the street level."

From the corner, Captain Torres said, "The ironic thing is, last compstat? Drug violence is down in the Northeast." In her smirk, Worth saw the Gina Torres he remembered from the academy. "How's that for community policing?"

"Regular crimedogs, Ray and Tony." Granger motioned for Worth to unbutton his shirt again. "Cleaning up the streets one degenerate dirtbag at a time. How's that feel?"

Worth shrugged. "Like a microphone taped to my chest."

"Good, that means it's working." Granger crossed two more strips of tape over the base of the mike bud and said, "Still reading okay?"

Another thumbs up-from the audio tech.

According to Levon Williams, Tony Briggs had been placed on emergency family leave effective this afternoon.

Ray Salcedo had posted for duty as normal, no doubt to maintain reasonable appearances.

The only real surprise was that the money drop wasn't going to be a drop after all.

It was going to be a handoff. Adding yet another twist Worth hadn't anticipated, Tony Briggs's call had been to set up a face-to-face meeting, in public, at a midtown bar.

Worth felt as though he'd reached the inner core of the bomb.

It was getting difficult to keep track of the final snarl of wires. There were lies spliced with truths. Interconnected triggers. Who knew how many variables? All with one simple, unstable, incontrovertible fact at the center.

"Russell James has obviously been taken out of the picture," the new guy said.

His name was Terry Farmer, a Special Agent with the DEA's Omaha District Office. He'd arrived at Central Station this afternoon.

"Which leaves a chunk of cash still unaccounted for, Tice's crew beefing internally, and now, suddenly, a power vaccuum," Agent Farmer said. "If Briggs and Salcedo are suddenly open to talking business, maybe we can work toward developing a line on their product source in Chicago."

Worth said, "What makes you think they want to talk business?"

Agent Terry Farmer looked at him casually. He had an average build, a level manner of speaking, and a vaguely outdoorsy air.

Worth looked at him back.

"Just speculation," Farmer said. "Either way, Officer,

here's your chance to convince some people you're one of the good guys here."

"Not that there are doubts, right?"

Farmer gave him a smile that could have meant just about anything.

"Okay," Detective Granger said. "Let's go run it down."

They all filed out: Vargas first, followed by Granger and Torres. Followed by Special Agent Farmer, who carried the duffel bag Granger's team had dummied up with department cash based on consultation from Derek Price.

The audio guy stayed behind, packing up gear.

Down the hall the rest of them went, to a meeting room filled with more cops. Detectives, officers, commanders. A sergeant from weapons and tactics. Terry Farmer's crew from the DEA.

In their midst sat an off-duty checkout girl, looking pale, out of place, and alone. Worth smiled and joined her at the table, a hell of a grocery bagger if he did say so.

---

There was a lot Tony Briggs could take.

Pain? No problem. Stupidity? Sure. Bullshit? Went with the job.

He'd soothed crack babies and been puked on by drunks. He'd taken his ration of shit from pencil-necks. Death, dismemberment, blight, decay: Welcome to his and Ray's little corner of the world.

But he couldn't take the sight of Aunt Joanie.

She'd made it all the way through until dinner before the weight of the day finally brought her down. The shock, the heartbreak, the disbelief. The flat-out indignity of it all.

Thirty years together, her and Eddie. Half a lifetime in the foxhole, back to back. It hadn't always been pretty, and it hadn't been perfect, but they'd stuck together through sunshine and shit. Thirty years of working, fighting, worrying, laughing, crying, raising their kids.

And it all came down to this:

Eddie, shot in the head. Her husband, shot to death sitting in his chair. Murdered in his office at two in the morning with his cheap little office whore.

Tony stayed with the family at Uncle Eddie's big house in Gretna until the place cleared out, long after dark. A little after 10 P.M., he left his mom and his cousin Carmen with Aunt Joan, his pager number, and enough Xanax to knock down a horse.

He made it back to the apartment by ten-thirty. He stripped down and took a scalding shower, and by 11 P.M., he was almost ready to go.

Tony dressed in jeans, a black sweatshirt, and mid-top boots. He laid out a selection of equipment on the bed. After debating a minute, he picked up a Beretta Tomcat, secured in a pocket holster.

It was a palm-size .32, easy to conceal. Good for tight spaces. He flipped the barrel and checked the load.

He took off the safety with his thumb.

Then he turned fast, leveling at the footsteps behind him.

Ray Salcedo stopped in the doorway, showing his palms.

"Yo," he said. "Go easy, Crockett."

Briggs grinned and lowered the gun. "You don't knock anymore?"

Ray was still decked in his patrol gear, mobile radio turned down low. He slipped his lock picks back into their leather sheath, snapped the flap, put the case back in its spot on his belt.

"I knocked for ten minutes."

"Guess I was in the shower," Tony said. "How was shift?"

"Nice and quiet."

"Catch any bad guys?"

"Gave 'em the night off." Ray strolled in, glancing at the bed. "How's your aunt?"

"Deeply tranquilized. You ten-seven?"

"Not yet. On the way now."

Tony nodded slowly. "So what's up?"

"I don't know," Ray said. "You want to tell me?"

Tony faced him and said nothing. No point insulting anyone's intelligence.

"You left the phone we've been using to call the Mullen girl in my truck," Salcedo said. "I checked the outgoing numbers before I posted on shift."

"No shit."

"Last call I made was last night."

"What's your point?"

Ray nodded toward the belly gun in Tony's hand. "Going out?"

Tony chuckled, tossed the Beretta back onto the bed. He pushed by Ray and went over to the dresser, grabbed his wallet and watch.

Ray said, "I thought we were on the same page."

"Don't worry, partner," Tony told him. "You still get your share."

"That's not what I'm worried about."

When Tony came back over, Ray stopped him. One hand to the chest, five fingers spread. Like stopping some punk trying to duck a scene.

Tony looked down at Ray's hand for a long time.

He finally looked at Ray.

# 31

The irony was that just about every piece of furniture in the whole damned apartment had come from Uncle Eddie at one point or another.

The bedroom set, the kitchen table. The leather recliners and the sofa sleeper. Not only the stereo system, but the cabinet where the stereo system lived.

So maybe he'd only gotten the forty-two-inch television. When you got down to it, Uncle Eddie had done pretty well by his favorite nephew over the years.

He and Ray made a mess out of all of it. Out of the bedroom, down the hall, into the living room. They chopped and gouged and grappled, Tony in his street clothes and Ray in his uniform, throwing fists and elbows where they could.

Ray caught him with a short uppercut. Tony's head popped up but he rolled with it, slamming his elbow into the back of Ray's head.

Right on the funny bone. His fingers went numb.

Ray stepped back and threw his weight. They went over the couch.

The bitch in the apartment below pounded on her ceiling. Tony pounded Ray in the ear. Then he got caught with his legs in a twist, and Ray found a gap.

He scrambled around, driving his knee into Tony's cheek. Once, twice, three times.

Tony took each shot full force. He couldn't make a move to evade. By the third shot, he felt his vision start to wobble.

He tried to roll over, but Ray had capitalized. He hooked up an arm lock and cranked it, powering Tony over, onto his face.

Tony reached across, grabbed Ray's thumb. He pretended he was twisting the cap off a beer bottle.

Ray punched him in the side of the head.

Right in the goddamned stitches.

When Tony didn't let the thumb go, he did it again.

"Motherfucker," Tony wheezed. He threw his head back but didn't connect with anything. He bucked, putting all his strength in it, and tried to twist.

Ray shifted his weight and drove him back down.

"Eddie wanted to be a player," he said. He used his leverage, driving Tony's face into the carpet. He was panting, but not as hard as Tony. "He got to be a player. Right? You said that shit yourself, man. Think about it."

Tony couldn't move. His whole head was throbbing, and his arm couldn't go over much farther without tearing out of joint.

He drove with his feet, but Ray hooked a leg and bore down. Tony's shoulder popped. Slowly, he began feeling the edges of the answer to the question he'd always wondered about but never had reason to ask.

Fair fight. No holds barred.

Could he take Ray?

"Okay," he said. He spat blood, dragging in a breath. Let himself go limp. "Fuck, dude. Okay."

Ray eased the arm hold a fraction. "Yeah?"

"Jesus," Tony said. "Yeah."

Ray held for a second, then let up a little more. After another pause, just for good measure, he said, "I'm getting off."

"Thanks for the warning," Tony said. "Don't get any on me."

Ray moved a hand to the back of Tony's head. He pressed down, let the arm lock go, and stood up.

Tony pushed himself up and hung for a second, resting on his hands and knees. He caught his breath, rolled his shoulder. Spat more blood, plus a tooth.

*Motherfucker.*

He grabbed the edge of the coffee table, pulled himself up to his feet.

Ray stood between Tony and the front door, working his jaw. He dabbed a bleeding cut at the corner of one eye with the back of a hand.

Tony straightened. Slowly.

He said, "Thought you had my back."

"This is me getting your back," Ray said.

They leaned against each other then, stood there, breathing like bulls. Tony grinned. It hurt.

"So what now?" he said.

"You tell me, partner."

It was a tooth from the bottom Ray had knocked out.

Broken off right at the gum line; Tony could feel jagged shards of enamel with his tongue. His mouth had filled up with blood.

He swallowed. Sighed. "It's been a long day."

Ray nodded. "I know."

"A long fuckin' day, brother."

"Ride with me to the station," Ray said. "I'll change up. We'll go get drunk."

Tony straightened again, looking away. He finally sighed. Nodded. "Okay."

When he saw Ray's hand move away from the butt of his service weapon, he added, "Hey?"

"Yeah," Ray said.

Tony head-butted him in the face.

Ray stumbled back. Without waiting, Tony dropped his good shoulder and rammed him in the gut, using his legs.

You had to hand it to Ray Salcedo. He recovered quick for a guy who'd been head-butted in the face. He lowered his center of gravity and spread his legs, instinctive as breathing, not only staying on his feet but gaining leverage again.

Tony sacrificed his position and jammed a thumb in Ray's eye. He finally heard the guy grunt, like he'd actually been hurt. He shot in like a high school wrestler, grabbed a leg, lifting and driving forward at the same time.

Ray twisted and tried to drop even lower. Tony stepped in front of his other leg and shoved.

They went down again, Ray headfirst, Tony riding his back, into the coffee table Eddie had given him. The table collapsed under their weight in a twist of chrome and a crash of glass.

"Booya!" Tony said.

He punched Ray twice in the kidney before rolling off, not wanting to get into more Greco-Roman bullshit on the floor. He planted his elbow in a pile of glass and sucked air through his teeth at the pain.

But he still made it to his feet first.

Now it was Ray on his hands and knees, slowly pushing himself up out of the rubble. Tony put a boot in his ribs and stepped back.

Blood streamed from his nose. He felt more dripping from his fingers. He stood there, out of breath again, sporting another new set of wounds.

"I changed my mind," he said. "We're splitting sixty–forty."

Ray made a strange gurgling sound.

Tony finally noticed the way he pawed at his collar. He said, "Ray?"

Ray lowered his hand. He gagged, and something wet hit the carpet. For a moment, Tony thought he'd vomited.

Then Ray sagged against the couch. Tony finally saw the scythe-shaped shard of glass in his partner's throat.

"Oh, shit." He hurried over, dropped down. "Shit. Hang on."

Ray worked his mouth without making a sound. The blood seemed to be falling out of his neck in sheets. Tony reached out and took the glass in his fingers; a new gout pumped from the wound, pouring over his hand.

"Hang on, partner." Tony looked at Ray, forcing eye contact. Ray's gaze had gone vague. "Just hang on."

His heart raced now. He didn't know what to do with all this blood coming out. Before Tony could stop him, Ray finally managed to pull the glass out himself.

"No! Shit. Goddammit."

It came in a hot flood now, bright red. Arterial. The front of Ray's duty shirt was soaked, dark blue turned black, silver badge turned red. Tony's hands were slick to the wrists.

He eased Ray back and pressed down on the wound. He tried to clench the flow off in his fist. Ray grabbed his free hand, but his grip had no strength.

Tony shook free and tore the comset off Ray's shoulder. His fingers were so slippery that he couldn't hold it. He fumbled the unit, picked it up again.

Ray coughed. A wet, congested heave.

It didn't take much longer after that.

For a long time, he stood there in the demolished apartment, looking down at Ray's body.

The carpet had soaked up a lake of blood. Tony was covered in the stuff; he couldn't tell what was his and what was Ray's. Ray lay there in the middle with his eyes still open. He almost looked gray.

At some point, Tony found himself in the bathroom, looking in the mirror. His nose was broken. He had a knot on his forehead, and his upper lip was pulped out on one side.

A sharp pain caught his attention. He looked all over, finally pulled a long sliver of glass out of his elbow. It was easy to grab, now that his hands were sticky. Ray's blood had already started drying in his fingerprints, the grooves of his palms.

At some point, Tony glanced at his watch and coughed out a laugh.

It hit him like a knife in the ribs, but he couldn't help it. It just seemed so utterly, impossibly fucked up.

All this, and it wasn't even eleven-thirty yet.

Standing there, numb, trying to decide what to do, Tony finally followed the only real urge he had:

He stripped out of his gore-soaked clothes and got back in the shower. Cranked the water on hot as it would go.

Tony Briggs hung his head in the gathering steam. He let the water run over him. Watching the runoff turn red and swirl down the drain, he thought of Ray, dead in the living room. He thought of Eddie in a tray at the morgue.

As the warm water slowly loosened the aches, Tony thought of the fake identities all three of them had kept on hand. Just in the unlikely event that everything went to hell in a hurry.

He thought of other things.

Pretty soon, he grabbed the soap and started scrubbing.

# 32

The Homey Inn sat askance in the bend where Saddle Creek turned, a lone cracker box with a covered porch and neon eyes.

It was the kind of bar Worth's dad would have liked on a Sunday afternoon: a dark smoky nook with lacquered tables, low ceilings, and newspapered walls, where they served warm peanuts in dog bowls and cheap champagne on tap.

An hour before last call on a Thursday, the place was half packed with college students, slumming office types, and the barflies who had been there since lunch.

They lucked into the booth least visible from the door. Back corner, half tucked behind a vertical air shaft and the scratch card machine. Worth took the view of the bar; Gwen wriggled out of her coat and hung it on one of the booth-side hooks.

"This still doesn't make sense," she said.

"Don't worry." He had to raise his voice over the thump of the jukebox. "Everything's set."

"Well, I don't know about you," she said, "but I'm ready for a drink."

She headed for the bar before he could ask her to sit tight. Worth kept his eyes on the door.

While Gwen was gone, he reached under his shirt and pulled the concealed microphone plug half out of its jack in the transmitter. He gave the plug a wiggle, just for a second. Then he jacked the line back in again.

His cell phone vibrated on the table. Worth flipped it open and said, "I'm here."

"What's going on with the wire?" Neil Granger said.

"What do you mean?"

"You keep cutting out."

"Really?" Worth moved around in the booth. His clothes would be rustling down the street, behind the coin laundry, where the tech van was parked. "I don't know. Nothing looks wrong. Is it off or on now?"

"It came back on a second ago," Granger said. "Look, just, I don't know. Sit still or something."

He hung up.

Worth folded the phone.

Gwen returned with two beers and two shots of whiskey, somehow carrying it all in both hands.

"I took the liberty."

"Clearly." He smiled, even though he was thinking of her injured kidney. "Dr. Mandekar wouldn't approve."

She crossed her heart. "I'll drink lots of water tomorrow."

Somebody from the YWCA had brought a few of her own clothes to the safe unit. Tonight she'd dressed in a baseball-style T-shirt, running shoes, and a pair of frayed jeans that rode low on her hips. The shirt fit tight and short, showing the name of some band he'd never heard of, a hint of belly button, a glimpse of thong underwear, and the difference in their ages.

At the SaveMore, Worth had noticed that guys didn't really seem to look twice at Gwen Mullen. Personally, he'd always considered her pretty but plain, beautiful underneath the surface in some way only a sensitive soul like his could appreciate.

Here, almost every male in the bar took some form of notice as she crossed the floor. A few females did the same, for clearly different reasons. For the briefest moment, Worth couldn't decide if he wanted to tear all her clothes off or ask her to put her coat back on.

Then she slid into the booth carefully, her movements slow and measured. He caught a look at the remnants of her bruises and remembered what they were doing here.

Gwen arranged the drinks in front of them. She raised her shot and said, "Here's mud in your eye."

Worth grinned, but he left the alcohol on the table. It was almost midnight. He unplugged the wire and watched the door.

Gwen knocked down her shot and placed the empty glass quietly on the table. She winced, ground her teeth together, and blew out a breath. *Whoo.*

She turned and dug in her coat, pulled out a cigarette, and lit one with a book of matches somebody else had left behind. While he watched the door, Gwen took a drag and sat back, sighing long and content, sending a jet of smoke toward the ceiling.

"God," she said. "Do you know, this is the first cigarette I've had in almost a week? I almost forgot I smoked."

His cell phone buzzed again.

"I'm here."

On the other end, Granger said, "So, just kinda look around. You don't happen to be sitting near a giant electromagnet, do you?"

"Not that I know of," Worth said. "Why?"

"Completely lost you now."

He fiddled, moved around, slowly easing the microplug back into the jack on the transmitter unit a little at a time.

"Okay, you're back. What did you do?"

"I just wiggled it," Worth said. "There must be a short."

Gwen pointed toward the bathroom and slid out of the booth. Worth tried to grab her hand, but she was already out of reach.

"Gwen," he said, but she didn't seem to hear him over the jukebox. Even though a few people at nearby tables glanced his way.

Granger said, "What was that?"

"Nothing," Worth told him. "What should I do about the wire?"

"Okay, hang on. Maybe we have time to . . . shit."

"What's wrong?"

"Incoming," Granger said, and hung up again.

---

Tony Briggs pulled into the cramped, crooked lot of the Homey Inn five minutes before midnight.

He spotted Grocery Boy's Ranger sitting alone, beyond the reach of the streetlamps. He parked alongside, killed the engine and the headlights, and sat tight for a moment, surveying the area.

For the time he sat there, nobody came in or went out. No traffic passed by on the street. All was quiet.

Tony hauled himself out of the car.

He felt like he'd been thrown off a balcony. His ribs were sore, hands bruised. Joints already starting to stiffen. His lower back felt loose and creaky from grappling with Ray on the floor. Salcedo had wrenched the shit out his shoulder, and Tony thought there might still be a piece of glass in his elbow somewhere. His torn stitches felt like barbed wire under the ball cap he'd put on.

On top of that, he couldn't breathe through his nose. The cold night air hit his broken tooth like a dentist drill. Tony instinctively covered the jagged socket and sliced the bottom of his tongue.

He took a deep breath. Clenched his fists. Spat a mouthful of blood.

*Maintain.*

Ten yards away, music thumped faintly. Neon buzzed in the windows.

Eddie had brought them here. Tony and Ray. They'd held down a dark corner booth and heard all about these Polacks in Chicago, a direct supply of Turkish heroin, and a franchise opportunity.

That was Uncle Eddie. He'd spent the week up there at some trade show, got bored by Wednesday. Went out looking to score a cocktail waitress and maybe a gram to party with back at the hotel.

Instead, he'd ended up in some dive off South Archer Avenue, drinking Zywiec beer with some guy who knew a guy. That was why he'd picked this place to pitch Tony and Ray in the first place: it was the only bar in town that served Zywiec on tap. Uncle Eddie through and through.

They'd killed five pitchers between them, closed the place down talking possibilities.

So much for that shit.

Tony spat another string of blood. Wiped his mouth.

Went inside.

---

While Gwen was in the bathroom, Worth got up and moved all her stuff onto his side of the booth. Coat, cigarettes, a small nylon purse.

A few of the same people at the same nearby tables glanced in his direction again.

He ignored them, dividing his attention across the barroom floor, between the front door and the bathrooms in the opposite corner.

After a couple minutes, Gwen came out, holding the door for the next girl waiting.

Worth looked to the front and saw Tony Briggs coming in.

He slid out of the booth and stood to the side. Partially to let Briggs see him, mostly to direct Gwen where he wanted her to sit.

She smiled at him, starting back to the booth.

Worth checked out Tony Briggs. He wore khaki pants, a black nylon jacket, and a black ball cap pulled down low.

The guy's face was a mess. Scrapes all over, a couple small cuts, a fat purple bulb for a lip. As Briggs neared, Worth noticed his nose was packed with cotton.

Gwen saw where he was looking and followed his eyes.

The moment she saw Tony Briggs, her smile faded.

Her expression went blank—eyes going dull and distant, face becoming smooth as stone.

They all met at the booth.

"Hey, kids. How's it going?" Briggs tipped his head to Gwen, gesturing toward his side of the booth. *After you.*

Worth put a hand on her elbow, steering her gently his way instead.

He felt her tense up the moment he touched her. Instant, reflexive. She pulled her arm away.

"Don't do that," she said.

More glances from the other tables.

"Yeah, come on," Tony Briggs said. "Don't be so controlling, man."

Worth could sense the change in Gwen from a foot away. It was the same change he'd witnessed at the safe unit, the night Briggs and Salcedo had braced them. That extra gear of hers: like a small animal backed into a corner by a larger one.

She pushed past Briggs, slipping into his side of the booth like it was nothing one way or another to her. *You don't control me, either.*

Briggs grinned, shaking his head. He slid in beside her.

That was the moment Worth decided two things.

First: something wasn't right about this.

Second: the wire stayed connected from now on.

He'd been trying to establish a pattern of malfunction, so that he could disconnect the wire when Briggs got here.

But no more games. Everything they'd been through these past days six days boiled down to these past six seconds. Briggs had taken control of the situation as simply as that.

All of a sudden, the guys down the street were the best advantage Worth had.

He sat down. "What happened to your face?"

"Hands on the table," Briggs said. "Both of you."

Worth put his hands in front of him. "Where's Ray?"

"Ray? He's on duty." Briggs nodded to the beer mugs and shot glasses on the table. "She's getting ahead of you there, brother."

"I decided I wasn't thirsty."

"Yeah? So you don't mind?"

Without waiting for an answer, Briggs reached out. He knocked back Worth's whiskey. Then he picked up the beer and drank it down. When it was gone, he put the mug down and made the univeral sound of the slaked: *Ahhh.*

"Thanks," he said. "I needed that."

"The money's in the truck," Worth said. "How do you want to do this?"

"Right. Business. That's good." Briggs motioned with his hand. "I need your keys."

"My keys? Why?"

"Because I said so."

When Worth didn't respond, Briggs put his hand in his coat pocket. He took out a small automatic pistol, put it in his left hand. He put his right elbow on the table, shielding the gun from view of the rest of the bar. He pressed the muzzle into Gwen's ribs.

Gwen looked at Worth. Her eyes widened slightly; other than that, her expression didn't change.

"Keys," Briggs said.

Worth dug in his own pocket and put the keys to the truck on the table.

"Thanks." Briggs picked them up and put them in his pocket. "Gotta go."

"You're taking my truck?"

"Yeah, okay. You're right. That's not fair." Briggs tossed his own keys on the table. "Better?"

Under the pounding noise from the jukebox, Gwen said, "Take that fucking gun out of my armpit."

Worth looked at her. She was looking at Briggs, but she was talking to him. To the wire. To the guys in the van.

Briggs just smiled. His swollen lips made something grotesque out of the expression.

But he took the gun away, put it back in his pocket, shook his head and said, "Baby, I like you."

"Really? I hope you die."

"You should come with me," he said. "I'll show you what you're missing."

She spat a laugh in his face.

"Hell, I'll even share the money with you."

"Not a chance."

"Have it your way." Briggs chuckled. "How 'bout a little kiss good-bye?"

Gwen looked right at him, gray eyes flaring. *Nothing you say or do means a thing.*

Tony Briggs dropped Worth a wink. "Take notes here, brother."

He leaned over and kissed her, fat lips and all. One hand went behind her head, pulling her in. One hand went under the table. Gwen sucked in a short breath, eyes widening again.

Over by the bar, some drunk fell off his stool, hauling

a tray full of empty beer mugs with him. The drunk hit the floor in a clatter of wood and the crash of shattering glass.

When Worth looked back, Tony Briggs was already out of the booth, head down, slipping away through the crowd.

# 33

"He's on the way out," Worth said to his shirt. "Taking my truck. Over."

"Matthew?"

He lost Briggs in the clog of people standing around the end of the bar. "Coming to you right now."

*"Matthew?"*

Gwen had an odd look on her face. Her eyes seemed frozen, vaguely perplexed. She opened her mouth and shut it again.

"Gwen, what's the matter?"

She looked down at herself. He heard a noise over the music and realized it was Gwen, staring at her lap, sounding a high, strangled note of distress.

Worth leaned forward quickly. The moment he looked over the edge of the table, his guts turned cold.

Just below her breasts, Gwen's T-shirt was soaked through with blood. The lap of her jeans looked slick.

"Oh, Jesus." Worth vaulted out of his side of the booth.

Gwen began to grasp at the knife handle sticking out of her belly. He gently pulled her hands away.

"No, sweetie. Don't grab it, okay?"

She made a high-pitched, awful sound.

It reminded him of the only animal he'd ever killed on purpose. The winter he'd turned twelve years old, on his best friend's uncle's farm: a cottontail rabbit with a .22 rifle.

"Medical," he yelled into his shirt.

Nobody had ever told him about the death squeal a rabbit made. After hearing it once, Worth had never harmed an animal again.

"I've got you," he said. "Look at me, sweetie. Here we go."

From what he could see, it looked like a short, fixed-blade tactical knife. Rubberized handle, olive and black. Briggs had thrust the blade in at an upward angle, beneath her lower ribs. Then he'd twisted, winding the now-sopping fabric of Gwen's shirt a half turn around the hilt.

"It hurts." Gwen was panting now. "It hurts."

"I know," Worth said. "Don't look at it, okay? Look at me."

Almost everyone in the bar was looking at him by now. Everybody but Gwen. Worth could tell by her pupils and her breathing that shock had set in.

In the distance, he heard Tony Briggs, shouting: "What's that guy doing?" Then: "He's got a knife!"

Within moments, the whole place became a minor swarm. Through the moving bodies, Worth finally caught his last glimpse of Briggs, turning and stepping out the door.

Then he saw the beefy guy in the Seminoles T-shirt

rushing toward him. The guy yelled something, grabbed Worth by the neck, and pulled him away from Gwen.

As she fell, Worth pivoted his weight and chopped the guy in the neck as hard as he could. Brachial stun, square on target. The guy shivered and folded up on himself.

Worth climbed over him, back toward Gwen. He felt weight piling up on his back, driving him down.

Through the tangle of feet and legs around him, he saw Gwen slump to the floor. He saw hands on her shoulders. He saw other hands on the handle of the knife.

"Don't pull it out!" He screamed the words with all the air in his lungs.

But they were lost in the clamor. He bucked and thrashed, sunk a fist in a groin. He bit an arm, drove his heel into a knee.

He shouted, "Medical! Now!"

It was some young guy in flannel who pulled the knife out. Just trying to help. While Worth struggled, helpess, Gwen spasmed and arched her back.

The serrated blade dragged a smooth gray loop of intestine through the gash in her belly. Her sodden shirt began to glisten with new blood.

"Back off! I'm a cop!" Facedown, arms and legs pinned, Worth shouted until he was hoarse. "I'm the police!"

The guy in flannel made a yelping sound and stepped back. The knife clattered to the floor, bounced once, and landed a foot from Worth's eyes. He saw five capital letters printed on the olive-drab handle in black marker: *EDDIE.* A random foot swept the knife out of view.

Gwen sat against the booth, hands limp on the floor

beside her, looking down at her stomach with a fascinated expression.

"Gwen, look at me!"

Somebody kicked him in the face. More weight piled on, pressing him harder into the grimy floor.

Worth screamed into his shirt. "Get over here! Jesus Christ!"

Later, he'd consider the irony that all the flailing and the dog piling had disconnected the audio line for real.

First came the sole of a construction boot, filling up his view.

---

Tony Briggs gunned the Ranger out of the parking lot, cornering onto Saddle Creek, black duffel bag full of Uncle Eddie's cash on the passenger seat beside him.

He'd avoid major traffic zones as far as he could. West to 50th, then south through the residential streets. He'd hop Grover to 42nd, then hit the interstate.

By the time anybody managed to sort through the pandemonium he'd left behind in the bar, he'd be long gone. He could ditch the truck at a rest stop or filling station. Boost another car, keep on going. With a quarter million in cash, plus the bogus IDs, he'd be able to lay low indefinitely.

Tony hadn't traveled half a block before a set of flashers turned on behind him.

*You've got to be kidding me.*

In the rearview mirror, he saw the black-and-white coming up on his tail, lights swirling. He couldn't believe the pure dumb luck. The unit must have been hanging out in the vacant car wash next to the bar, waiting for last call.

What, no violent criminals? These Northwestern jerk-offs didn't have anything better to do?

He dug the .32 out of his coat pocket and considered how to play the situation. He didn't want to waste a fellow cop on purpose, but he wasn't stopping here. Somebody in the bar had called 911 by now; in another few minutes, the Homey would be crawling with radio cars and EMTs.

Tony checked the mirror again.

Make that two sets of flashers behind him. The squad units drifted apart while he watched, straddling the center line between them. They took up both lanes, flanking him. One of the units hit the spotlight; the beam hit the rearview mirror, half blinding him.

Unbelievable.

Up ahead, Saddle Creek fed into a roundabout. Tony entered and followed the circle around. One of the squad units followed him in, hitting the siren once. *Bweep.*

The other unit swung around, cutting off the return lane.

Could there be some kind of alert out on Grocery Boy's truck?

No. Too quick. Unless . . .

A third cruiser rolled into play from the south, blocking the last turnout onto 50th Street.

Tony scrambled, trying to assess. He pulled the wheel left, hugging the turn. As he came around nearly full circle, he saw something curious.

A white van with no markings barreled out from behind the laundromat down the street. The van roared across 47th, across the parking lot of the car wash, across 48th, and into the parking lot of the Homey Inn.

As the van skidded to a halt, Tony pictured Matthew Worth, back in the bar, sitting on the other side of the table. Looking smug. Pieces clicked together in his mind, trying to fit.

The unit following him tapped the siren again. *Bwee-wheep.*

Tony checked the rearview again. He looked over his shoulder. Bottom line: It didn't matter *why* he suddenly found himself inside a barricade.

*Gangway, douchebags.*

He punched the gas.

At least Grocery Boy's pickup had some guts. Tony took the last curve of the roundabout hard, tires whining, gathering speed. He aimed the nose of the Ranger at the rear quarter panel of the cruiser up ahead.

The spotlight hit him in the eyes as he closed the distance. Tony hit the cruiser right where black paint met white.

The force of the impact rocked the truck, swinging the tail end around. The Ranger broadsided the cruiser with a long screech of steel on steel.

Tony jammed the gas pedal to the floor. He banged up over the curb, head hitting the roof of the cab. But he made it through, straightened the truck, and roared back down Saddle Creek in the direction he'd come.

He blew past the Homey, where people were already spilling out into the lot. The back doors of the white van stood open: He saw guys in black coats fighting their way into the building, initials OPD and DEA in reflective white letters on their backs.

The units following him out of the roundabout had gone to full sirens now. No more warnings.

Tony sped on, planning alternate routes in his head. Saddle Creek widened and turned south at the bottom of the hill; it was a major artery, meandering on a diagonal all the way through midtown.

His new best friends would be all over the radios. Once somebody assessed the basic situation at the bar—about two minutes from now, Tony speculated—they'd try to set up snares at the nearest interstate on-ramps.

He swerved to avoid oncoming traffic, shooting through the stop sign at the three-way intersection where Saddle Creek crossed Hamilton. Tires screeched, horns blared. Sirens howled.

Three cruisers behind him now. He saw a fourth speeding down the north branch up ahead; he didn't know if the unit was responding to a radio call for the Homey or angling to intercept him.

It didn't matter. Tony grimaced and bore down. He reached the junction on a collision course with the cruiser and faded to the right, plowing into the front end of the oncoming unit just head of the front wheels.

The squad car spun. Tony jumped another curb, clipped the stop sign there, and fishtailed into the southbound lane.

One of the units behind him stopped to help the car he'd hit. That left two on his tail, red stoplights ahead. Tony floored the gas, bore hard to the left, and pounded across the median into the oncoming lanes.

Cars swerved. Traffic parted.

He ran straight down the wrong side of Saddle Creek, trading sideview mirrors with a Plymouth Grand Voyager in a glittering spray of glass. Unit number one stayed on him. The other ran parallel, across the median, slowly drawing ahead.

At Leavenworth, Tony cut back over, shooting behind unit number two. Both squad units braked and swerved, but there wasn't enough street left between them. They piled into each other.

Tony let out a whoop and sped on, approaching the very SaveMore where Grocery Boy and Gwen Mullen had cooked up their little scheme.

He couldn't help glancing at the big glowing letters over the front of the store. They seemed to tower there, encircled in a hazy red corona.

At that moment, Tony wished more than anything else that he'd done them both.

The Mullen girl for Uncle Eddie; that had been his thinking. But it wasn't right.

He should have done them both. He should have taken them outside, behind the building, knelt them down in the dark. Two bullets: one for Uncle Eddie, and one for Ray.

He snapped back to attention just in time to see the little Honda pull out in front of him. Young girl at the wheel, not even looking.

The stupid kid saw him coming too late; her eyes flew wide. No time to swerve. Tony stood on the brakes.

Everything slowed down.

The car stopped dead in front of him. He could see the girl flailing her arms. Somehow, even as he braced for impact, she managed to find the reverse gear. The little Honda scooted back up into the parking lot.

Tony couldn't believe it. *Attagirl.*

Then the truck suddenly lost traction. The tires were screaming, shedding long smears of rubber; then, all at once, the street seemed to glide out from under him.

*Hell no.*

In that yawning moment, Tony had time to identify the problem: Dirty snow piles on either side of the parking lot entrance had melted into thick pads of ice.

He had time to feel the truck bounce over the curb, time to feel the wheel slip out of his hands. He had time to see a wall of pebbled concrete approaching fast. He even had time to think: *I'm going to hit a goddamned grocery store.*

Ray Salcedo would have liked that one.

# 34

"Dude. That's Supercop's truck."

"Bullshit."

Curtis Modell pointed. "That's his license plate, man."

His brother said nothing. LaTonya Wells shook her head and said, "This ain't even good."

All around them, shoppers and other employees continued filing out into the lot, everybody craning to see what on earth had rattled the store to its rafters two minutes ago.

Worth's maroon Ford Ranger had rammed head-on into the southeast corner of the building. The front end had crumpled halfway to the cab, creasing the hood into a sharp peak. Steam hissed; engine fluid splattered the ground. Nuggets of windshield scattered the sidewalk.

Two squad cars had already arrived: one behind the truck, one parked at an angle in the exit of the lot. Both held spotlights on the truck, illuminating the scene in bright light.

Sirens filled the air. More cop cars arrived. Suddenly,

they seemed to come from everywhere, descending on the parking lot of the SaveMore like black-and-white bugs. Whirlpools of red and blue swirled against the side of the building.

Somebody said, "Is that thing going to blow up?"

Before anybody could speculate, a brace of uniformed police officers came toward the crowd. They all made pushing gestures with their hands.

"Everybody back."

"We need you folks back."

"Back inside the building now. Here we go."

Sorensen, the night manager, walked out toward one of the cops. The cop nodded his head, steered Sorensen around by the arm, and herded him back with everybody else.

Behind them, a bullhorn sounded, loud and electric over the chatter of the crowd: *Step out of the vehicle. Hands first.*

The driver's door wrenched open.

LaTonya said, "That ain't Supercop."

They all saw the guy stumble out, blood streaming down his face. He staggered a few feet into the spotlight, doubled over a moment, then straightened again. He looked around like he couldn't get his bearings.

All at once, he seemed to shake off the cobwebs. He turned and started hobbling toward the crowd.

*"Stop,"* the bullhorn said. *"Stop right now."*

Somebody said, "Is that a gun?"

The officers working the crowd drew their weapons, shouted warnings. Some woman screamed. The bloody stranger held his ribs with one hand, raising his other.

He did have a gun.

So they shot him.

It sounded like firecrackers. *Pop pop pop.* The guy fell down like he'd tripped on something, writhed on the ground a moment or two. Then he coughed and stopped moving. Right there in front of everybody.

Curtis Modell said, "Holy *shit.*"

He turned to his brother, but Ricky was gone. Everything went nuts. Standing on his tiptoes, looking over the crowd, Curtis glimpsed Ricky in the distance, heading back into the store.

"Dude," he called out. "Where the hell are you going?"

If Ricky heard him, he didn't respond.

Curtis tried to break away, but he never quite managed. Somehow, he found himself stuck in the parking lot, helping the cops move people back from the scene, working to keep the gawkers at bay.

"Your face is looking much better."

"Think so?"

"No question about it."

As Dr. Jerry Grail moved his hand toward the middle desk drawer, Worth closed his eyes. Jesus. Couldn't he see it coming by now?

"Have a look for yourself."

"I swear, Doc. You and that mirror."

Grail smiled. "Humor me."

Worth gave in, picked up the mirror, held it in front of his face. Two black eyes, fading. Assorted cuts and scrapes, all gone to scab.

"I see a man on the mend," Dr. Grail said. "What do you see?"

Worth slid the mirror back across the desk. His ribs still hurt when he leaned forward. "I see a guy who didn't take a knife in the stomach."

"You say that like you wish otherwise."

"I wish a lot of things."

Grail nodded along. "Let me ask you. Do you hold yourself personally responsible for the actions of every officer in the department?"

"Of course not," Worth said.

"I see. Only in the case of Officer Briggs, then."

Worth sighed. "I hold myself responsible for putting people in dangerous situations. For my own actions."

"Do you believe your actions could have prevented those situations?"

It was physically painful, sitting here, but not because of his few straggling injuries. All in all, he would have rather been back on the floor of the Homey Inn, getting stomped by the mob.

"You mean, do I think that if I'd behaved differently, there might not be a crew from *Dateline* outside your office building right now?"

Grail smiled. "If you'd like to put it that way."

In the past two weeks, most of the major news outlets had been to town. Everybody seemed to love the story: a disgraced officer, a battered checkout girl. Crooked cops and organized crime. A bloodbath in the frozen heartland. Worth assumed it must have been a slow month.

"Yes," he said. "I think that if I'd acted differently, none of this would have happened."

"If Officer Briggs and Officer Salcedo hadn't been doing what they were doing." Grail counted the ifs on his fingers. "If Mr. Tice hadn't been doing what he was doing. If Russell James hadn't been violent and abusive. If Miss Mullen had come to you sooner."

"If she hadn't come to me at all."

Grail stopped pursuing that avenue. "How is Gwen?"

She'd almost died twice in the hospital. Once from

the damage caused by her stabbing, once from the septic infection that started at the wound site and spread through her blood like fire.

At the moment, she was hooked up to a ventilator and a dialysis machine, still suspended in a drug-induced state of unconsciousness while the machines and the medicine did their work. But they said she was recovering.

Worth said, "The doctors seem happy."

"That's wonderful."

"It's lucky," he said. "But yeah."

Grail tapped his notepad with his pen. After a long minute of silence, he said: "Would you mind if we changed gears for a minute?"

"Sure," Worth said.

Grail took a sheet of paper from the case folder. He handed the sheet across the desk and leaned back in his chair. "I received that several days ago."

It was the letter from the department's public information office, announcing that the Fallen Brothers memorial, previously scheduled for last week, would be postponed until an undetermined date in the future.

"Right." He handed the letter back. "I got one, too."

"I'd hoped to discuss it during our session last week," Grail said. "But our conversation never quite seemed to turn in that direction."

"Was there something to discuss?"

"I don't know," Grail said. "Your brother is among the officers to be honored. Do you have any feelings about the postponement?"

"I think the department has a national media story on its hands, funerals to figure out for two dirty badges, and a grand jury investigation in progress." Worth shrugged. "I don't know how else they could have handled it."

"Forgive me," Dr. Grail said. "How was Kelly killed, again?"

"Doc, come on."

"I'm sorry. Just refresh my memory."

The guy knew exactly how Kelly had been killed. They'd been over it before. Several times, in fact. A fifteen-year-old kid, playing dead in the street, earning his colors on the first cop who stopped to render aid. Worth could see one of the newspaper clippings in Grail's case folder from where he was sitting.

"Doing his job," he said.

"Right, yes." Dr. Grail nodded. "You've phrased it that way before."

"You know what else?"

Grail seemed genuinely interested.

"He wouldn't have wanted a memorial anyway."

Dr. Jerry Grail ran his finger around his watchband for the eleventh time. Worth had been counting.

They went on like that for the rest of the hour. At the end of the session, Worth snuck out the back of the building, hoping to slip past the television crew.

The bastards had posted rear sentries at the door.

---

Running the grinder, Vince hadn't heard anybody behind him.

The thing made so much noise he couldn't even hear himself think. Which was just how he liked it. He'd ground up enough goddamned limestone these past couple weeks to pave the road all the way out to the highway.

"I saw Matthew in the newspaper," she said.

At the sound of her voice, he actually felt his heart jump in his chest. Vince turned.

Rita stood a few feet behind him, arms folded, hair blowing around her head in the breeze. She wore one of his coats from the back stairway at the house. It was about ten sizes too big for her. They stood there looking at each other until Vince finally cleared his throat.

"Hi."

Rita looked off toward the burn shed. Then she pulled the coat a little closer around her.

"I saw pictures of that girl, too. On television. Gwen Mullen?" She shook her head slowly, like she'd heard a sad story somewhere. "They showed photos of what she looked like, after that boy hit her."

On the word *boy,* her eyes flickered back toward the shed. Just for a second.

Vince let out a long whiskey sigh. He wanted to walk over there and scoop her up. He wanted to promise her anything. He stood there like a dumb animal.

"She was all bruised," Rita said. "All up and down."

"That's what Matty said."

Rita finally looked at him. "I want you to tell me something. I'll know if you're lying."

"I won't lie to you."

"Did you do it for the money?" She took a step closer. "Vince? Or did you do it for your brother?"

If there was a way he could say it that erased every doubt, he would say it exactly that way. But he couldn't think of one. He raised his hand, shielding the sun. So she could see his eyes.

"Didn't know about the money until it was done," he

said. "Can't tell you I didn't do it, babe. But I didn't do it for the money."

He couldn't tell if she believed him. If she didn't, he couldn't tell that, either. She just stood there, looking into the distance.

"Two things," she said. "Two things I will not have in my life."

"Anything."

"That," she said. She pointed to the bottle poking from the hip pocket of his coveralls. "And this money. Not one dollar of it. Do you understand?"

Without hesitating, Vince took the bottle, threw it in the grinder, and flipped the switch. The machine made a deafening racket for about four seconds as it chewed up the glass. Rita covered her ears.

When it was over, he left the machine running, raised his voice, and said, "Be right back."

While Rita stood there, holding his old coat closed with her hands, Vince took the four-wheeler into the scrap yard. Way in, almost to the middle. Where he'd stashed two hundred and sixty-four grand in the trunk of a '65 Ford.

Even at full throttle, he couldn't get to it fast enough. It seemed to take a goddamned year to get back, the bag in his lap, grinder still running patiently.

She was still waiting when he got there.

---

Curtis Modell couldn't take it anymore.

He knocked a case of green beans out of his brother's hands, turned him around, and shoved him into the walkway between two half-unloaded pallets for Aisle 12.

The case hit the stockroom floor and broke open. Cans rolled all over.

"Jesus." Ricky jerked his arm away. "What the hell?"

"Enough," Curtis said. "You been acting like a goddamn spook for weeks. What's your deal already?"

Ricky straightened his apron. He looked pissed.

Like Curtis really gave a rat's ass. He folded his arms and waited. A couple of the other guys stopped working.

"Ooooh."

"Cat fight."

"Kick him in the nuts, Ricky!"

Laughs.

Curtis just stood there. His brother was a gonad, but something was eating him. One way or another, he was going to spit it out.

Ricky finally got that look on his face. It was the look he got whenever he'd done something stupid and didn't want anybody to know about it.

He dropped his voice and said, "Dude, I gotta tell you something."

"What?"

"Not here."

"Why?"

"Meet me out by the Dumpsters in an hour. Don't let these assholes see you, either."

Jesus, what a goober. Curtis said, "Fine."

An hour later, he slipped out the back and found his brother smoking a cigarette in the garbage area. Ricky didn't smoke.

"Okay," Curtis said. "Just tell me. What'd you do?"

"I didn't do shit," Ricky said.

"Then what's your problem?"

Ricky took a deep breath. He flicked the cigarette away, turned to Curtis, exhaled like an air brake and said: "That night Gwen went to the hospital?"

"Yeah?"

"When I went over there?"

They'd both known something was wrong when she hadn't shown up for work two nights in a row. Gwennie never missed a shift. No matter how bad the son of a bitch had tuned her.

So Curtis had covered with Sorensen while Ricky took the Blazer over to Gwen's place. She'd walked into the store two minutes after he'd left.

"When I got there?"

"Just spit it out."

"Door was standing wide open," Ricky said. "She must've wandered out of there in a daze, man."

"So?"

"So I went in."

"And?"

Ricky looked all around. He dropped his voice, leaned in close. Curtis listened.

"Bullshit," he said.

Ricky shook his head.

"Are you serious?" It wasn't really a question. He knew by the way the guy was acting. "Holy shit."

"Tell me about it."

Curtis couldn't believe it. He didn't even know where to start.

"You mean all this time . . ."

Instead of finishing his sentence, he made a fist and

slugged his brother in the shoulder. Hard as he could, points of his knuckles.

"Asshole," Ricky said, stepping away. "What's your problem?"

"What's *my* problem?" Now it was his turn to check over his shoulder. His turn to whisper. "Why didn't you tell me?"

"Because you're a dumbass."

"Dude, *you're* a dumbass."

Curtis thought of that time, when they were little, Ricky had gone a week without telling anybody he'd found a dead kitten in the air-conditioning unit. He'd been convinced everybody would think he'd done something wrong. Nobody had ever been able to figure out why. Ricky was just that way. Always had been.

"I was going to," he said. "Okay? I shut the door, hauled ass out of there, came right back here to find you. But you weren't around, and Gwen was already up in Sorensen's office with Supercop. So then I was like, okay. You know? Like, man, just leave me *out* of it."

"You couldn't tell me later?"

"I got weirded out."

Unbelievable. Curtis thought about it.

"So that means . . ."

Ricky nodded his head. "Yeah."

"And Supercop must have . . ."

"I know."

Curtis shook his head. "Holy shit."

"Yeah," Ricky said. "That's what I'm saying."

Just then, the back door punched open. Light spilled out into the loading zone. Dave, one of the part-time night guys, came out with a fat garbage bag that smelled like cold spaghetti.

"Hey, Curtis. Get the lid? This is heavy."

Curtis reached out and lifted the lid to the nearest bin. He wrinkled his nose as Dave heaved the sack in. It landed in the bottom of the bin with a heavy, wet plop and the sound of broken glass.

"What's that?"

"Ragú sauce." Dave sighed. "Dropped a whole case, man. Looks like somebody got murdered in Aisle Nine."

Curtis glanced at his brother.

Ricky didn't say a word.

# 36

It turned out to be the warmest November on record. All across the Midwest and the plains, weather maps posted unseasonable highs. Religious groups talked about the end times. The golf courses stayed open.

The Tuesday before Thanksgiving, late in the afternoon, Worth answered the doorbell and found John Pospisil on the front stoop.

"John," he said. "Hey, there. You back home?"

"Nah," John said. "Just a trip to the bone doc. Liz had some errands, so I had her drop me by the house. Figured I'd check the place over."

Worth realized he hadn't seen John since the night of the break-in, weeks ago. He looked healthy and rested. The big external brace had come off, and he was down to the crutches and a padded boot. He was freshly shaved, and his cheeks had a ruddy tone. Worth wouldn't have sworn to it, but he thought maybe John had even lost a few pounds.

Worth opened the door wider, stood aside. "Come on in."

John shook his head. "I can't stay."

Worth couldn't help noticing the way John wouldn't look at him directly. After holding the door a minute, he finally said, "John, is everything okay?"

"Got a call from that detective this morning," John said. "The one who was over here. Sheppard?"

"Roger Sheppard, yeah." Worth nodded. "Is there something wrong?"

"They want me to come in and give another statement. See if I remember anything else, I guess."

"Oh." Worth shrugged. "That's not surprising. I wouldn't worry about it, John, it's probably just routine."

"Thing is," John said, "I did remember something else."

With that, he leaned over his crutches and said what he'd come to say. As Worth listened—as the significance of what John was telling him slowly sunk in—he realized that he should be feeling something. Panic, for a start.

When he was finished, John looked off toward the yard.

"You've always been a good neighbor," he said. "Guess I wanted to hear what you had to say for yourself."

At that moment, Worth realized that not only didn't he feel panic, he didn't feel much of anything.

After three solid weeks of reporters and meetings, lawyers and hearings, hours upon hours of sworn testimony, he'd finally found the bottom of his tank. He felt empty.

And he didn't have another lie left.

So he stood there at the door and told John Pospisil everything. Every last detail, starting with the night he found the body of Russell James.

Worth left out nothing. He offered no color, no spin. He just puked the whole thing out at John's feet.

It felt like purging a gut full of toxic waste. Like coming up for air. When he was finished, Worth knew only two things for sure:

He wasn't a cop anymore. And he felt better than he'd felt in as long as he could remember.

"Do whatever you need to, John." Worth nodded. "It's okay. I understand."

John leaned on his crutches, gazing off toward the splintered remains of the big old maple tree.

"Always have been a good neighbor," he said.

---

Three days before Christmas, the state grand jury officially cleared Worth of any criminal wrongdoing in the deaths of Officers Raymond Salcedo and Anthony Briggs.

Two days before Christmas, Dr. Jerry Grail sent registered letters pronouncing him fit for a return to active duty, effective day one of the new year.

Worth didn't kid himself.

He spent Christmas day at Elmwood Manor and ate processed turkey loaf with Dad. One of the other residents rolled up and down the halls, bawling carols in a demented baritone.

"I arrested that guy," Vince Worth Senior said. He thought he'd arrested everybody there. "It's tough for an old cop in a place like this. They all want to kill you."

"Nobody wants to kill you, Dad."

"Be a good kid and get me some rum."

"Eat your cranberries."

Late in the afternoon, it snowed. Fat flakes the size of

half-dollar coins fell gently outside. He wheeled the old man up front, to the picture window bordered in red and blue lights.

Dad sat and told stories while they watched the snow. Worth knew half of them weren't true, but he listened anyway.

At one point, he found himself talking to his poor bewildered father about Tiffany Pine. He often thought of her around this time of year. Especially when it snowed.

"Wish I knew what to tell you, son." Vince Worth Senior sighed. "It's a goddamned black world."

"Yes, sir."

"That's why I worry about your brother."

Worth said, "Who, Vince?"

"Hell no, not that sonofabitch. Matty."

"Oh." Worth didn't bother correcting him. "Right."

"You need to be looking after him out there."

"I am, Pop." He patted the old man's hand. "Don't worry about us."

"Goddamned black world. I could tell you things."

Worth didn't want to get him wound up, so he stopped talking.

They sat together and looked out the window, watching things turn white again for a while.

# ACKNOWLEDGMENTS

Two people played key roles in the writing of this novel. First: Dr. Mark Wurth, chiropractic wizard, who returned me to the walking-upright-and-sitting-in-chairs branch of the evolutionary tree. (Worth . . . Wurth . . . one of several eerie, unintended coincidences associated with this book.)

Second, but in no way second: Carol Doolittle—my mother—who kept our household running during the perfect storm of deadlines, sick kids, hospital stays, and assorted scheduling complications that was January 2006. Thanks, Mom. Sorry for all the bad words.

Thanks to Anthony Neil Smith, Victor Gischler, and John and Amy Rector, who offered keen comments on the manuscript. Special thanks to the Omaha Police Department for the ride-along. The bad cops in this book are strictly mine.

Extra-special thanks to super-agent David Hale Smith. And to my steely-eyed editors: Shannon Jamieson Vazquez, who shaped this book up, and Danielle Perez, who came in with the lens and the polishing cloth.

And to Jessica, 24/7, always.

# ABOUT THE AUTHOR

Sean Doolittle is the author of *Rain Dogs*, *Burn*, which was the winner of the gold medal in the mystery category; of *ForeWord Magazine*'s 2003 Book of the Year Award; and *Dirt*, which was an Amazon.com Top 100 Editor's Pick for 2001. He lives in Omaha, Nebraska, with his wife and children.

Don't miss Sean Doolittle's

other electrifying thrillers

# BURN

*and*

# RAIN DOGS

Please turn the page for a preview of RAIN DOGS.

On sale now from Dell Books

"Sean Doolittle is a cult writer for the masses—
hip, smart and mordantly funny."
—Laura Lippman

# RAIN DOGS

"A terrific novel."
—Dennis Lehane

SEAN DOOLITTLE

Author of *BURN*

# RAIN DOGS

**On sale now**

The offices of Tyler & Tyler sat next to a taxidermy shop with a stuffed coyote in the window. The taxidermist had the bigger awning.

Standing curbside, Tom Coleman considered the attorneys he knew. None had a grip like George Tyler Jr.'s: blunt, callused, crusted with sun spots, knuckle hair like steel wool. He almost said uncle.

"You made it, Tom."

"Sorry to drop in on you." He was supposed to have arrived three days ago. Tom wasn't completely sure what he was doing here now. Yesterday had been his daughter's fifth birthday, and he'd spent it in a twenty-dollar motel room. Today he felt a dead coyote watching him through cloudy glass. "I should have called."

"Never mind that, son. Glad you're here. How was the drive?"

"Long," Tom said. "But fine."

"Any trouble finding the place?"

"No trouble."

Tyler must have been pushing seventy, but he didn't seem to notice. His weekday business attire appeared to run toward stiff dark blue jeans and Tony Lamas. Tom had caught him on the way out, zipping a windbreaker against the sunny March chill.

"Well, welcome to the Heart City." Tyler nodded down the empty sidewalk, the quiet street. Downtown Valentine. "Don't guess it's quite the speed you're used to in Chicago."

As Tom started to respond, a big eighteen-wheeler rumbled past, heading for the highway junction at the end of Main. He started again and was defeated by a pickup pulling an empty horse trailer.

He gave up and nodded at the key ring on Tyler's finger. "Is this a bad time? I can come back."

"Do what? Nah. I was just headed down the street for a bite. You hungry?"

Tom wasn't. Hungover. Getting thirsty. But not hungry.

"Hell, it's early for lunch." Tyler clapped him on the shoulder. "Let's go on in. We'll get the boring stuff out of the way."

It sounded like a plan.

■ ■ ■

There were papers to read and sign. Tom pretended to read them and signed.

They sat in Tyler's office, one of three small rooms off a small reception area that smelled like new paint. Tyler had a scarred wooden desk cluttered with file folders, a bookcase of legal volumes, a few trout flies in shadow boxes on the walls. They had the place to themselves.

"I'll have Judy get you copies. She comes in Thursdays."

"No rush."

"That one at the bottom." Tyler pointed to another sheet. "There you go."

Tom scribbled his signature one last time and slid the entire folder back across the desk. His grandfather's executor took the folder up, tapped the spine on the desk, and set it aside.

"I wish he'd gotten a few more years," he said. "Your granddad."

"He wasn't too old." Tom felt like he should say something else, but he didn't know what.

"Besides the trick pump, I don't know anything would have killed him. He was a character."

"Is that the legal term for cranky old bastard?"

Tyler barked a laugh. "Tough as a whip and half as personable, George Senior always said. But I liked him. He was a good man."

"To tell you the truth, Mr. Tyler, I didn't really know him all that well."

As a kid, Tom had spent one summer out here, in the Sandhills, hours west of the Nebraska he knew. He'd earned an allowance doing chores on a cow/calf operation his grandfather had owned at the time. This was several years before his grandmother gave in early to the same cancer that killed Zevon and McQueen. He'd been eleven or twelve years old.

Beyond that summer, twenty-odd years ago, he'd only seen the man on a handful of occasions. Most of what he knew about Parker Coleman he'd gotten through stories from his dad and uncles. He hadn't even attended the funeral.

"You could say this is unexpected."

Tyler nodded. "That's more or less the way your dad put it."

"Oh?"

"We spoke a bit on the phone the other day."

"I see."

"Guess they were thinking of coming out to surprise you. Your mom thought you might use some help settling in."

Tom sighed. It was a six-hour drive from Lincoln; he'd already told them not to bother. "I should have called."

Tyler now wore a small, humane smile. Tom knew what was next.

"Son, I can't say how sorry I was to hear about your little girl."

"Thank you."

"I have a niece in Dallas. She and her husband lost a boy the same way."

"I'm sorry to hear that," Tom said. "I truly am."

"It's an awful thing."

"Is there anything else I need to sign?"

Tyler lingered a moment and shook his head.

"Nope, we're done. One last thing." He picked up a plain white envelope and handed it across. "Your granddad left instructions to pass this along when the time came. Guess that's now."

Tom held the sealed envelope to the light. He tore off an end and slipped a single sheet of lined notebook paper from inside. The paper still had an edge of fuzz where it had been ripped from a spiral binding. He unfolded the page and saw lines of spiky blue ink, one running bulk of a paragraph. The man had written it just over a year ago.

*Thomas,*

*You're burying your little one today. Expect your heart is broke and I'm goddamn sorry as hell. Like to say I wish I was there but I don't. Older I get the less I can stand people. Guess this river is probably the best place for an old rain dog like me. Maybe you don't want a goddamn thing to do with it. Anyway, you get the land and the buildings and the truck, do what you want. I'm in the ground either way. Don't have much else to say. Good luck to you, boy.*

*PC*

He read the note a couple of times. When he was finished, he didn't know how he felt. He didn't know how he was supposed to feel. He looked up and found George Tyler Jr. watching him.

Tom said, "Truck?"

"Sorry?"

"There's a truck?"

"Your granddad's pickup. Didn't I mention it?"

Tom couldn't remember if Tyler had or hadn't.

"Well, there's a truck. Can't promise it's much of a truck, but there's a truck."

"Oh."

After a few moments of silence, the attorney rose. He opened a drawer, took out another ring of keys, and said, "Guess you're probably anxious to go have a look at the place."

There wasn't much to look at for most of the drive.

Tom followed George Tyler Jr. almost twenty miles along the tar-patched stretch of highway leading east out of town. They finally turned south at a town called Sparks. Tom saw the sign, but he didn't see the town.

Tyler took a county road through an open gate, bouncing over a handful of iron bars set parallel over a trench in the ground. Tom remembered his grandfather calling them autogates; they were designed to keep livestock from crossing. Ranchers installed them all over this area where fence lines paused for road.

The road turned to gravel, then bare dry sand, narrowing as it curled through pasture toward lower ground. Grazed scrub turned to taller grass.

Then trees. They entered a tunnel of elms and oaks and hackberries, all beginning to bud with new leaves. Within the next couple of miles, Tom saw paper birch growing next to tall fir and pine.

According to the brochure he'd taken from a wire

rack in the front office of the motel, this leg of the Niobrara flowed twenty-eight miles through a state park and a federal wildlife refuge. Ecosystems jumbled in the river valley, from western to eastern forest and prairie between.

According to the brochure, if you liked getting away outdoors, the Scenic Niobrara River was for you. Wildlife abounded. Waterfalls cascaded. A child could navigate the diciest of the rapids between the put-in below Cornell Dam and his grandfather's place at the end of the run.

The wildlife Tom had spotted from the car consisted of polled steers and a rabbit. A smashed turtle. A few birds. He hadn't really been looking. Every mile or two now, they passed a weather-beaten shingle for one of the other outfitters along the bank.

Tyler took a cut off the main road, and they came to a pine rail arch. A big splintered sign welcomed them to Coleman's Landing. An arrow labeled CAMPGROUND pointed toward a right fork; the arrow pointing left said ARRIVAL CENTER—CANOE/KAYAK/TUBE RENTAL * FIREWOOD * CONCESSIONS * GEAR & GIFTS.

Tom heard the river, and then he saw it, flat water tumbling over a ford of jagged bedrock and driftwood limbs. They followed a bend around a curtain of trees to a parking lot topped with crushed rock. Tom could smell the water when he got out of the car.

"I've never been here," he said. "Pretty."

"Water's low," Tyler said. "Awful drought, last few years. Folks were hoping for a big snow this winter. Didn't get one."

"Oh."

"Not sure who belongs to that one." Tyler indicated a third car parked in the lot: a rusted Subaru Brat with a camper shell and no hubcaps, IN TRANSIT tags instead of plates. The Sube sat near what appeared to be a mini school bus that had been painted silver, hitched to pull an aluminum trailer.

"Which one's the truck?"

"Truck ain't as nice as either of those." Tyler nodded at the bus. "And that's the only one belongs here. Take a load off if you want. I'll go see what's what."

Tom didn't feel like waiting around in the parking lot. He went with Tyler up a cedar chip path.

The main building sat back on a small rise overlooking the ford; it looked to Tom like a cross between a farmhouse and a ski lodge with a long covered deck added on. He saw a couple of sheds and what looked like a small bunkhouse farther back in the trees.

He also saw a row of canoes turned up on the ground outside one of the sheds, aluminum keels glinting in the sun. The shed's sliding door had been rolled open; loud classic rock drifted from inside.

A guy in cutoffs emerged with a coil of rope in the crook of his elbow. He wore flip-flop sandals and a red bandana pirate-style on his head. He saw them coming and stopped what he was doing.

"Afternoon," Tyler called.

The guy raised a hand. Up close, he aged a decade from Tom's initial guess. His eyes looked pink, slightly shot.

"You work here, son?"

"Little as possible." A grin. "What can I do for you guys?"

Tyler glanced at Tom. "Sorry, I didn't get your name."

"I'm Duane."

"Duane who again?"

"Foster. If you're looking for the owner, he's not here right now. I just got here myself."

"Just got here from where?"

Foster narrowed his eyes. "Omaha. Is there a problem?"

Tom didn't know why he felt like he should jump in. "I'm Tom Coleman."

"Hi."

"Your boss was my grandfather."

"Was?"

"Heart attack," Tyler said. "Three weeks ago. I'm sorry, son, I thought Park's employees had been notified."

Foster looked at the loop of rope on his arm. He looked out at the river. He looked at Tom.

"Damn," he said.

■ ■ ■

Before dark, Tom left Foster at the bunkhouse smoking a joint in a hammock strung between two old elms.

His new truck was an old F-150 with creaky suspension, rust holes in the fenders, and a red paint job long faded pink by the sun. They'd found it parked at one of the campgrounds, weeds already growing up around the tires. The truck looked like hell but seemed to run fine. At least it started on the first try.

He found a narrow stretch of old buckled pavement

and kept to it, winding into the Sandhills. In the valleys, big dunes rose up around the cab, scrub-covered hulks that blotted the view of all but the road ahead.

Tom climbed to a high point and parked in the bunchgrass alongside the road. He pulled his flask and climbed up the bumper, onto the warm hood. He leaned back against the windshield and looked at the darkening sky.

It felt like nothing but sky here. No buildings, hardly a tree—just a kingdom of grass in all directions, a world of sky meeting the low horizon all around.

He still remembered the feeling he'd had here as a kid. A vague terror somewhere in his blood.

He remembered a summer rainstorm that rolled in late one afternoon. He'd been out on the range fixing fences with his grandfather, miles from anything, when massive black thunderheads the size of continents seemed to rise out of the prairie and cover them over fast. He'd felt the dark sky lowering as if to crush them; he'd cowered reflexively, grinding his teeth and gripping his elbows as they'd waited out the pounding storm in the truck. Tom remembered his grandfather smoking Winstons and humming to himself as the thunder rumbled over them.

On clear days, blue sky towered like an ocean. Tom remembered that he used to avoid looking up; he remembered the irrational, overwhelming sense that he might float up, untethered and helpless, until he disappeared into the clouds.

Somehow, back amongst these strange rolling dunes, looking up into this sky for the first time since that summer as a boy, the idea of floating away didn't seem so bad.

He thought about Melissa. She'd already been to the cemetery before he'd left town; he'd recognized the fresh clutch of white Gerber daisies she'd left on the grave. He wondered how she'd spent the rest of the day.

He'd finally called, from a filling station on the Iowa side of the Quad Cities, just because he couldn't shake the feeling that he should. He'd left the number to his grandfather's place on her machine, but he doubted she'd use it.

Tom wondered what he'd tell her if she did. *Found a great job. The sky's the limit.*

Stars begin to flicker in the purple nothing above. His dad always said they were better out here. Tom tipped the flask and watched, knowing the truth.

They were the same here as anywhere. He was just in a different spot.

If she called, he guessed he'd tell her he'd moved.